A Lost Heart
By
Iris Bolling

Siri Enterprises
Publishing Division
Richmond, Virginia

This is a work of fiction. Names, characters, places and incidents are either the product of the author's imagination or are used fictitiously, and any resemblance to actual persons, living or dead, business establishments, events, locales is entirely coincidental.

A Lost Heart
Copyright©2010 by Iris Bolling

All rights reserved. No portion of this book may be reproduced in any form without the prior written consent of the publisher or author, excepting brief quotes used in reviews.

ISBN-13: 978-0-9801066-4-0
ISBN-10: 0-9801066-4-8
Library of Congress Control Number: 2010913441

Cover and page design by: Judith Wansley
Cover model: Stephen Howell

The Heart Series
By Iris Bolling

Once You've Touched The Heart
The Heart of Him
Look Into My Heart
A Heart Divided
A Lost Heart

www.irisbolling.net
www.sirient.com

Acknowledgements

Thank you my heavenly father. Raymond, Chris and Champaine, thank you for your love, support and patience.

Judith Wansley, thank you for sharing your talents, your kindness and your unyielding dedication and belief in the dream.

Roz Terry, LaFonde Harris, and Gemma Mejias: the roots to my tree, thanks for always answering the telephone. Kathy Six, and Cathy Atchison, thank you for your time, knowledge and encouragement.

To the beautiful people, Monica Jackson, Sakeitha Horton, Justin Wansley, Jason Wansley and Stephen Howell, may God's blessings always be with you.

To Beverly Jenkins and Gwyneth Bolton, thank you for sharing your knowledge and experience.

To my mom, Evelyn Lucas, my sister Helen McCant and brother Albert "Turkey" Doles, family is the strength that binds us forever and always.

To the book clubs: SiStar Tea- ARC Book Club, New York, Patricia Nolan-Euphoria Book Club, Miami, Fl., Jackie Chew and Phyllis Williams-Onyx Book Club, Ft. Lauderdale, Fl., Pricilla Johnson-APOOO Book Club, Deatri King-Bey, Shelfari-Black Romance Online Book Club, Nikkea Smithers-Readers With Attitude Book Club, Richmond, Va., Shaun Robinson-Sisters Book Club of Richmond: Thank you for your support book after book. You make us what we are.

A special thank you to Victoria Wells for putting up with my phone constantly calling her number. God don't make mistakes, he put you in my life for this purpose.

To Margie Corder, an angel right here on earth, thank you for being a part of my life.

To all of my readers, your wait is over, Brian's story is here. Enjoy book five of The Heart Series as JD's and Brian's friendship is tried and tested, but endures the test of time.

Dedication

This book is dedicated to, Shannon Pilgrim Purnell, one determined sister. Believing is achieving.

A Lost Heart
Prologue

Boredom had set in sooner than expected. After five years with the Federal Bureau of Investigations and four years with his own company, Thompson Security Agency, the silence was about to drive Brian Elliott Thompson crazy. He was literally about to lose his mind. It was the twelfth day of his release from the hospital, after more than a month long stay. His friends believed he needed more rest. He, however, believed it was time to return to work. Not to the pile of paper work staring back at him from his desk, but to his real job, protecting the Attorney General of Virginia and his childhood friend, J.D. Harrison. That's what he should be doing, not sitting around shifting through paperwork. He was so tempted to push the stacks of paper off the desk, but that would cause, his secretary more work.

Patiently waiting for a return call from JD, Brian stood and stared out of his office window. Below was the view of the very building he would be guarding once JD was elected Governor of the Commonwealth of Virginia, the Executive Mansion. A grin slowly appeared on his face as the memory of the day James Brooks, JD's campaign manager, stood at that window and declared, he was setting him up in business to protect JD and his family once they moved into the Governor's Mansion. James knew then that JD was heading in that direction. He wanted Brian to be free from the bureaucracy of the Bureau to conduct protection for JD and his family as he saw fit. It was an honor to be given such a detail, especially since the man he was protecting was one of his closest friends.

Shaking his head, Brian thought of their friendship. There were very few people he considered a friend and JD Harrison was one. The fact that he'd put that friendship in jeopardy, to this day cause him internal turmoil. Looking back on the situation, he had no one to blame but himself. Kissing a man's wife was wrong, and even worse if you called that man a friend.

As if on cue, the bruises on his back began to ache, but he refused to take any of the medication the doctors prescribed for the pain. It was over a month ago that a gang invaded JD's home while his wife and two children slept in the bedrooms upstairs. Brian was able to get Tracy, JD's wife and Jasmine, their two-month-old daughter out of the house. However, when he went back in to get JC, their three-year-old son, he was shot four times in the back. A man who stood six-three and was two-hundred ten pounds of solid muscle, was brought down with four bullets in his back, like a leaf falling from a tree. From what his friends and family had told him, for weeks no one was sure he would be here today. After a month in the hospital and a few weeks on house recovery, the pain let him know, he was still alive. The pain from the bullet wounds he could stand, the pain of possibly losing his friend was unbearable. Even though he and JD were not on speaking terms at the time of the shooting, there was no way he would have allowed harm to come to JD or his family. Primarily, it was his professional integrity and his personal pride that would not allow him to give less than one hundred percent to the job every day.

Secondly, JD's family was his family. He loved his friend's children as if they were his own. And as for his wife, Tracy, well he loved her a little too much.

The door opened and then slammed before Brian could turn towards the sound—his reflexes were slow. That was not a good sign.

"What are you doing here?" the woman asked angrily.

Recognizing the angry face seething at him, Brian sat in the chair behind the desk, before Pearl could see evidence of the pain surging through him. Pearl Lassiter had become his champion since the shooting and seemed determine to make his life miserable by making sure he healed properly according to her rules. "I own the place," he mockingly replied.

"Really, do you have a will?" Frowning, he looked up at her. "I just want to make sure I get something out of caring about you one way or another," Pearl snapped out the response.

"Thanks for the confidence in my recovery. Do you want something this early in the morning?"

"Imagine my surprise," she began sarcastically as she walked towards him, "when I stopped by your place to make sure you'd had breakfast and had taken your meds, before I came to work, only to find you gone."

"I'm sure you were, but as you can see I'm fine."

She sighed, "Have you had breakfast?"

"No."

She placed a McDonald's bag in front of him, "Breakfast steak burrito. Have you taken your meds?"

Opening the bag and pulling out the contents he looked at her, "Thank you."

"I'll take that as a no. I did not find them at your place, so I am going to assume you were at least smart enough to bring them with you."

"Unlike other times, your assumption is correct," he stated as he bit into the burrito and smiled.

She placed her arms across her breast. "Would you take them now while I'm here?"

Sitting back in the chair he replied, "I'll take them when I need them."

Putting the back of her hand to her forehead in frustration she sighed. "Brian, I don't have time for this today. JD has to fly out in an hour and I need to know you are okay before we leave."

"Where are we going?" He asked eagerly, thinking he might have something to do after all.

"We are campaigning in Northern Virginia. Avery and Gwendolyn Brooks are hosting a fundraiser."

"I'll give JD a call to see what time we are leaving."

"We? What are you going to do if you go? You can't take anyone down if something were to hop off." Seeing the look of denial in his eyes, she softened her words. "Look, I know you want to protect your friend, however, at the moment, you are physically unable to do that. Give your body the time it needs to heal and you will be back on the job in no time. You'll probably be better, if that's possible." She added that last statement to give him the compliment she felt he needed.

"Thanks for the moment of reality and the pep talk. It doesn't help my boredom, but I hear you. Go meet with the posse. I'll talk to you later."

Pearl smiled, relieved. "I'll go as soon as you take your meds."

He looked at her as he pulled open the desk drawer, "Where is Dr. Kildare? Shouldn't you be harassing him this time of morning?"

"His name is Dr. Theodore Prentice and he has had his dose for the morning," she replied flirtatiously, "You jealous?"

Glaring at her he laughed, "Been there, done it, had fun, we moved on." He took the pain pills, and swallowed them down with his coffee. "Satisfied?"

"Yes, I am." She opened the door to leave. "I'll call you later."

"I don't like him."

She stopped and turned back to him. "You're jealous."

Taking a seat, he smiled, "Only when you wear those short skirts."

Pearl shook her head. "Now I know you're getting better. You're flirting again." She laughed and walked out of the door.

Sighing as the door closed, Brian checked the computer for security updates on his clients. Presently he had four VIP clients that had top government clearance. Each had different levels of coverage, but none as high as JD. It was a foregone conclusion that in a few years Jeffrey Daniel Harrison would be the Democratic candidate for President of the United States. Until that happens and Secret Services Units are assigned, it was Brian's job to keep his friend and his friend's family free from harm. Under normal circumstances, JD would not make a move without him by his side, but not now. Since he could not protect his friend, he'd made sure that his top man, Samuel Lassiter was heading up the detail. Anyone going after JD would have to go through Hurricane, as Brian called him, and that would not be an easy task. Samuel was fully capable and just as dedicated to protecting JD as he was, but it did not ease the disappointment of not being next to his friend. Then there were Tracy and the children. Magna Rivera, whom he was fortunate to get from the District of Columbia Gang Task Force, and Ryan Williams, whom he literally recruited from the streets, were handling the detail on them. To get through those two women, you had better bring an army fully armed with heavy artillery.

Yes, he had good men and women working for him, but it wasn't him and that was the problem. Since high school, he was the protector of not only JD, but their other high school friends, Calvin Johnson and at times Douglas Hylton as well. It was hard being placed on the side-lines. Like it or not, there wasn't a damn thing he could do about it, for now.

JD sat at the desk in his home office looking out the window as his wife Tracy and their three-year-old son JC played tee-ball. As his son hit the plastic ball with the matching bat, he smiled at the child-like giggles that echoed into his office. The scene only fueled his anxiety over the situation at hand. Brian had a son that he doesn't know about. He was missing out on not just seeing his son grow up, but on seeing his development as well. Promise or not, that was something JD could not be a party to. The question was, how would he let Brian know about his son without flat out telling him. The day he ran into Caitlyn Montgomery, Brian's college girlfriend, replayed in his mind. The shock alone, threw him, but discovery of Brian's son turned him upside down. A week had gone by and JD was still at a loss as to how he would handle the situation. Replaying the scene in his mind, he tried to remember exactly what he had actually promised.

He and Tracy were standing at the podium holding hands and waving to the crowd of over one thousand supporters that had showed up to hear him speak at their Founders Day Celebration. More than pleased with the turnout he whispered to Tracy, "I didn't think Nickelsville had this many people living here and I'm more surprised to see a few of us here."

"At least you had heard of this town. Today when we stepped foot off the plane was the first time I had heard of this place. According to the history on the internet, this town had an interesting beginning. A wealthy family by the name of Nickels owned quite a bit of land along the borders of Virginia and Tennessee. It seems one of the Nickels sons fell in love with and married a black woman. During those

times, that was a no-no. He and his wife were shunned from Tennessee. He moved his family to the far end of the family's property line, which happened to be in Virginia. Over time the young couple had a number of daughters, but no sons. It's said that by marrying a black woman he cursed the family's name, for several generations no sons were born to carry on the name, only daughters. Years later, one of the daughters married a Becker. The town manager, Jacob Becker is a direct descendant from that family. Of course over time, property was sold on both sides of the border allowing the development of the town we are in here, in Virginia, and the town across the street which, is now known as Nickelsville, Tennessee. If we go across the street on Main Street, we will be in Tennessee."

He looked at his wife. She always amazed him with her knowledge. "I guess we better stay on this side of the street then."

As they walked through the crowd shaking hands, a young boy approached him. Pulling on his pants leg the boy called out, "Mister, Mister" and looked up at JD with the most excited eyes. JD looked down at the boy who appeared to be ten or eleven and smiled. He bent his six-two frame down to the boy to speak. "Hello," he shook the young boy's hand. "What's your name?"

"Elliott, what's your name?"

The boy's speech seemed young for his size. But JD dismissed the thought a moment later after considering the possibility that the education system in this rural part of the State might be lacking. "My name is JD."

"That's not your real name. My mommy says a name can say a lot about the man you are going to become."

JD smiled, liking the boy immediately, "You're right, my name is Jeffrey Daniel Harrison."

Proud of himself the boy smiled and continued. "My mommy say's you are going to be our new governor and then president."

"Your mommy said that?" The boy nodded his head. "Where is your mommy?" JD asked standing.

"Over behind the tree."

JD stood and took the boy's hand, "Let's go find your mom so I can thank her for the kind words."

Tracy smiled at her husband, "Looks like you have a new friend."

"Yes I do," JD laughed, "He looks familiar to me for some strange reason. We're going to find his mom."

"Come on," the young boy said. "I'll show you where she is."

JD and Tracy followed the boy through the crowd shaking hands along the way. As they reached the area, where the boy had indicated his mother would be, a woman stopped the young boy. She was very slender with blonde hair, beautiful blue eyes, and a welcoming smile. "Elliott are you bothering Attorney General Harrison?"

"No Ms. Margie. I'm taking him to meet my mommy."

"Mr. Harrison, I can take him to his mom," the woman with the southern accent offered.

"It's no bother at all." JD replied. "I would like to meet her. She has a wonderful son."

"Well, if you are sure it's no problem, she is passing out buttons at the third tree over yonder."

"Thank you," JD replied with a smile as they continued on the short journey.

As they walked closer to the tree, Elliott called out to his mother, "Hey mommy look who I have."

The woman turned to JD just as he was looking up from the boy and shock was a mild response to the look that appeared on his face. He looked down at Elliott who was smiling proudly at his mother and then his glaze returned to the woman.

"Caitlyn?"

The woman's shocked expression was a less intense match to JD's as she stammered, "Hello JD." If Caitlyn *could have crawled under the tree stump she was standing next to she would have. For the entire day, she had volunteered to work on the outskirts of the event just to keep this very thing from happening. Now she had to face her past.* She extended her hand to Tracy who was watching the looks transpire between the two, wondering what was wrong with her husband. "Hello, I'm Caitlyn, Elliott's mother."

"It's nice to meet you," Tracy smiled then looked up at her husband.

"Caitlyn, what—"the words did not seem to form.

Sensing Jeffrey and this woman needed a moment Tracy took Elliott's hand, "How about you show me where I can get some ice cream," she said bending down.

"Okay, come on." Elliott took her hand then turned to his mother. "Ya'll coming Mr. Harrison and Mommy?"

"No Elliott, I'm going to stay and talk to your mom for a minute." Waiting for the boy and Tracy to leave the area, his intense glaze fell on Caitlyn again. "How old is Elliott, Caitlyn?" He asked mindful of where he was and other people watching.

She stepped closer to him so they would not be overheard, "He is about to turn eight and to answer your next question, no, Brian does not know he has a son, JD. And you can't tell him."

"Mr. Harrison..... Mr. Harrison." Mrs. Gordon called out from the doorway.

At the sound of his housekeeper's voice, JD's attention returned to the present. "I'm sorry Mrs. Gordon, what did you say?"

"Mr. Thompson is on the line for you."

"Thank you," he sighed. Talk about timing. Taking a moment to gather his thoughts, he picked up the receiver and answered. "Hey Brian, what's up?"

"I hear you are on your way out of town. Why you leaving a brother behind man?"

"The four walls getting to you?" He smiled hearing his friend's irritation.

"Man, you know I'm not used to staying still. If I don't get some action soon, I swear I'm going to go crazy."

JD thought for a moment. "You know," he sat forward as the plan formed in his mind. "I could use your help on something."

"Name it man, I'm game for damn near anything."

"Well, it's not a big deal, and there will be no action, but it would help."

"Talk to me man."

"I need an advance security check done on a location I plan to revisit. It's a small town in southwest Virginia. I promised this little boy I would come back through for a visit with his family. The town is nice enough, but there may be some security issues due to its close proximity to Tennessee. You know the folks there don't like me very much. It would be great if you could go there, be the advance man on this visit."

"JD, I tell you I'm bored and you want to send me to Hicksville, Virginia?"

Laughing JD pressed on. "It's not that bad man. Tracy and I were there and it was nice."

"If you were just there why are you going back?"

"I got a little attached to this boy and gave my word that I would come back to see him with Tracy and the children. It's imperative that everything is in place. Look, I know this is not what you normally do, but I figure it will keep you out of trouble for at least a week."

"A week? Doesn't Calvin normally do this kind of stuff?"

"Yes, but he is wrapping up the Munford case and can't get away. B, look, normally I wouldn't ask you to do something like this, but I'm planning on taking my children with me. I need to know they will be safe."

"Alright man, but you're going to pay for this big time. I'm talking transportation, hotel, meals, and if there are any decent women around, you're paying for them too."

"You know I can't pay for any woman, man. I'm a politician."

"I'll put it down as food for my soul. What's the name of this God forsaken place?"

"Nickelsville, Virginia." JD gave Brian all the pertinent information for the assignment. He was certain once Brian hit the town; there was no way he would not run into Caitlyn or Elliott. Looking up he said a silent prayer, asking the Lord to forgive his little indiscretion, but he had his friend's best interest at heart.

Tracy was standing in the doorway of her husbands' office waiting for him to complete his call. "So, you're sending Brian to Nickelsville?"

JD turned to see the woman that had stolen his heart five years ago and she still looked like the nineteen-year-old college freshmen he'd met back then.

Shrugging his shoulders he looked a little perplexed, "I'm not sure what the outcome is going to be."

Walking over to where he sat behind his desk, Tracy slid easily into his lap and wrapped her arms around his neck to console him. "One or two things will happen. Brian will understand and be thankful you sent him in that direction or," she hesitated, "he will beat you to a pulp for sending him there."

"Thanks a lot," they both smiled at each other.

"It will work itself out. You two are brothers in your hearts. The question is where Caitlyn Montgomery stands in all of this."

Shaking his head JD thought back to the time during college when Brian had fallen in love with Caitlyn. "When we were in college I thought Brian was going to marry Caitlyn, but then she disappeared. Since then, Brian hasn't let any woman get close to him."

"Maybe their coming together will bring closure for both of them."

"Maybe," JD replied as he pulled his wife closer wondering if he had done the right thing.

Brian cursed when he hung up the telephone after arranging for the trip. First, there was no hotel in the town JD was sending him too, just Margie's Bed and Breakfast. Then there was no major airport near the place, which meant he would have to drive the six hours, 350 miles, trip to Nickelsville. If he wasn't bored senseless he would have called JD back and told him a thing or two. But the more he thought about it, the more he warmed to the idea. When he was in school at the University of Virginia in Charlottesville, college mates always talked about how relaxing the Blue Ridge Mountain area was. The memory of UVA never came without a thought of Caitlyn. Now, like always, he wondered why she disappeared or where she might be. One night when he was in the hospital, he thought he heard her voice, smelled her scent, felt her gentle touch. The next day when he awakened, there were no signs of her. Shaking the thought from his mind, he grabbed his keys. "What the hell. A drive in the country could do me some good." Brian locked up his office. At six the next morning he began a journey meant only for him.

Robert Canter stood looking out the window onto the meadow. This was his new sanctuary. All his trophies were buried here. Well the trophies he'd collected since leaving Roanoke. That was a close call, but, he changed his demographics, his method of operation and his target audience. Hell, the way he saw it, he was helping to reduce the number of people on the public welfare system. Most of the parents in his targeted areas had more mouths than they could feed anyway—he knew his mother did. This was his way of helping the system that could not help him. The manner in which it came about was different, but hell the result was the same. Now, in addition to satisfying his special desires, he was well compensated for his actions. The cartel curtailed his actions to some extent, but hell he didn't mind waiting until they were through with the targets—until now. The ass they were working with was an amateur and afraid of his own shadow. Finding a way to eliminate him without pissing off the cartel would help his life flow a lot smoother.

The place was so serene, with a river as a backdrop, trees hanging low shading the area surrounding the cabin and a porch that seemed to wrap around the house nestled in a remote area of southwest Virginia. The two-story cabin could only be seen once you were literally in front of it. Ironically, the decision to end a young boy's life was being contemplated in that idyllic setting. The area surrounding the cabin looked peaceful, but the residents of the house were anything but at ease.

"One bad apple can and will spoil the whole batch if it is not removed." Robert Canter stated as frankly as he could without losing his temper. "The boy is a fighter and he is getting out of hand. When one begins to fight back, the others will follow. Of the five, his will is strongest. It is conceivable escape could be on his mind even now after ten years."

"They don't last as long as they used too. It seems the innocence fades quicker now." The amateur sighed with regret as he thought. "Our profits dropped last year. I don't know if it's the economy or if our clients are finding other forms of entertainment. Either way, it has to change. Do we have any prospects for replacement?"

"I have one or two in my sights."

"Two from this area would be dangerous." The man shook his head. "We don't want to cause suspicions. Stick with one. Let your people know that we have an addition to the main auction and prepare to ship him out."

"You don't want me to take care of them? Dead men tell no tales."

The man standing at the window looking at the boat dock in the back, turned to ensure his orders were understood. "No bodies," he stated adamantly. "According to your boss, that's the reason you had to move here and deal with me now," the amateur argued. The last thing we need is for JD Harrison to come to this area searching like he did in Roanoke." To ease the harsh tone of his order, he added, "Think of the commission you will get from the sale. Start the bids at $50,000. Make it interesting."

Canter watched as his boss boarded his boat to leave. His boss just did not understand. Money wasn't always a motivator.

Chapter 1

The trip to Nickelsville was less eventful than Brian had anticipated and his mood, once he arrived, was a direct indication of just how dreadful it had been. The countryside traveling up interstate 64 through Charlottesville and Roanoke was breathtaking. The Blue Ridge Mountains seemed to line the passageway forever. A city boy could only take so much of mountain scenery, nice or not. About four hours into the trip and listening to the same CD over and over because the alternative radio station was not an option, Brian prayed for something to break the monotony. Be careful what you ask for. About five hours into the six-hour drive, a herd of cows was being moved from one side of the pasture, across the road to another, as the owner explained in his slow drawl voice, "It should only be another thirty minutes or so."

"Is there another road I can take into Nickelsville?" Brian asked, trying to be pleasant.

"No need for another road. This one here is just fine." The owner of the herd replied in the same slow motion the cows were moving in and an accent Brian wasn't sure was from this country.

If he weren't in so much pain, Brian would have laughed at the response. But his back felt as if it was on fire from the long drive. All he wanted to do was stand and stretch his legs. Besides, arguing with the man would only extend the delay. To give his back a little release, Brian walked around the vehicle awhile, then eased back into the car to wait, and he waited, and he waited a while longer. It took the owner and several farm hands just about an hour to get the cattle across the road. His sigh of relief must have been heard outside the vehicle for the farmer turned and tilted his hat to him. Brian waved bye to the man and pulled away. Looking back, there were no cars behind him. "Huh, what's up with that?" he thought to himself.

Driving into town, if that's the name you would give an eight block city radius, with one stop sign and no traffic lights, there was a gas station with two pumps, and a mechanic shop where a few men with jeans and straw hats stood talking and drinking beer. They looked at the strange vehicle, nodded their heads acknowledging his presence, and continued on with their conversation. Brian turned right as the voice from the GPS system instructed. There was a Post Office, at least that's what the sign said, but it did not look like any post office Brian had ever seen. Next to that was Becker's General store with the old fashioned Coke bottle sign on the front. Brian had to smile at that. The only other time he had seen the old Coke bottle was in a picture of his Big Mom. Looking around as he drove slowly through the town, there were two men sitting in rockers on the front stoop of a store-front playing checkers. Across the street was the sign he was looking for, Margie's Bed and Breakfast. Relief surged through his body. His back was still screaming and if that wasn't bad enough, it was the beginning of June with the temperature in the high nineties. To make matters worse, it seemed the air conditioner in the rental vehicle was playing games with him.

Parking the black SUV in front of the building, Brian stepped out of the vehicle and stretched his six three frame. He looked around and noticed people stepping out onto the front porch of the few buildings that were around waving at him. He turned in the other direction looking down the street, all four blocks and noticed a few people looking out of the windows waving. He smiled and waved back thinking, small town USA where everybody knows your name. He turned and took the three steps leading to the porch of the place he was supposed to be. There was a sign on the door stating;

I had to run out for a minute. I will return real soon. Go on inside and have a cold glass of lemonade and some brownies.
Margie.

Brian frowned. What kind of person would leave the door to their business open to strangers? He followed the porch that wrapped around the building, and was surprised to see tables and chairs, some rockers on a deck overlooking a lake on the back. Walking further around, he came back to the front and surveyed the area and nodded at some folks walking by. Reading the note again, he tested the door and sure enough, it opened to the ringing of a bell signifying someone had entered. He shook his head, then stepped inside. First, he smiled, then he broke out into a full fledged grin. It seemed like he had stepped inside a 1960's Andy Griffin television show. There was a reception desk directly in front that seemed to be in the center of a curving staircase leading to what he assumed was the second level of the building. Looking straight back through the establishment, he could see the deck and the lake out back. It was a beautiful view. He stepped into the archway on the right. The room was set up like a restaurant with about twenty chairs and tables covered with red and white checkered table-cloth. The chairs were draped with white chair covers with bows on the back. Red and white checkered curtains rustled gently in the breeze coming through the screened windows. Near the front of the opening, on the left, was an honest-to-goodness old time juke box with round 45" rpm records inside. Brian wondered what type of music was in there. He turned back towards the entrance. On the counter was a book register open to today's date. On the desk, behind the counter, was a flat computer monitor, a very nice executive chair, a radio to the right of the monitor and an empty pet basket on the floor.

Brian took a step towards the restaurant and called out, "Anyone here?" he waited a few moments, but there was no answer. Stepping back into what he assumed to be the foyer he walked over to the room across the hallway and there were sofas and recliners positioned for socializing in a room large enough to host a medium sized function. A fireplace sat in the middle of the room separating the room into two small areas. Beside the fire place, he noticed a small table with a plate of brownies covered with saran wrap and a envelope sitting up. He walked over. The envelope had his name on it. Opening it, he read the note: *Have a glass of lemonade and some brownies. I'll return real soon.* Smiling at the simplicity and trusting ways of the owner he decided, why not. Taking a cup, he opened the refrigerator that sat next to the table, filled it with lemonade, took several of the brownies, and then took a seat near the window in one of the recliners while he enjoyed the refreshments. Checking his watch it was a little after noon. He put his feet up and waited.

At some point Brian must have dozed off. When he opened his eyes, he looked across the hallway. Several people were in the back of the restaurant wiping down tables and setting up chairs. The cook most certainly was somewhere nearby for the fragrances of home fried potatoes, greens and ham were definitely in the air. Looking at his watch it was a little after one. He stood and stretched then flinched at the discomfort in his back. Apparently, the trip had worn him out more than he thought. He never slept during the day.

"Well hello there. Man, when Lil Joe told me a big black man just walked into my place, he sure wasn't lying, you're a mighty big fellow. Why I told him the only big black man I knew was that Mr. Harrison fellow that came through a little bit ago. He was a mighty nice fellow. Lil Joe told me you work for the Attorney General. Do you know him well? Now, don't think I'm prejudice or anything like that, thinking every black man knows every other black man. I know that's a little over the top, but you two do look a little alike. Come to think of it you look a lot like little Elliot too. Oh, look at me carrying on and on. I haven't even introduced myself. I'm Margie, Margie Nickels. I own this place." She extended her hand.

Shell shocked, Brian hesitated. Never in his life had he heard anyone talk that fast with the weirdest accent and the friendliest smile. Taking her small hand in his, "Brian Thompson," he replied.

"Well now, Mr. Thompson, welcome to Nickelsville. I had Lil Joe take your bags from your SUV and carry them on upstairs to the best room I have. It has a nice view of the town from the front and on the back side, you can see the mountains. In the winter time, they are just beautiful with the snow and everything on top. Of course, you are not going to see that any time soon. We just came through the cold weather and now we are all just ready for the warm temperature to settle in. Now come on with me and let me get you settled in your room. It seemed like you were a wee bit tired so I didn't want to wake you." She turned from the doorway and began to walk towards the foyer to the stairs. "You know I had to get Lil Joe to move the king size bed out of Momma's old room to put in the front room for you. There was no way in the world you would have fit in that double bed." She was halfway up the stairs before she realized the man was still at the bottom looking up at her. "Is something wrong Mr. Thompson?"

All Brian could do was look at the petite blonde woman whose mouth was going about a mile a minute. In his mind, he was thinking every time a black man followed a pretty white woman up a flight of stairs in this part of the country they were hung, shot or their body parts were never found. Of course that was only in the movies, but still. Just then, the door opened and a man with long blonde hair and piercing blue eyes, dressed in an officer uniform walked through, taking off his hat as he entered the establishment. Brian estimated the man to be about six-three, a formidable build and around his late thirties or early forties. *Here we go*, Brian thought. "Good afternoon, Mr. Thompson. Welcome to Nickelsville." The man extended his hand and smiled. "I'm Sheriff Joseph Wade. Around these parts they call me Lil Joe. You drove all the way from Richmond and seemed a little tired so I didn't wake you when I was here before. I took your keys and moved your bags in upstairs. I took the liberty of locking your firearm inside the vehicle. We don't have a problem with having guns around here. We just like to keep them locked away from the young'uns, you know." The man smiled, but Brian did not say anything. The Sheriff looked up at Margie, then back to Brian. "Well, I thought I would stop back in now to say hello."

"Nice to meet you Sheriff," Brian replied still a little shocked by the reception he was receiving from these strangers.

Waving her hand, "Oh, you don't have to call him Sheriff, just call him Lil Joe." Margie stated as she resumed her steps. "Come on up now let me get you settled in. Lil Joe go on into the kitchen and tell Suzie Mae to fix you a little lunch and I'll be right back now. Mr. Thompson, now you come on with me."

Brian looked hesitantly towards Sheriff Wade and nodded. "Sheriff."

"Mr. Thompson. Lil Joe will be just fine. We're a little informal around these parts. You have a good afternoon."

When he reached the first landing, Brian turned and looked down at the sheriff, who was still standing near the door looking curiously up at him. The staircase split, allowing him to go down steps which led into the room he'd fallen asleep in or continue up the steps. Following Margie's voice, he followed the steps going up trying to catch every other word the woman was saying, because there was no way in hell he could catch all of them. As he came to the second level of the building, the hallway was wide with double doors at the end of each. Directly in front of him was a wall lined with pictures of old white men some in confederate uniforms. Raising a brow, the thought that he should have his firearm crossed Brian's mind, just in case any of them stepped out of the pictures. Turning to the left, he followed the direction Margie had walked and met her at another set of double doors. Taking in his surroundings, he looked down the hallway. There were two double doors on one side, across the hall from his room there was a double doorway and further down the hallway on the other side of the stairs there was another room, making a total of six rooms. At least he assumed they were all rooms.

Opening both doors, Margie stepped aside to let him in. "I'll put you here. This room is a little smaller than the one I put Mr. Harrison and his pretty little wife in when they were here. But I thought they would enjoy the romantic room at the end of the hall. They seem like such a nice couple, mighty nice people, I tell you, they certainly were." She stepped inside the room showing him around. "Now, the bathroom is right in here." She pushed a door open. "It has a shower and a nice claw tub in there. My friend Cat says that is the rage right now for city folks like yourself. This here is your walk-in closet, oh, and this is your entertainment station." She picked up a remote control and pushed a button and the wall next to the door he was standing near, slid sideways to reveal a flat, wall mount television with a DVD player and a mini bar area. "Unfortunately, we don't get a lot of cable stations around here, but we have a good variety of movies you can look at. Now over here," she walked to the other side of the room, "is just in case you might want to take your meals in your room. Just let Suzie Mae know when she comes through to do your room and she will have it sent right up to you. But you may want to eat out on the deck, it is just beautiful out there at night when the sun is setting. Well, here let me give you this. This is the key to your room, there's only one other, and Lil Joe keeps it locked away. Right now, you are our only guest, so you have the run of the place. Now, I'll be right down stairs if you need anything." She walked over to the door, "We do dinner around four o'clock and you are more than welcome to join us downstairs. Suzie Mae is a wonderful cook, but you're welcome to go over to Jumbo's to have your meals if you like. Just tell him you're staying with us and your meals will be on the house. Now, is there anything else you think you might need?"

The woman had said so much in a short span of time that it took Brian a moment to realize she had asked him a question and was waiting for his response. "Um, no, I'm good."

"All right then, I'll see you once you get settled. If you need anything just come on down-stairs."

Standing in the middle of the floor shell-shocked from the welcoming, all he could do was shake his head. "You ain't in Richmond anymore." He chuckled. Looking around, the room wasn't bad, not at all. It was a good size room, about the size of a large suite at your better known hotels. The entertainment area was actually state-of-the-art.

The decor was elegant country, that's about the only way Brian could explain, the white linen bed coverings with black and red cord trimmings, matching window curtains and pure white carpet. White, not cream, not egg-shell, it was white. Brian immediately sat on the bed and took off his shoes.

Memories of his Big Mom, that was what he called his great-grand mother and the woman that had raised him, telling him to take off his shoes when he walking in the living room, came to him. The carpet in the living room of the small two-bedroom bungalow house was egg-shell. Shoes leave imprints and dirt. He jumped up off the bed, he'd forgotten he had on jeans. Jeans can leave a stain on the white bedspread. At least that's what Big Mom would say. The thought brought a smile to his face. His Big Mom worked two jobs to make sure his dream was obtainable. Losing his mother at the hands of a drug dealer she was testifying against, had made him want to become an FBI agent. His mother had agreed to testify against her main supplier. It broke his Big Mom's heart when her only child turned to drugs. When she'd tried to change her ways by agreeing to testify, she lost her life. She was in protective custody when the FBI agent left her alone at the safe house for what-ever reason. When he returned his mother's throat had been cut. It was that single event in Brian's life that had him determined to protect anyone that was trying to do the right things in their life. He made two promises to his Big Mom. One, he would never do drugs. That's one of the reasons taking even prescription drugs bothered him. Two, he would do a better job of protecting people than the FBI agent had.

Putting his shoes in the corner near the window, Brian pulled the curtains back taking in the surroundings of Main Street Nickelsville, VA. A lopsided grin touched his face, as another memory crossed his mind. Caitlyn as she talked about the small town she was from. Then he remembered another promise he'd made. He'd promised Caitlyn he would always be there for her. Damn, the room was making him crazy, he hadn't thought about his Big Mom in years. And Caitlyn, well she was never far from his mind.

To keep his sanity, he pulled the bedspread down and neatly folded it at the end of the bed. He sat on the side and pulled out his cell phone. He had some words for JD. Pushing the button, nothing happened. He looked down at the phone. The bright red banner read, "No Service." He was supposed to have a network of people around to make sure his calls went through. Where in the hell are they? He walked over to the window, still nothing. He opened the window. Bars began to appear on his phone indicating he now had service. "Ain't this some shit," he had to laugh at the irony. Here he was, as city as a person could possibly be, in a town with a Sheriff, named Lil Joe, a hostess that had to be a relative of Mary Tyler Moore and a town that doesn't have cable or cell phone reception. Brian pulled out his brief-case to get the information on the contact person for this trip. A day should be all he needed to do a security assessment. Hell it only took five minutes to drive from the beginning of town to the end. The concern was the Tennessee border. It seemed some members of the ever growing pain in the ass Tea Party, a very volatile portion of the Republican Party, did not like the idea of a Black candidate for Governor of Virginia. If JD was planning on returning to the area, security plans had to be made. After reviewing his notes, he threw the notebook on the bed. A quick shower, change of clothes, and then he was in search of Jacob Becker, Mayor of Nickelsville, VA.

Chapter 2

The shower took longer than planned. For the first time in his life, he was tempted to take a long bath in the tub that was large enough for him and a few other people. There were four shower heads in the walk-in slated shower stall, with three different settings. After a short debate, Brian decided on the shower, but would definitely try that tub before he left. The shower was so invigorating he didn't want to get out. The power at the third level setting massaged his back, leaving it more relaxed than it had been since before the shooting. After his shower, Brian wrapped one of the big bath towels around his waist and walked into the bedroom.

"My Lord in heaven. Boy where did you get a body like that?" Suzie Mae stood in the doorway with a basket in her hand that almost fell to the floor. She had seen tall well built men in her day. But never had she seen a man with shoulders that went on forever, pecks as thick as a tree trunk and a stomach that looked like it had been carved by the same people that did Mt. Everest, chiseled like a Greek God.

Stunned, Brian reached for his shirt, feeling naked in front of the five foot black woman who had to weigh a good two hundred pounds with the biggest cheeks he had ever seen. "You don't have to cover up for my sake. Lord have mercy, let me just stand here and look at you." She did just that then exhaled, "Okay you can put your shirt on now. You made my day. Hell, you've made my year," she laughed. "Look here honey, Becky over at Jumbo's sent this welcome basket for you." She sat the huge basket on the table near the door. "Now, Becky's a sweet girl, but can't cook worth a damn. So I would stay away from the cookies and stick to the fruit. If you want some real food come on downstairs, I'll fix you right up." She looked over at him one more time and smiled. "Thank you son." She turned walking out the door, still thanking the Lord.

It took Brian a moment to gather his senses. When he did, he walked over and put the lock on the door. Finding the woman in the room took him by surprise, but her reaction was funny as hell. Stepping back into the bathroom, he looked in the full-length mirror and raised an eyebrow.

"You still got the women talking to the Lord." He smirked, and then got dressed.

Walking down the stairs Brian took a quick glance at his watch. It was two-forty-five. That should be plenty of time for him to meet with Becker, review the plans for JD's visit, then take a look around the town. With any luck, he would be on his way back to Richmond by this time tomorrow.

Margie wasn't at the desk, when he walked downstairs, so he walked around the corner into the restaurant. There were a few people sitting at tables eating and talking until he walked into the room. Everything went quiet. A thick boned young black girl dressed in too tight jeans and a too low cut tee shirt looked his way. You would have thought the sun had just reigned down upon her and graced her with a kiss, her face lit up so bright.

"You must be the man Suzie Mae is going on about. Look at you. Looking like somebody's sugar daddy, just ready to be licked up. She walked away from the table, up to him and gave him a good looking over. There was no shame in her game. Her wide grin indicated she liked what she saw. "I'm Leslie, friends call me Redbone. You can see why. How long you gonna be around?"

The girl was standing so close to him, he could see clear down her blouse and what a view it was, looking like two overstuffed pillows waiting for his head to lay between. Normally, he would enjoy the scene, but he was on a mission. Giving her a crooked grin, he ignored her question and asked one of his own. "I'm looking for Margie. Is she around?"

"My—my—my, you have a smooth voice to go along with those good looks, sounding like my Johnny Gill. Can you sing?"

The way she stretched the word smooth almost made Brian laugh. "Is Margie around?"

"No, but I can sure help you with whatever your little heart need honey," she offered as her lip parted and her tongue emerged as if ready to taste him right then and there. "I bet you taste like caramel."

Brian was used to bold women, but this one was in a league all to herself. "You have a thing for candy?"

"I sure do baby, especially with a toffee brother like yourself."

"I'll have to pass—today. Is Suzie Mae around?" He asked before this young girl got both of them in trouble.

"Suzie Mae," Redbone yelled. "Suzie Mae," the girl bellowed again, never taking her eyes off Brian. "I bet sucking you would be like tasting sweet caramel from a stick—yummy. Brian could not do anything but laugh. "Pretty white teeth too, nice thick lips. You know how to use those lips, don't you?"

Unable to resist any longer Brian replied. "I do. I also know how to use my hands to turn your little behind over my knee and spank you if you don't behave yourself."

"Ouch—spanking. I might like that," she grinned.

"Why in God's name are you calling me? And get your frisky behind out of that grown man's face." Suzie Mae snapped Redbone with the hand towel when the girl walked away still looking over her shoulder at Brian. "Don't mind my granddaughter. I'll try to keep her away from you. Now, what can I do for you, standing there like a lollipop ready to be licked?"

That was it, the last straw, Brian had to laugh. "Does this speaking your mind thing run in your family?"

"We ain't ashamed of letting a man know we like what we see. If that's what you mean," Suzie Mae shrugged her shoulder and laughed.

Brian nodded still smiling, "That's what I mean. Suzie Mae do you know where I can find Jacob Becker?"

She pointed out the window, "Right over yonder in the courthouse."

Brian looked out the window, he didn't see anything that resembled a courthouse. There was a row of store fronts, one was marked Becker's General Store, next to it was what he thought was a furniture store, and a barber shop. "Which building?" he asked sure he was missing something.

"The one right there between the grocery store and the barber shop."

Brian frowned. "Where the furniture is in the window?"

"That's it, son. But that's not a furniture store, that's the post office in front and then you walk to the back. That's where the court-room is. What you want is the City Manager's office. Well that's going to be right up stairs in the back. See when you go in, walk through the post office, past the courtroom, and take the steps on the left. That will lead you right into Judge Becker's office. His secretary, Cat, will be there. Real quiet girl, she's his daughter-in-law. I'd never know why such a sweet girl married in that family but I guess everybody needs love."

"Okay," Brian cut the woman off. The last thing he needed or wanted was a history of every person in the little town. "Through the post office, past the court room, stairs to the left will get me to Jacob Becker."

"That's right son." She smiled, "You got it."

"Thank you Suzie Mae," he said and walked towards the door.

"Well, where you going son?" she asked with a confused look.

Brian returned the look, but hoped he was able to restrain his frustration. "I'm going to see Jacob Becker."

"Oh he ain't there. They close down at three every day. You won't talk to them until nine tomorrow morning."

It took every ounce of his will to keep from losing his cool. He inhaled and stepped back inside the door. "Nine o'clock tomorrow morning?"

"That's when they open back up." She turned to walk away, as if she expected him to follow. "Come on over here and let me fix you a plate of food."

Flabbergasted, Brian stared at the retreating woman. Who in the hell closes down an office at three o'clock in the day, he wondered. He walked back into the restaurant.

"You ain't in Richmond no more," a man at the one table said as he smiled up at him from his plate. "This ain't the big city young fellow. Everything around here run at it's own pace. Come on over here and sit with me while you eat your dinner."

Brian couldn't believe what was happening. What kind of business close at three o'clock in the day? And who in the hell eats dinner this early? He wondered. One thing he could say, the people were friendly. So what the hell, he'll have dinner with the old man. He took a seat in the chair across from the man.

"Lil Joe said you one of those big city FBI agents. Is that true?" The man spoke with a slow drawl that was different from Margie's faster dialect.

Hell, did the Sheriff do a full background check on him, Brian wondered. "Yes sir, I was."

"Said you got shot a few weeks back. Is that true?" Brian raised an eyebrow that answered that question. Man, people around here sure are nosey, he thought. As if the man had read his mind he said, "Hell, we ain't got nothing else around here to do but get into each other's business," he laughed. "Ain't that right Clem?" he yelled across the room.

"That's right Bart." Brian turned to see another older man sitting at a table across from him.

"That's Clem over yonder. He's an old coot. I'm his younger brother Bart. I'm an old coot too, but I'm nicer."

Brian laughed at the two old men that looked as big as lumberjacks, with long dirty blonde hair that reached their shoulders, piercing blue eyes and identical frowns. It was very clear they were related. "If you are brothers why aren't you eating dinner together?"

"Huh, I ain't sitting at no table with a man that shot me in the ass with a buck shot. Brother or no." Clem mumbled.

"Should have got your slow ass out the way," Bart replied as he continued to eat his food.

Brian was laughing when Margie walked up from behind him. "I see you met Clem and Bart. Don't you let them get you in a brawl, or Lil Joe will have you in a cell right along with them." She had a jar in her hand. "Listen," she patted Brian on the shoulder, "Marybeth over at Dr. Becker's' heard about you being shot and all so she sent you this cream. I'll tell you there ain't nothing like it. You rub it on your back, or you may want to get some-one to rub it on there for you since you can't reach it and all. And I swear on my mommy's grave, bless her heart, that stiffness and pain you got in your back will go away in no time. People around here get shot all the time and they swear by it." She picked the jar up, "Now, I'm going to put this up in your room and this evening around six o'clock I'm gonna send Suzie Mae up to put this on your back. Then Marybeth said for you to rest for about an hour or two. Then take a shower and wash it off real good. Get in the bed around eight o'clock, get you a good night's rest and you will be good as new come morning. You enjoy your dinner now." Just like that, the woman was gone.

"That went a little too fast for you son?" Clem asked in a slow drawl identical to his brother's.

Brian could not get pass the point where everybody in town seemed to know who he is and what he need. "I think I got it."

"I swear by it. Used it when that fart sitting at the table with you shot me in the ass."

"That was over a year ago Clem." Bart replied, "Just shut-up and let it go." He looked at Brian as Suzie Mae put his food on the table. "Now tell me some of your FBI stories."

An hour later, Brian and the folks from the restaurant had retired to the room across the hall. They all sat around captivated as they listened to Brian talk about his time with the agency. Just like that, Brian was now one of their own.

Chapter 3

People often asked her why she had two names. Caitlyn Montgomery-Becker would smile and say, I wanted to stay connected to my family. The truth was her marriage was a sham. Her husband Dr. Colin A Becker treated her and her son well, was very generous and one of her best friends. There was nothing she wouldn't do for him, or he wouldn't do for her. But their marriage was the result of two old-school parents, whose children had disappointed them. Their parents' professions would not withstand the scandal if the truth of their children's behavior was ever known. Therefore, the marriage was arranged to cover indiscretions.

Caitlyn Cheyenne Montgomery was born to a family with a proud heritage and her father, the honorable Fredrick Theodore Montgomery never let her forget it. Nor did he ever allow her to forget what her role in this family was; to fortify the family's status—by any means necessary. Not wealth, for the family had more money than the government, just status. But because she was not born a boy, she was constantly reminded of her personal debt to him and tried all she could to make up for the misfortune. She understood the importance of carrying on the family's name. In homage to her father, Caitlyn did everything in her power to appease him in all areas of her life. Since she had the misfortune of being a girl, she had to be the prettiest, daintiest, and, of course had to behave with the utmost propriety in all things. It goes without saying that her intelligence and confidence had to be that of a man, for you see according to her father, man was meant to lead; after, all he was made in the image of GOD.

The beauty and grace part was easy. Her mother, Beverly Montgomery was a descendent of Native American Indians. The olive-toned skin coloring, straight, black, waist-length hair and the tall, slim, bone structure came naturally. Caitlyn's skin tone was not as her father would have liked, it took on more of his dark coloring, making her a rich cinnamon brown. But she did have one feature that made her unmistakably a Montgomery; the very, light brown eyes. On some of her relatives, Caitlyn thought the eye coloring made them look like voodoo queens and as a child, some of her father's relatives had frightened her. However, on Caitlyn with her skin coloring, the high cheek-bones, slanted eyes and long lashes, the eye color was alluring. Her looks were what caused most of the problems in her life. She'd learned long ago to accept it and move on.

Walking into the house, Caitlyn considered her existence reasonable for an only daughter that had disappointed her parents so much, that they did not want to have anything further to do with her. The home, her father placed her in was considered one of the best in the small town of eight-hundred and two. There were two wings to the house. She and Colin had adjoining bedrooms that were located on the east wing and her father-in-law, Judge Jacob Becker's room, was in the west wing.

Her routine was simple. She was up at seven each morning, went to work at nine, came home at three, and went to bed at nine. Then the next day would start over. The times in between three and nine brought her the most joy and kept her smiling each day. At three-thirty each day, the school bus would pull up in front of the house and drop off Elliott Brian Montgomery-Becker in front of the house and she would be there to greet him. Their daily snack was the same, creamy peanut butter, grape jelly and a glass of milk. She would spend a portion of the afternoon doing homework and then his choice of activity. Right now, he was into fishing, but some afternoons they would do her favorite pastime—riding her beautiful bay pony from Chincoteague Island, Queen, that she loved. Six was family dinner time. Seven-thirty was bedtime story time for Elliot then lights out at eight. Those were the moments of her days that made her life worth living.

They had a good life, one of the largest properties on the outskirts of town, thoroughbred horses, cattle, farm hands to handle them, and a lake at the end of the property filled with fish. Everyone in town envied her happy life. What no one knew, with the exception of Colin, was that the idea of living a happy life had ended with her sophomore year in college.

Normally, before coming home, Cat, as her friends called her, would stop by to see her close friend Margie Nickels, but today, she felt restless and couldn't quite put her finger on why. When she walked through the front door, her husband, Colin, was coming down the stairs.

"How was work today?" He asked with his sweet southern drawl that made him appear to be more sophisticated then he really was.

Colin looked just like a young Rick Fox, the ex-NBA player, with striking good looks. His skin was barely brown, in fact he could pass for a white man with a tan at times, light brown eyes, a style unmatched by anyone within a hundred miles and a women-grabbing smile. Only Colin's choice was not the opposite sex. The day before they married Colin told her of his preference and at the time, it was music to her ears. The thought of having to fulfill certain marital duties with a man she did not love frightened Caitlyn. His confession eased her concerns. To keep up appearances and both their family's good names intact, he agreed to marry her. Out of respect, he did not date anyone in the area and never stayed out at night. The people in Nickelsville were just like the people from her hometown, warm and welcoming, but narrow-minded when it came to certain things.

Colin's father, Judge Becker knew of his extra-curricular activities, but didn't deal with them and ensured Colin's discretion by holding his inheritance of the town and just about everything in it, over his head. Close to two hundred and twenty million dollars in income and land valued four times that, would be an incentive for just about anyone to stay in line. As for her, Colin never showed her anything but respect. They would talk from time to time about her happiness, but she always assured him she was content and that was enough.

"Not much action going on," Caitlyn replied to his question. "Becky Joe hit Tully with a frying pan and he wants your father to charge her with attempted murder."

Laughter erupted from Colin as he stood in front of her. "How many times has he made her black and blue? Now the tables have turned. The people in this town never fail to amaze me."

She returned the easy smile. "You're going out?"

"I'm going to stop by and check on Mable. Just to make sure she is taking her high blood pressure medicine, as she should. I'll be back in time for dinner."

"Give Mable my love," she said as Colin walked towards the door.

"I will. Did you stop by Margie's today?"

"No," Caitlyn replied as she placed her purse on the table near the door. "I came straight home. I think I'll take Elliott to town for ice cream later."

A concerned frown formed on his face. "Is everything alright with you?" He asked taking a step back inside the door. "You seem a little troubled."

Caitlyn turned to him. "I'm fine." She jokingly pushed him out the door onto the porch. "I'm just a little restless today, that's all."

Colin worried about Caitlyn. He was able to live at least a portion of his life the way he wanted, but Caitlyn didn't have that option. Her life centered around Elliott and nothing else. He often wondered whatever happened to Elliott's father. From what Caitlyn told him, the man was a senior in college with a bright future ahead of him. She did not want to interfere in his chance to be successful, therefore, she never told him about his child. Often Colin wondered if the man loved Caitlyn as much as she apparently loved him. It was a shame that a beautiful caring woman like Caitlyn would spend her life in a loveless marriage. She was too good of a person not to have love in her life. There were times he wished he could love her the way she deserved, but it was just not in the cards for him. So he did all he could to make her life as comfortable and carefree as he could.

"How would you like to take Elliott to Washington for a short trip? We could make it educational, visit the White House, The Capitol, the museums, and maybe even catch a baseball game or two."

She smiled at him, "I'm sure Elliott would love that."

Pleased, he was able to make her smile, he kissed her cheek. "I'll look into planning it for when school ends."

"That would be nice. Thank you Colin."

"I'll do anything in the world for you and Elliott, Cat."

The smile reached her eyes, "I know."

He looked up the road and pointed. "There's the bus." He walked down the steps to his car. "I'll see you later."

Caitlyn turned towards the bus, which had stopped in front of the house. A blast of energy, going by the name of Elliott Montgomery-Becker burst around the front of the bus. Caitlyn waved at the driver, then stretched her arms out and gathered her son up into a loving hug. "Hello my Elliott. How was your day?"

"Hi Mommy," He giggled as she swung him around.

"It's so good to have you home." She put him back on the ground. "Let me look at you." She stepped back and looked the smiling child up and down. Shaking her head, she held out her hand, "I think it's time to measure you again."

The boy took her hand and eagerly followed her up the steps to the front porch. "Do you think I've reached five feet yet?"

"I don't know. Five feet is very tall for an eight year old. But we will check right after your snack and we'll see. How's that?"

"Ok," the child replied a little dejected.

Caitlyn stopped and looked down at her son with his head hung down. "Elliott, a man is never ashamed of who he is. A man always carries his head high, even a little man like you." She got down on her knees and held her son in front of her at arm's length. "You are who you are. Your job is to be the best Elliott you can whether you are three feet tall or seven feet tall."

Elliott's eyes grew as big and round as a saucer. "Wow! Do you think I could do that Mommy? Can I be seven feet tall?"

Caitlyn stood and continued walking through the foyer towards the kitchen. "I don't know about seven feet, but you will definitely reach six feet one day." She pushed open the double swing doors leading into the kitchen with Elliott in tow.

Elliott climbed onto the bar stool at the island in the kitchen and watched as his mother prepared his afternoon snack. "Mommy is my daddy tall?" He asked with his elbows propped on the counter top and chin resting in his hands.

Caitlyn turned to him, so startled by the question the jar of smooth peanut butter almost slipped from her hand. She placed the jar on the counter, then reached into the refrigerator for the grape jelly and bread. Pulling a butter knife from the drawer, she exhaled slightly as she made the sandwich. "Colin is six feet one. So yes, I would say that is tall."

"Not my father Colin, Mommy," the boy replied as he bit into his sandwich. "My real daddy—is he tall?"

Caitlyn looked into the inquisitive eyes of her son and saw his father's eyes staring at her, waiting. They had not talked about his real father since the day she told him who his father was. The funny thing was, his father had been heavy on her mind today that's why Elliott's question rattled her. They were both thinking of Brian. The last time she'd had that intense feeling of doom was the night he had been shot. The next day she read about the shooting on the internet. She knew he'd been released from the hospital a few weeks ago. Could he have had a relapse? As soon as she got a free moment, she would check the internet for any news. For now, she had to deal with her son. "Elliott, do you remember that was our secret? No one else can know."

Elliott nodded his head up and down as he drank his milk. "I remember Mommy. I didn't tell anyone. But is he?"

Caitlyn smiled as she thought about Brian. *She was in the library studying for her first college exam. Being a loner was not new to her, as she had grown up an only child to parents that had a very active social life. From a very early age she was left home alone while her parents attended one social function after another. Other than her roommate, Shania, she really did not know anyone one on campus at the University of Virginia. Besides the few people she'd met tended to tease her because she did not know the latest fashion, music or movies. It seem only one or two people had ever heard of where she was from and laughed when she tried to explain. So hanging out in an isolated area of the student center the night the first step show of the semester was not a problem for her. Besides, it gave her a good view of the show without being in the crowd. One thing she* looked forward to when she came to college was pledging to a sorority. However, it didn't seem like it was going to be easy since she wasn't too popular on campus. But that did not dampen her excitement about pledging. She was keeping her options open. The DELTA's with their red and white, the ZETA's, in their blue and white and of course the AKA's with their pink and green were all stepping tonight. Her decision wouldn't be based on their performance. It will be based on the community service each of the organizations provide. However, this would be the first time she ever witnessed an actual step show. Afterwards, she'll settle in and study for her exam. Excitement was beginning to build up within her as the show began. The KAPPA's were first up. She may not know the latest dance steps, but the synchronized moves sure did look good and she began clapping as each team performed.

"Why don't you go downstairs with them?" the man asked startling her. "I'm sorry," he laughed. "Looks like you are enjoying the show." Caitlyn looked over her left shoulder and then she realized she had to look up. When she did she almost wished she hadn't. The man had to be almost as tall as the cubical dividers in the room and shoulders just as wide, at least that's what he looked like to her. He had on a black tee shirt that stretched across his chest and circled his biceps like a halo. All of that was great, but his eyes were strikingly sensual. They were brown, big and twinkling. She just stared at him for what seemed like a few hours, but was actually only a minute, and then she recognized who he was. The smile threw her off. It was the guy from the disciplinary hearing with Jerry McClintock, the one that never smiled, he just always stared at her when he thought she wasn't looking. The look always made her stomach feel like butterflies had taken up residency there. Little did she know that man was going to become her best friend and later her lover.

Even now, she would not change one moment of the time they spent together.

"Was he Mommy?" Elliott's voice full of food penetrated her thoughts. "Yes Elliott. Your father is very tall. He is six feet two inches tall, to be exact."

"Wow! Will I be that tall Mommy?"

Caitlyn shrugged her shoulders, "I don't know. You have to eat all your vegetables to get to be as tall as your daddy."

Elliott looked down at the saucer holding his snack and frowned. "I don't have any vegetables, Mommy."

"This is a snack. You'll have some at dinner."

"Can I have some now? I want to start getting tall right away."

Caitlyn smiled at her son. "I think vegetables at dinner will be soon enough. You know what else helps a little boy grow tall?"

"What?" the boy replied eagerly.

"Ms. Margie's home-made ice cream." She nodded her head at the boy's shocked expression. "That's right. I've been told by a number of people that not only does it make little boys grow tall and strong, it can also put hair on his chest."

"Is that why Grandfather Jacob has hair on his chest?"

Caitlyn laughed, "How would you know Grandfather Jacob has hair on his chest?"

"He showed me one day."

A startled Caitlyn stared at her son for a moment, then dismissed the comment. "Well, Grandfather Jacob does eat a lot of Ms. Margie's ice cream." She put her elbows on the counter top with her face resting in her hands in front of her son. "You know, I think we should go to Ms. Margie's after dinner and get some of her ice cream. What do you think?"

The child's smile spread from ear to ear. "Yeah."

Caitlyn stood. "Well, the sooner you do your homework and I cook dinner, the sooner we can go to Margie's."

Elliott gulped down his milk and ran from the kitchen to do as his mother asked.

Marybeth, Colin's assistant, was sitting at her desk near the window staring at the window across the street. The FBI man who was sitting at the table talking to Bart sure did look familiar, but she just could not put a finger on why. Hell, she knew he hadn't been here before. The whole town would have known if an FBI man had come, just like now. She sighed again at the puzzle, just as Colin walked in.

"Good afternoon, Marybeth. Anything happening I should be concerned about?" He walked to the back, took off his suit jacket and replaced it with his white coat, then walked back to his office. He had taken a seat and was looking at a file when he realized Marybeth had not responded to his entrance. Normally, she would be running down everyone's business to him by now. He stepped back into the front part of the office and noticed she was still in the same position from when he entered. He walked over to the window and looked out over her shoulders. "What are we looking at?"

Marybeth sighed, "The FBI man."

Colin looked down at her, then out the window again. "What FBI man?"

"The one over at Margie's talking to Bart."

Colin looked towards Margie's' place and noticed the man sitting in the booth. "Is there something wrong with him?"

Marybeth looked up excitedly, "Well, you know I'm not one to gossip, but they say he was shot five times in the back a few months ago. And it's been paining him something awful, so I sent some salve over by Margie for his back. You know to ease the pain. According to Lil Joe, he doesn't like taking his pain pills. Anyway, it's something about him that so familiar, but I just can't put my finger on it."

"Well, you always did say that all of us look alike," Colin stated as he walked back to his office.

Marybeth blushed and thought about how badly she used to talk about Black people. "Now, Colin, I thought we had put all of that behind us. That was my thinking before I got to know you. And now, I can tell you apart from the others."

Colin looked up and frowned. He knew she had come a long way from thinking every Black person in the world was bad. But, she still had a ways to go and he just could not help himself. "What others Marybeth?"

"Well, I know you apart from Suzie Mae's people. And I know you don't look nothing like the FBI man. Why, you have some good blood in you too. That's where you get your goodness from. That FBI man is black through and through. You can look at him and see that."

Colin didn't know if he should laugh or yell at the silly woman. Yes, he had a mixed family, but his mother and father were black. His mother's skin coloring was just so close to white, people often wondered. But that was his father's doing. His father did not marry for love; he married to improve the color of his family. To Colin, he was trying hard to erase the history of his ancestors falling in love with and marrying a black woman. "So, since he is black through and through, he's not a good person?"

"No, now I didn't say that Colin."

"You said, I got my goodness from the white blood in me. If the FBI man doesn't have any white blood in him, where would he get any goodness from?"

"Well, it could be his mother raised him to be good, like Suzie Mae's family. Well, except for that granddaughter of hers."

"Your son seems to like that granddaughter of hers," Colin replied before thinking.

Marybeth turned beet red in the face and stormed out of the office.

Colin exhaled, then walked out to the front area. "I'm sorry Marybeth. But at some point, you have to learn to accept the fact that there are good people and bad people in this world. Their skin color has nothing to do with it. You have to accept people for who they are. Look at you. I love you because you are a very, nice person. A little on the prejudiced side, but I accept that because it is a part of who you are."

Still a little miffed by Colin's comments, she huffed. "You know my son did not have anything to do with Redbone being pregnant."

"I can only go by what the two of them said. But that's not our concern and I should not have made that statement. Would you accept my apology?"

"I reckon I could."

"Thank you," Colin replied, then walked back into his office.

"I think I'm going to take a walk over and talk to the FBI man and get to know him a little better." Marybeth called from the front.

"Before you go, get Mable on the telephone. I want to check on her sometime this evening." Colin thought to warn her that people don't like being questioned, black or white and especially FBI agents. But he thought, maybe she would learn a lesson if she asked the wrong question and the agent really got on her. He smiled at the thought and decided not to give the warning.

Chapter 4

It must have been the fresh air coming through the windows, but whatever it was, Brian was going to find a way to bottle it up and take it home with him today. He had never slept past five in the morning. Now, there were many days that he was still in bed long past noon, but that was when a female body was next to him. This morning he was so relaxed, it was like he'd had an all night love making session, releasing all pent up frustration. He sat up in bed preparing to cringe from the pain in his back, but then realized there was no pain. He twisted left and then right—no pain. An instant smile appeared on his face. He tentatively raised his arms over his head and rested his hands behind it. He had not been flexible enough to do that since the shooting. He closed his eyes relishing the thought of getting back to real work.

For the first time in a while, he felt at peace. Closing his eyes, he remembered a moment during the night when he thought he heard Caitlyn's voice. Suzie Mae was rubbing the salve from the doctor's office on his back and sending thank you's up to the lord for bringing this fine specimen of a man into the world. That was all he remembered as he dozed off to sleep. It was then that he dreamt of Caitlyn. Her sultry voice and sweet laugh was so clear, it was as if all he had to do was open his eyes, and she would be there. Shaking his head, Brian opened his eyes and cleared his mind. Thinking of Caitlyn, the sound of her voice and the gentleness of her touch, seemed to ease his soul. This time it did not bring anger, as it had in the past. Actually, there was a feeling that she needed him. Maybe it was time to try to locate her to find closure. Before, he could not bring himself to search for her after what he; experienced during his first search. But, now he felt that maybe it was time to hear her side of the story. Not sure how, but it was time to find her.

Since he'd been in town the longing for Caitlyn seemed to have intensified. Maybe a shower would help. Under the spray of the shower, happy thoughts of the first day he'd laid eyes on Caitlyn filled his mind. This time he didn't fight the memory.

As a resident assistant at the university, from time to time Brian had to participate in disciplinary hearings. This day, Caitlyn Montgomery had to testify before the disciplinary board for an incident involving none other than Jeremiah "Jerry" McClintock IV, better known as one of the future presidents of the United States, if his father, US Senator Jeremiah McClintock III representing the good old state of Texas, had anything to say about it. But first he had to find a way to help his son Jerry overcome his weakness; beautiful black girls.

The room resembled a mini courtroom, with the seats divided down the middle, a swing gate that led to an open area with two tables on both sides and a long table on a riser where the panel members would declare judgment. At the Senator's insistence, no one but the family of the parties involved in the incident would be allowed at the proceedings. In fact, at the Senator's request, all witnesses had been sequestered until they were asked to testify, which he had no plans of allowing. If he'd had his way, this farce of a hearing would not go longer than ten minutes. The advisory panel consisted of the dean of students, three professors from different departments and three students from the council. Their task was to listen to the accusations and make a recommendation to the school on any disciplinary action.

Caitlyn and her parents were seated in the chamber on one side of the room. On the other side of the room the seats were filled with Jerry's relatives, all fifty of them.

The members of the board filed out from a door at the back of the room and took their seats at the table. The members were as diverse as could be expected with one female professor, two male professors, two female students and one black male student. The man sitting in the middle, the dean of students, called the hearing to order.

"It is my understanding," he began in his nasal voice, "this was to be a closed hearing at your request Senator McClintock."

The Senator stood and smiled. "Yes sir. That is correct."

"Then who pray-tell are all these people?"

The Senator looked around with a peaked eye brow and smiled. "Well sir, this is Jeremiah's family. They are all here to support him in this matter."

"Is his mother in that crowd?"

"Why yes. My lovely wife Elizabeth is here. "He turned to the crowd." Stand up honey."

An attractive woman, dressed in a two-piece delicate pink suit with her hair neatly arranged in an up do, stood and smiled. "Good Morning your honor."

"Good morning," the dean replied. "You may stay. Everyone else can wait outside."

"Excuse me Dean." The Senator took exception to the Dean's dismissal. "These are Jeremiah's relatives. They can vouch for his good nature."

"This is not a court room. No characters witnesses are needed."

"I strongly object to that Dean."

The dean stared at the Senator defiantly. "Senator, look to your right. There is a young woman and her parents. If she is comfortable with just them, your son should be as well." He waived his hand. "You requested an empty chamber and so it shall be. Now will you instruct your family to leave or shall I just evoke a recommendation of suspension for your son?" The Senator turned to his relatives and at once everyone stood and walked out. "Thank you so kindly Senator. You may have a seat next to your lovely wife. Now let us proceed. Ms. Caitlyn Montgomery."

Caitlyn stood wearing a black business suit, crisp white collar blouse, black pumps and, no outfit would be complete without, pearl earrings and necklace. Her hair was brushed back and wrapped in a neat ball at the nape of her neck, no makeup, only a touch of lip gloss. "Yes sir." The smoothest voice stilled the room.

The Dean cleared his throat and whispered to the professor sitting next to him. "I have to find the boy not guilty, because the sight of her is giving me thoughts." He straightened and cleared his throat again. "Um, please come up front." When she reached the front he smiled. "Thank you," then he took a moment. "Jeremiah McClintock IV, would you come down front also?"

Jerry walked forward in his tailor suit, crisp shirt and political winning smile. "Yes sir."

The dean looked at the two students and they would indeed turn heads. "This is not a courtroom, however, I do expect the truth from each of you. No embellishments. Do each of you understand?"

"Yes sir." They said in unison.

"Good. We may be able to get through this with as little bloodshed as possible. You may stand at the tables. I'll take a moment, for the Senator's benefit, to describe the panel to show there is impartiality. We have one of Jeremiah's professors, Professor Burbanks and his dorm director, Mr.

Thompson. We also have Caitlyn's professor, Dr. Kane and her dorm director, Professor Wyatt. Professor Taylor and Professor Arkmed are not associated with either student and neither am I. As you all know I am Dean Steinbeck. We are here to make a determination on if disciplinary action should be taken in this case and if so what that will entail. Because of the nature of the accusation, it may be forwarded for legal action if necessary."

"Dean Steinbeck..." the Senator stood.

"Have a seat Senator. This will not take long." The Senator sat back down and exhaled.

"Ms. Montgomery, since we know Jeremiah's parents, the Senator and his lovely wife, Elizabeth, would you mind introducing your parents so the panel will know everyone here."

"Yes sir." She turned and smiled, then turned back to the panel. "These are my parents, Judge Fredrick T. Montgomery, and my mother, Beverly Montgomery."

"Thank you Ms. Montgomery and your mother is lovely also." Some members of the panel smiled. "Mr. McClintock, you are accused of making unwarranted advances on Ms. Montgomery. According to the complaint you broke into her dorm room through a window. At which time you began to remove your clothing with the intent to have sexual intercourse with Ms. Montgomery."

"Which he categorically denies," the Senator offered.

The Dean placed the papers he held in his hands on the table and looked incredulously at the Senator. "The expediency of this hearing would work well for your son if you sit down and remain silent, Senator."

The Senator huffed again then sat back down. The Dean looked at Jeremiah, "Son do you understand the accusations?"

"Jerry," nodded his head, "Yes sir I do."

"And you do understand that Ms. Montgomery does have legal remedies available to her."

"Yes sir." The boy acknowledged.

"Good," the Dean nodded his head, "this will make things simple. Ms. Montgomery, will you share with the panel in your own words, the incident that took place in your room on last Thursday."

"Yes sir. On the night in question, I was first approached by Mr. McClintock and his friends at the library. He asked my name. I did not think he was speaking to me so I continued reading. Mr. McClintock then came over to the table I was studying at and took a seat beside me. I moved over because he was rather close. He grabbed my arm and said there's no reason to be afraid of me I won't hurt you. I just want to know your name. I then told him my name. He then said that's a very beautiful name, almost as beautiful as you are. I said thank you and moved down. He then touched my hair and asked is this all your own hair. I said yes and pulled my hair away. He then said it was so smooth and silky. I never thought a black girl could have hair this soft and long. I became uncomfortable with the comment. So I said thank you then stood and gathered my things to leave. He asked where I was going and I told him back to my dorm to study. He then said don't leave yet, I was just getting to know you. He then stood and said, let me walk you back to your dorm. I told him no thank you, then walked away. Later that night I was awakened by one of my dorm-mates banging on my door. When I opened my eyes, Mr. McClintock was in my room removing his shirt. I screamed and ran to the door to open it, but before I could get there he grabbed me from behind and said don't open the door. I was so shocked and frightened at the time I did not listen to his words. That's when my dorm-mates kicked the door down. In hind-sight Dean Steinbeck, I believe Mr. McClintock was as frightened as I was."

"Caitlyn," her father called out her name with a firmness that caught everyone's attention. Turning to look at her father, Caitlyn did not say anything further.

"Is that all Ms. Montgomery?" the Dean asked thinking the girl wanted to say more.

Caitlyn hesitated for a moment. "Yes sir."

"Mr. McClintock your version of the night in question."

Jerry looked over at Caitlyn, "It was pretty much the way Caitlyn—I mean Ms. Montgomery stated. I was infatuated with her. To be honest, in a way I still am. I mean Dean, look at her. She is beautiful. But I swear to you I had no intention of having un-consensual sex with her. I am quite persuasive when it comes to the opposite sex and I intended to persuade her that it would be a mutually satisfying experience for both of us." He looked over at Caitlyn and smiled, "I still believe that." Caitlyn looked at him as if he had lost his mind, then Jerry turned back to the panel. "However, when I saw how frightened she was I attempted to gather her in my arms and console her. I did not intend to do her any harm. I told her that before everyone came barging in. I did take off my shirt because it ripped when I came through the window. If at any time Ms. Montgomery had said no, I would have gone right back out the same way I came and no one would have been the wiser." He turned to Caitlyn again, "I sincerely apologize for the actions I took. But in my own defense, you are almost irresistible and I really would like to go out with you."

The Dean looked at Jerry as if he could strangle him with his bare hands. This boy had a brilliant future ahead of him. Why would he do something so stupid to put it all in jeopardy? The Dean turned to the panel. "Mr. McClintock, this is not a time for you to try to get a date with Ms. Montgomery. I believe that ship has sailed. Does anyone have questions for either of the students?"

"Yes," Mr. Burbanks one of Jerry's professors replied. "Ms. Montgomery, you stated when Mr. McClintock approached you and asked your name you did not answer—why?"

"I did not think he was speaking to me." Caitlyn replied.

"Why not? Was someone else at the table with you?"
"No."
"Then why did you not respond to his question? Do you think your ignoring him could have ignited the situation or could it be you were being coy as some young women have the tendency to do?"

Caitlyn gave a condescending smile. "I don't have time to be coy, professor nor do I see the relevance of your questions. However, for the sake of expediency I'll attempt to answer them. I did not think he was speaking to me because most students on this campus do not. As for your second question, I'm not connected to the inner workings of Mr. McClintock's mind and would not be at liberty to ascertain what would ignite him to take the actions that he did. As for your last statement, I can't speak for other young women, but I don't have time or the tendency to be coy."

"Ms. Montgomery," Brian cleared his throat, "What were you about to say earlier?"

Caitlyn looked to the Dean's right at the far end where the question came from. "Well," she started but stopped suddenly.

"Ms. Montgomery," the Dean called out, "did you hear Mr. Thompson's question?"

"Are you Brian Thompson?" She asked with a worried look on her face.

"I am."

She frowned, "Do you play football with Mr. McClintock?"

He sat forward and captured her gaze. "I do."

"Do you believe you should be on this panel?"

"Do you think it's wise to question a panel member's integrity?" he asked still holding her eyes captive.

"Please answer the question Ms. Montgomery," the dean insisted.

Slowly she pulled her gaze from him and looked at the dean. "What was the question?"

"Stay focused Caitlyn," her father instructed. Caitlyn heard her father's demand and stood up straight.

Brian understood Jerry's' reaction to the girl—she was stunning. Nothing on this earth could have prepared him for Caitlyn Montgomery. The fresh face, prim, and proper, dark skinned sister with the body of a goddess and the face of an angel caught him completely off guard. It was his senior year at the University of Virginia. He was a black athlete that had a pro football career ahead of him if he wanted it, but he didn't. Upon graduation he would be reporting to Quantico Virginia for 20 weeks of training with the FBI and he couldn't be happier. When Jerry came to him and requested he be a part of the panel on his behalf, Brian's first instinct was to say no. But he liked Jerry. He also knew his teammate was destined to be in the political eye. This type of accusation could ruin him. Then Jerry explained to him how this girl affected him with her sultry look and sensual voice. Brian laughed at him at first, but Jerry actually seemed to believe the girl had put some type of spell on him. He was just that enchanted with the girl he couldn't help but try to get her to go out with him. After Brian gave Jerry a piece of his mind about no means no, he agreed to be a part of the panel. Jerry wasn't a bad guy, he just wasn't used to women saying no.

When he first walked in the room Brian's only purpose was to do what he could to help Jerry out of the situation with as little bloodshed as possible. Then Caitlyn Montgomery came to the table and every vein in Brian's body came alive. Jerry was right, she was enchanting in the form fitting suit showing the most incredible brown legs Brian had seen. Even with her hair pulled into a tight bun, he could imagine it down the way Jerry had described. Then when she spoke Brian's body began to vibrate from the beating of his heart. He cleared his throat to cover the moan that escaped. The fact that she was only a freshman surprised him the more she spoke. She was composed, confidently eloquent in her speech. The way she squirmed each time her father spoke, bothered him. But when she responded to Professor Burbank's questions, he knew the girl had a little backbone and that pleased him. Then she turned her eyes on him and for a moment Brian was mesmerized and so was she, he could feel it. This was one woman he had to stay away from. She was dangerous in many ways. Staying away, may not be too difficult, taking into consideration the way she was frowning at him.

"My question was simple. Earlier you were about to say something more regarding Mr. McClintock and you stopped. What were you about to say?"

She hesitated and looked over at Jerry. For a moment, Brian thought she was going to turn to her father, but she looked back up at him. "It was just that Mr. McClintock wasn't rough or cruel in anyway."

"Caitlyn," her father warned again.

Caitlyn stopped talking. Brian could see a battle taking place in her mind through her body language and her eyes. "Ms. Montgomery did you bring these charges to the panel?"

"The charges were brought on my behalf by my father."

Brian continued holding her stare, "Do you believe Mr. McClintock would harm you in the future?"

Caitlyn's father stood, "The question is irrelevant. She has no way of determining what may be in another person's mind."

"Judge Montgomery, this is not a court of law. Any question can be asked and is expected to be answered.

The look the judge gave Brian would have stopped most men in their tracks, but not Brian. "Ms. Montgomery, do you believe Mr. McClintock would harm you in the future?"

Judge Montgomery cleared his throat and Caitlyn flinched. "I honestly can't say," she replied pulling her look from Brian's grasp.

For some reason Brian understood her actions and let the questioning of her go. "Mr. McClintock, do you know the punishment for attempted rape in the Commonwealth of Virginia is two to ten years in the penitentiary. The punishment for breaking and entering with the intent to cause bodily harm is also two to ten years. No woman, man, or action is worth your future or your freedom. Knowing the consequences, will we ever see this type of behavior from you again?"

"I have a new understanding of how my actions affected another person. My life has been and will be dedicated to helping others, not causing them any harm. The university can be assured this type of behavior will never be demonstrated again." Jerry replied grateful to Brian for his question. A sigh of relief could be heard from the Senator and his wife.

"Eloquently spoken Mr. McClintock, however, I'm not sure your charm and knack for public speaking is sufficient under the circumstances." Professor Wyatt stated. "You entered another person's domain. If your intent was as innocent as you indicated, you should have simply knocked on Ms. Montgomery's door and asked her out. If her response was no, that should have been the end of it. Dean Steinbeck, it is my opinion this student did not respect the decision of another student and should be disciplined."

The room was silent. A pin would have been heard dropping on the carpet. Dean Steinbeck did not want to punish the boy for being arrogant. He desperately wanted a way out. "Does anyone have any further comments or questions?"

Judge Montgomery stood, "Dean Steinbeck," he said in an authoritive voice. "I believe if Senator McClintock is willing we could dispense of this matter without further deliberation.

The Senator stood, "I'm open to negotiations on this matter. What do you have in mind?"

"Is there a place we could speak in private?" Caitlyn's father asked.

Relief showing in his manner, Dean Steinbeck stood, "Certainly, this way." Senator McClintock, Judge Montgomery, and Dean Steinbeck exited through the door the panel members had entered through earlier. The others in the room took a seat to wait.

Judge Montgomery took the meaning of a bargaining chip to a level Brian did not know existed. His solution was to have Jerry marry Caitlyn. The Senator categorically refused to even consider the possibility. He had plans for his son. Marrying him off to "a hick town judge's daughter" was not one of them. As a result, Judge Fredrick Montgomery sold his daughter down the river for a position on some board in his locality and a monetary settlement.

Leaving the hearing all Brian could do was shake his head. He was happy for Jerry, the outcome was just what the senator wanted. But for Caitlyn, it was clear from the look on her face how belittled she felt. He remember going into the lobby where his girlfriend Gwen was waiting. When Caitlyn and her parents walked out of the room he could not help approaching her father about the decision.

Brian walked over to where the Judge was talking to Caitlyn. "Mr. Montgomery, I'm Brian Thompson from the panel. Sir, I'm just curious what did the senator offer you?"

Judge Montgomery looked at him with as much respect as you would give a roach. "This is a private conversation. Step back while I finish talking to my daughter." He turned his back on Brian. "Sign this document Caitlyn. This will put me on the planning board for the county. Do you know how much power comes with that position?"

"What's the agreement?" Brian asked.

The judge turned around. "Why are you still standing here?"

"I'm just wondering what was worth your daughters pride?"

"I'm her father. Now step away."

"You're not acting like a father. You're auctioning your daughter to the highest bidder."

"Boy you don't know how to work in the political world. When you got them by the balls you squeeze." His chest puffed out, "This little incident with Caitlyn is going to be worth something. In addition to the cash settlement, I get a position on the planning board." He nodded his head like that meant something to somebody. "That's how you make people in the political realm pay."

"You're selling your daughter for money and an appointment? What kind of father are you? "This is your daughter. You are supposed to protect her at all cost."

"Mr. Thompson," Caitlyn touched his arm. "It's okay. I'll sign it."

"No you will not," he yelled down at her then turned back to her father. "How much is your daughter's honor worth Judge?"

"I don't like your tone. You dare to speak me this way. You have no idea who I am or what I am capable of."

"I don't give a damn who you think you are. I asked you a question. How much?"

"He agreed to pay the remainder of Caitlyn's college tuition and for law school."

"Not to mention the position on the planning board." Brian said sarcastically.

"Boy, I've been dealing with people like this all my life. Putting that boy behind bars isn't going to teach him anything. But you hit them in their pockets, that'll hurt them." Judge Montgomery boasted proudly.

The look Brian gave the man conveyed exactly what he was thinking, this was a despicable little man. "You can't be serious. You'll sell your daughter's honor for money. It would have been better if you demanded he marry her."

"I tried that, the senator wouldn't accept."

"Daddy?" A shocked Caitlyn cried out. "You didn't."

"Of course I did. You were raised to marry for connections in the political world. It's your job to advance this family."

Brian reached for the man's throat before he could think of what he was doing. "Brian don't." Gwen grabbed him trying to pull him back.

"Please don't," Caitlyn cried.

"Call security. I want him arrested and thrown off this campus," the judge stated as he adjusted his suit jacket.

"No Daddy."

He looked from his daughter to Brian. "You don't want him arrested, then sign this paper." With tears in her eyes, Caitlyn looked at her father then back at a furious Brian and she knew what she had to do. She signed the paper.

Brian could see the hurt in her eyes as she signed the papers. "You're a pompous ass to put your daughter in this situation."

"You think so?" the Judge asked as he reviewed the document. "You're really going to like this. "Caitlyn you have really disappointed me. I didn't send you here to consort with hood rats." He looked at Brian. "You stay away from my daughter. Caitlyn come with me."

Brian didn't like seeing the young girl so distraught with the situation. He could see the distress on her face. "I'm here if you need me for anything. I'll always be here for you."

Caitlyn looked from her father to Brian. She bowed her head with tears in her eyes. "Thank you Mr. Thompson. I have to go with my father."

"I know," Brian said.

"Come along Caitlyn."

That was the day Judge Fredrick T. Montgomery became Brian's enemy.

On a Friday night during the third week of class, Brian decided cramming for the first exam of the semester was more important than attending the Greek step show. Hell everyone knew the Q-dogs and the Delta's were going to win the crowd over—they always did. Upstairs in the student center, there were several areas setup as study cubicles. Whenever he was bored in his apartment, he would come here to study. The place was usually empty, but tonight as he walked towards the back, he saw a lone figure standing in front of the windows looking out over the circle. She was dressed in a black skirt, yellow sweater and of course her signature heels. This time she was wearing something different. She was wearing a smile as she watched the step show below. The action transformed her face. She wasn't prim and proper now. She was breath-takingly beautiful. She put her hands up to her mouth and giggled. The sound was so delightful, Brian couldn't help but laugh with her, her giggle was just that contagious.

"Why don't you go downstairs with them?" he asked startling her. "I'm sorry," he laughed. "Looks like you are enjoying the show."

A little surprised at first, Caitlyn looked shocked, then she shook her head no. "I couldn't do that," she said as she turned back to the window watching the action below.

"Why not?" Brian asked as he placed his books on one of the tables and walked over to stand next to her.

She shrugged her shoulders, shaking her head at the same time. She turned and gave him a half of a smile, with her eyes twinkling as she spoke. "They don't like me very much." She turned back to the window.

There was something in the way she made the statement that made Brian think, there was nothing stuck up about the girl. And yes, this was a young girl, prim and proper from the way she dressed and carried herself. There was something else about her that shocked him as he stood close to her. She was not wearing any make-up. None. No eye shadow, no foundation, not even lipstick. Her lips looked that good with no lipstick. Damn. He knew what she said was true, but was surprised she acknowledged it. "Why?"

"Why what?" she asked still smiling at the antics taking place below.

"Why do you think they don't like you?"

She sighed, folded her arms around her waist, and stared back out the window. He could tell this was not something she wanted to talk about. "No one talks to me. My roommate comes and goes without as much as a good morning. I'm sure it's all connected to Jerry McClintock." She shrugged her shoulders, "But it's okay, I'm used to being alone."

Brian was watching her lips so intently he did not realize she had stopped talking. "You're probably right. Are you an only child?" Brian asked quickly to cover up his actions.

"Yes," she replied then smiled. "Just like you."

Brian was so surprised by her response that he laughed. "Yeah. Just like me. How did you know I was an only child?"

"Well, you kind of stay to yourself. A lot of people try to cling to you, but you don't really click with any of them. Full rage parties could be going on around you and you can partake or not. You have a lot of associates, but no friends on this campus. You can take or leave people."

"You're very observant. I detect a bit of an accent. Where are you from?" Brian sat on the table next to the window just to have a reason to keep her talking.

"I'm from Northampton County Virginia, a small town called Cape Charles. I'm sure you never heard of it. My father practically runs the place. I'm sure you remember him."

"Yes. I remember the not so honorable Fredrick T. Montgomery. I think it would be best not to talk about him. As for hearing of Cape Charles, no. I haven't."

"Where are you from?" she asked in a tone that clearly indicated she was happy to be talking to someone.

He extended his hand. "Brian Thompson from Richmond, VA."

She smiled and extended her hand. "I'm Caitlyn Montgomery. It's nice to meet you."

Turning off the water, Brian leaned against the shower wall with his eyes closed. He remembered the feel of her small hand in his. The immediate rush of desire that engulfed him when they touched was rushing through his body at the memory. He reached up, turned the shower back on to the coldest temperature he could find.

Chapter 5

Breakfast was a sin. It had to be. Anything that tasted that good, had to be on the wrong side of the law. Smiling, he looked up at Suzie Mae, "I think I'm taking you home with me."

Suzie Mae laughed. "Many men have tried honey and they couldn't hold me down."

"Oh I could hold you down Suzie Mae. You best believe that," Brian teased back as he stood.

"I bet you could honey—I just bet you could. Don't tempt me now." Suzie Mae laughed and walked away.

"Good Morning Mr. Thompson." Margie said with a bright smile. "It's a mighty nice morning wouldn't you say. I take it you're heading over to see Judge Becker. Cat came by last night and I told her you needed to meet with them. She said anytime would be good. So she'll be expecting you."

To Brian's surprise, he caught every word she said this time. "I appreciate that Margie and please call me Brian."

"Well alright then Brian," she smiled. "I'll make sure your room is cleaned by the time you come back. Do you think you will need another day?"

"I don't think so. But I'll know more after talking with the Judge."

"Well you go on over and get with Cat to make an appointment before the Judge gets away from you. He travels a lot you know. With handling all the court matters for several counties. Sometimes it's a little hard to catch up with him."

"Thanks for the heads up. I'll go over now." He started to walk out the door, but stopped and turned back. "By the way would you tell Marybeth the cream worked wonders and thank her for me. I may not see her before I leave."

Margie smiled brightly. "I certainly will. That will just make her day and give her something to brag about for a month of Sundays."

Brian smiled. He was beginning to like the people around here. He walked out on the porch of the B&B and looked up and down the street. His opinion of the little town had changed somewhat since he arrived. Pulling out his cell phone, he dialed Samuel's number. He wanted to get a report on things.

"Hello," Cynthia's voice sailed smoothly through the phone line.

"Hey prego. What's going on with you?" Brian's smile spread wide across his face. Cynthia was Samuel's wife and the closet thing Brian had to a sister. They grew up together with a love hate relationship, but when the time came they were and would always be there for each other. She was pregnant with her fist child and was due any day now. Brian had no idea who was carrying on the worst, Cynthia because she felt fat or Samuel who was a nervous wreck because Cynthia would not take it easy. It didn't matter how many times his mother, who had twelve children, told him that Cynthia was fine. And that staying active was healthy, Samuel didn't care. All he knew was the woman he loved was carrying his first child and he wanted keep both of them safe.

"If you value your life you won't go there with me today," Cynthia replied. "Where are you anyway? I called your house and when I didn't get an answer I called your cell phone. It said, "The customer you are calling is unavailable."

"I'm in Nickelsville, VA."

"Where?"

Brian laughed, "Nickelsville. It's a small town in southwest Virginia near Tennessee."

"What in the hell are you doing out there?"

"JD. I was pissed when he asked me to come, but now," he looked around, "I'm glad I came. It's not such a bad place. And..." he trailed off.

"And what," Cynthia laughed.

"Well, I feel like I'm supposed to be here for some reason. If nothing else the people have been really nice. Hell, the nurse here even gave me something for my back. I swear it wasn't drugs, but I am not feeling any pain right now. So you know I'm bringing some of that home with me."

"When is that going to be? You know Samuel is off somewhere with JD and you're not here. What happens if I go into labor?'"

"You going to push that little sucker out just like every other woman on earth with children have done. You don't need me or Samuel for that."

"But you promised to be here."

"Then don't have it until I get back."

"It. My baby is not an it."

"You're right. As big as you are it's probably a whale." Brian laughed. "I'll call you later and tell you when I'll be home. Bye." He hung up the telephone before she could begin cursing.

Still smiling when he crossed the street Brian nodded hello as he walked by the two men playing checkers in the same spot they were in when he pulled into town yesterday. He walked into the doorway that said Post Office, and was headed in the direction of the stairs, Suzie Mae had told him about when a voice called out. "Well hello there big fella.

You must be the FBI man everyone is talking bout. How you doing this morning? Is your back feeling better?" Brian stopped and looked around. He did not see anyone. "I'm over here behind the counter on the ladder."

Brian looked to his left and up. On the ladder was a woman that he thought to be around forty on a ladder reaching for something on the top shelf. He ran over and helped her with the box she was pulling out. "Let me take that for you ma'am."

"Why thank you son. I sure appreciate that. I'm LillyMae, Suzie Mae's mother. You must be the man her and Red was talking bout all night long. I gotta say I certainly can see why. You're a good looking heap of a man. Yes you are?"

"Thank you ma'am," Brian smiled at the compliment.

"You looking for Jacob?"

Brian noticed she was the only person to refer to the Judge by his first name. He guessed age gives you certain liberties. "Yes ma'am I am."

"Well that little sucker is off somewhere, GOD only knows where. You need to talk to Cat, but you're going to have to go to the house. Since Jacob won't be back until later today and there was no court business, Cat decided to pick her son up from school and spend the day with him. But she won't mind you stopping by. She's the one you need to talk with to get anything done around here."

"Then I'll go have a talk with Ms. Cat."

"Here, let me give you the directions."

Following the directions given to him by LillyMae, Brian pulled off the main road into the drive way that led to the private estate. On the right, he could see horses grazing and further out cows. On the left was grass, deep green grass that went on for miles over hills. It seemed soft enough to make you want to lie out in and sleep under one of the trees. As he drove another mile or two around the winding road, he saw the house come into view. All he could think about was the house from the TV show Dallas, Southfork Ranch, with tall white columns and the dramatic double door entrance. "Damn, places like this do exist," he smiled. Pulling up into the circular driveway, with a running water fountain in the center, he could see the river not too far off in the distance with a pier that extended out into it. He could imagine what it would be like to grow up in a house like this. Stepping onto the porch, that seemed to go on forever, he could hear voices inside. The main door was open with the screen door allowing air to flow through, as were all the windows on the front of the house. There were white rockers on the front porch, a few tables, cushioned wicker chairs and a double seat swing at the far end. This was truly a luxurious country setting.

Brian rang the door bell. As he waited, curiosity took over. He walked to the end of the porch on the right and sure enough, the porch wrapped around the house. "This is alright," he said aloud. He walked back over to the door and rung the door-bell again turning around to continue taking in the scene of rolling hills, and water, his back was to the door when he heard a little voice.

"Hello."

Turning, Brian took a step closer to the door. "Hello," he said looking down at a little boy that stood maybe four feet behind the screen door. "I'm looking for Jacob Becker."

"My grandfather isn't home. But my mommy is here."

"May I speak to your mommy?" Brian asked.

"Sure, come on in. I'll get her." The boy unlatched the screen door and pushed it open with his back turned calling out to his mother. "Mommy." He turned back and Brian froze. "My mommy will be here in a minute. She's making us some cookies."

Brian was stunned, he could not speak, nor could he take his eyes off the boy. He was a miniature version of himself. Brian was uneasy when he bent down to the boy. "What's your name?" his voice shook.

The boy extended his hand, "Elliott Brian Montgomery-Becker. What's your name?" he smiled.

Taking the small hand in his Brian was rendered speechless again. The boy had his name, just backwards. Time stood still as he continued to stare at the child. For a moment he felt disoriented. Brian took the boys hand and an odd feeling began to consume him. "My name is Brian Elliott Thompson," he said almost in a whisper.

The boy's eyes grew wide as he looked at the man surprised, "Ahhh, wow. That's my daddy's name."

The shocked look on Brian's face was nothing compared to the excited look on the boys face. Suddenly something foreign lodged in his heart, something he hadn't felt in years. Tears filled his eyes as he asked, "Ho-how old are you Elliott?"

"Eight. How old are you?"

Brian laughed, a nervous laughed, but he just didn't know what else to do.

"Who's at the door Elliott?"

Brian heard the voice before he slowly raised his head to see Caitlyn appear from the room behind the staircase with a dish towel in her hand. If the boy's appearance surprised him, seeing Caitlyn shocked the hell out of him. "Caitlyn?" came out in an inaudible voice.

"Mommy guess what? His name is the same as my daddy's."

"Brian? Oh my God, Brian!" Caitlyn dropped the cloth ran and threw herself into his arms.

Ten years rushed through his mind, as he closed his arms around the woman. Was this a figment of his imagination? If it was, he never wanted to wake up. Shocked beyond belief, Brian pulled Caitlyn into his arms and merged her body and lips to his. He didn't think, couldn't think and became less in control of his actions when her mouth opened to his. Their tongues danced to the familiar rhythm of the past. His hands roamed feverishly feeling every inch of her just to

A Lost Heart

make sure she was real. Then his fingers cradled her head, holding her lips secure to his, clinging to the blistering heat generating between them. If he died that moment, Caitlyn in his arms, life would have been worth living. He moved her shoulder length hair from her neck to touch the sensitive area behind her ear. One of them moaned as they plunged deeper and deeper into the kiss of lost lovers. Neither could or wanted to let the other go. Not after years of longing, wanting, not knowing.

"Wow. You must be my daddy. Mommy never kissed Colin like that."

Brian's mind snapped when he heard the little voice next to them.

At the top of the stairs, finding Caitlyn in a rather passionate embrace, put Colin on notice that his life was about to change. At first he was shocked, but then he realized as he looked from Elliott to the man, this must be the FBI agent—Caitlyn's FBI agent that was in town. His heart sang with ecstatic joy for her. He was standing there watching this man passionately mauling his wife and he couldn't be happier. For nine years, she had been denied real love. Now it seemed as if her fairy tale might happen after all. Colin had no idea how he was going to make it happen for her without screwing up his life, but on this, he would find a way. Colin was about to turn to leave, giving the family some privacy, when suddenly the man angrily pushed Caitlyn away.

Brian looked at the boy, whose hand he was still holding, then back at Caitlyn. "Am I Caitlyn? Am I his father?" The shock of the moment had rendered Caitlyn temporarily speechless. "Answer me." Brian yelled.

Elliott pulled his hand from his father's and grabbed his stunned mother's waist, hugging her tightly. The boy's action bothered Brian, but at the moment, he couldn't get past seeing Caitlyn and the thought that he might have a son. He tried to control his temper, speaking normally at first, but then his voice began to rise again. "What in the hell are you doing here? Is this where you have been hiding for the last nine years? Do you know I spent two years of my life looking for you?" Brian advanced on her, "Do you? I spent the night in jail jeopardizing my career with the bureau when your father had me locked up because I refuse to leave his property until he told me where you were?" He bit out continuing to advance on her. "No wonder I couldn't find you, you were living southwest of hell." He stopped yelling and stared, then asked almost in a whisper, "Why Caitlyn- Why did you leave me without as much as a good bye?"

Caitlyn parted her kissed swollen lips to speak, but he yelled again, "Why-damn it - Why?"

Caitlyn jumped as she held Elliott.

"Well, good-GOD man. First you kiss her senseless, then you're yelling at her like a caged animal just been released from captivity, come to think of it, that's the way you kissed her too." Colin said as he hurried down the stairs. "Give her a moment to get herself together. She'll answer your questions."

The two lost lovers turned to the stairs. Brian's look was furious, while Caitlyn was still shell shocked from seeing the man. Colin assumed this was Brian Thompson. Colin walked passed Brian over to Caitlyn. He rubbed her shoulders affectionately. "Cat, are you okay?"

Caitlyn looked from Colin to Brian and knew life as she had known it was about to change.

"Who in the hell are you?" Brian asked, not liking the man touching Caitlyn or the fact that she was letting him.

"Colin Becker, her husband," he extended his hand, but knew immediately the gesture would not be returned when he saw the blood drain from the man's face.

Brian frowned and stumbled backwards. "Husband," he repeated as if the word burned his throat. Damn if he didn't do it again. He kissed another man's wife. He shook the thought from his mind, then glowered at Caitlyn. "How long?"

"Brian, I..."

"How long?" He yelled cutting Caitlyn off.

"Don't yell at my mommy?" Elliott yelled, pulled away, kicked Brian, and began pounding his fist into his father's stomach, as tears streamed down Caitlyn's face.

Caitlyn wrapped her arms around her son pulling him back from a stunned Brian.

He looked from Caitlyn to the boy, then back to Caitlyn. "I'm sorry son," Brian said as he stared at his very angry child.

The tears wouldn't stop as Caitlyn and Brian just stared at each other. "You made my mommy cry."

Brian could not believe his eyes as his gazed returned back to the boy. Moments went by with no one saying anything. Colin walked up behind Caitlyn, "I'll take Elliott out back. You two need to talk."

Elliott still clung to his mother and Brian continued to stare at the boy. "Elliott, come with me," Colin said.

"No. I'm staying with my mommy."

"Your mother is going to be fine. Your father would never hurt her. He's just a little angry." Colin took Elliott's hand and looked at Caitlyn. "You have nine years of explaining to do. " Caitlyn looked over at Colin with tears in her eyes. "It's time," he said with the most sympathetic smile. He gave her an encouraging nod then left the room with Elliott.

The boy looked back and held the eyes of his father until they lost sight of each other.

Brian looked from Elliott back to Caitlyn and sneered, "Nine years," he shook his head in disbelief. "I didn't think you could hurt me any deeper than you had when you disappeared." He snickered and exhaled, "I was wrong." In a chilling voice, Brian said through the fogginess of tears threatening to fall. "I shouldn't be surprised." He shook his head. "Is Elliott the reason you never returned to school?"

"Brian, please let me explain."

"Is that why?"

"Yes."

Brian staggered backwards not believing what was happening to him. But he did remember what her father said to him. "I wasn't good enough to be his father. What was it your father called me? A hood rat. Is that why you took him away?"

"No Brian," Caitlyn cried out in despair, "It wasn't like that."

Angry and a little perplexed, Brian exhaled struggling to bring his temper under control. "Let's get the legalities out of the way first, shall we. Is he my son?"

"Yes."

Hearing the response caused a lump to form in Brian's throat. "Why? Caitlyn Why?" he asked looking hurt and confused.

She reached out for him, but he pulled away. All she wanted to do was comfort him. Never in her life had she imagined this moment would hurt him so deeply. But the evidence was there in the drops of moisture from his eyes. "Were you ever going to tell me?"

"I did tell you," she cried out.

Brian frowned up, "What?"

"When you were in the hospital, I stayed with you one night and I told you all about Elliott and his life. I didn't want anything to happen to you and you not know about your son."

"Did it ever occur to you to just damnit tell me. I was drugged to the high heavens while I was in the hospital. Did you think to hang around until I was, oh I don't know conscious?"

"Yes, but,"

"But what?" He put his hand up and closed his eyes to control his anger. "You know what, that's not important any longer. I want to get to know my son. You are going to cooperate or do I need to take you to court. Oh wait, I forgot, your father the Honorable Fredrick Montgomery, might block that." He laughed a chilling laugh, "Oh but contrary to what he may think his influence is nothing compared to mine." His look was menacing to say the least.

"I want you to get to know Elliott." Caitlyn cried, "But please let me explain what happened."

For years, he wanted to know what happened, why she disappeared. Hell, just this morning he wanted to know. Now he just wanted to get to know his son. Brian walked over with clenched jaws. "The next words I want to hear from you, is where I can find my son," he spat out.

Regardless of how angry Brian was, Caitlyn never feared him. She knew without a doubt he would not hurt her or Elliott. However, reasoning with him was another matter. "Brian with everything that has happened today, it would be best to wait until later to talk to Elliott. He may not want to talk to you today."

"Why the hell not?" he barked out.

"Oh I don't know." She raised her voice. "It could be he is as stubborn as his father," she replied taking a step closer, daring him to challenge her.

The act almost—almost made him proud. He'd taught her that. He'd taught her how to step defiantly to anyone that tried to bully her. But she was not supposed to use it against him. "Today Caitlyn," his Adam's apple bobbed, "Today. Now where did your husband take him?"

"Brian I beg of you don't force this today. Give it some time, just a little time." Caitlyn pleaded as she wrung her hands together.

"I've given it nine years without knowing Caitlyn. I think that's long enough. Now, are you going to get your husband

and my son or do I have to tear this place apart? And you know I will."

The flaring of his nostrils was a sure sign that the talking was over. This was the immovable Brian. There was no changing his mind or reasoning with him. Caitlyn lowered her head and turned to walk away. Brian desperately wanted to tell her to hold her head up high, as he had done so many times before, but he couldn't—he was still too damn mad. Why, he wasn't sure, but he'd figure it out later. He turned and angrily pushed open the screen door to stand on the front porch.

Colin stood in the open doorway staring at the back of the formidable man that had his arms folded across his chest and looked as though he was ready for battle. Well, if that was what it was going to take to find Caitlyn some happiness then so be it. Colin stepped out onto the porch where Brian stood. In his lazy southern drawl, he looked at Brian and said. "You may kick my ass today but you are going to hear me out." If it was possible it seemed the scowl on the man's face was more intense when he turned with an arched eyebrow.

"Excuse me?" Brian stood with his legs apart and arms folded across his chest.

Colin wanted to laugh, because Brian Thompson was exactly as Caitlyn had described him—someone you did not want as an enemy.

The man standing before him was Caitlyn's husband. Brian took a good look at the man who had stolen his woman. He was a little over six feet, slim and if Brian wasn't mistaken a little on the sensitive side. He wasn't a bad looking brother if you went for the light bright, red men with hazel eyes and cherry lips. Funny, he never thought Caitlyn did. Nevertheless, the man was married to his woman. He didn't know how it came about, but that was what the man had done, stolen his woman. That was the only way Brian could justify his anger at the man standing in front of him. Honestly, the man should be pissed with him. He did after all kiss his wife. "I didn't know she was your wife when I kissed her."

Colin had this knack of raising one eye-brow when he was puzzled about something, like now. "It's quite alright, I assure you. Caitlyn is more your wife than she has ever been mine." Colin stood in his white linen suit, with his hands in his pants pockets and his blazer opened. A cool breeze brushed over them and Colin was grateful for it, for Mr. Thompson sake. "I believe it is in everyone's best interest that you and I talk."

"Talk? You came out here to talk?" Brian glared at the man. "What kind of a man are you? I was about to take your wife where she stood. And you came to talk?"

Colin displayed that slow lazy smile of his and shrugged his shoulders. "Mr. Thompson, I assume that's who you are, you and I are bound by a history not of our own making but one we have been forced to live by none-the-less."

Brian tilted his head to the side giving Colin a look of total confusion because that's what he was, confused. "You want to come at me again?"

"Allow me to explain. The reason you and I are standing in this position at this day in time is not due to anything you or Caitlyn or I did. We are here because of two old men who like to play God in other people's lives." Colin took a non-threatening step towards Brian, "But it seems, yours and Caitlyn's fate is more than they can handle. Hallelujah, I say." Stepping back he sighed, "Unfortunately, I'm not at liberty to tell you all that took place nine years ago. That's for Caitlyn to handle. However, I implore you not to leave this town until you know the entire truth behind Caitlyn and Elliott being here. From what I could see, your feelings for her still run rather deep. I can tell, you see, by the vein throbbing in your neck as you try to keep from strangling me. Which I have no doubt you would be able to accomplish. And since I have no desire to die on this day, I will now take my leave to check on my wife whom you kissed senseless and your son. Do I have your word that you will stay?"

Brian contemplated the man's words. There was nothing malicious or even angry in his tone. This situation was getting weirder by the minute. "You have my word that I will not kill you at this moment. I give you nothing more."

Colin chuckled, "Well, I'll take that as my cue to leave while I'm still breathing. Elliott is walking out back. I suggest you take a few minutes to think about what this first conversation with your son will be. Calm down a bit." Colin tilted his head a bit and motioned with his hands, "He's a fine young boy that loves his mommy. Remember, he has no part in the crime that was committed against you and Caitlyn."

When Colin walked back into the house and closed the door behind him, Brian could not decide if he liked the man or hated him. He apologized for kissing the man's wife or did he? It didn't matter because the man said it was quite alright. What in the hell was that about? And what in the hell did he mean about two old men controlling our fate. There were too many unanswered questions and he wasn't leaving until he got some answers.

Attorney General JD Harrison, his chief of staff, Calvin Johnson and his campaign manager James Brooks were reviewing travel plans in the hotel suite in McLean, Virginia where JD had just given a rousing speech before members of the Congressional Black Caucus. Samuel walked over to him. "Your blackberry chimed."

JD looked up, taking the phone from the head of his security detail. Samuel knew whom JD wanted to take calls from no matter what he was doing or who he was with. He looked at the number and exhaled. The world was about to explode. Glancing at Calvin, JD shook his head. "All hell is about to break out."

Calvin laughed curiously, "What's up?"

JD pushed the button to answer the call. "What's up B?"

"You know what's up! You damn well know. How long have you known she was here and not tell me?"

"B..."

"B my ass. You are supposed to have my back. We were supposed to be boys. Down with each other no matter what. Is this your way of getting back at me over Tracy?"

"NO Brian. We are boys—always will be."

"How in the hell are we boys and you keep shit like this from me. Who made you GOD to play with my life like this? I'm not Tracy, you don't control what I need to know."

"Brian, give me a minute to explain." JD pleaded.

"Everybody wants a damn minute to explain. Did you give me a minute to explain when you saw me kissing Tracy—did you?"

"Brian that was my heart reacting."

"This is my damn heart too." Brian yelled and disconnected the call.

"Brian—Brian!" JD yelled then looked at the blackberry. The call was gone. "Damn," he expelled and cut off the phone.

"What's going on?" James was now standing concerned.

JD exhaled and began to laugh nervously. "Whew. He is pissed."

Calvin sat on the edge of the table with arms folded. "He saw her?" He asked curiously.

"Saw who?" James asked.

JD took a seat, held his head back, and continued to laugh. "He saw Caitlyn."

"Who is Caitlyn?"

"Apparently—his heart," JD replied.

"He said that?" Calvin asked as he took a seat to listen.

"He didn't just say it. He yelled it. I'm surprised you didn't hear it across the miles."

"He's mad?" Calvin asked.

JD held his head up and glared at Calvin, "Mad is understating it a bit."

Calvin held JD's stare. "He is going to kick your ass." They both started laughing uncontrollably.

James looked from one to the other, then sat back in his chair. "It's good to see you two are finding humor in this. How mad is Brian. How far is this going? And why?" James was JD's campaign manager, brother-in-law and friend. He was also a friend of Brian's. The last time the two men were on the outs with each other it affected all of them.

JD looked at Calvin, then to James. "Do you remember how pissed you were when you found David Holt in Ashley's condo?"

James' jaw flinched. That was four years ago and it still pissed him off to think about it. "Oh hell," he sighed.

"Yeah, well that is going to be mild compared to this." JD looked at Calvin again. "What do you think?"

"Depends. Does he know about his son yet?"

"Son," James sat forward. "What son?" He looked from Calvin to JD. "Start talking and don't stop until you get to the end."

Something was wrong. Elliott did not know what or understand why he felt the way he did. But he was sure something was wrong. His daddy was real mad at his mommy—that's all he knew. Colin tried to get him to talk about it, but he just didn't feel like talking. Walking out the back Elliott was going to the one place he could always think when he saw his grandfather docking his boat. "Well hello there Elliott. How are you boy?"

"Hello Grandfather," Elliott replied with his head down walking by him.

Jacob Becker looked at his son who stood on the back deck. "What's wrong with Elliott," he all but growled at Colin.

There wasn't much love left between the father and son since his mother died. That was the day Colin promised his mother he would not break all ties with his father. It was the only reason he was still in Nickelsville. To his father's way of thinking, he was there for the inheritance. That was the furthest thing from the truth. For all the connections and control Jacob Becker had, he never knew just how well off his son was. And Colin intended to keep it just that way until he was ready to make a change. He had a feeling that day was not far away. "It seems the sins of the fathers are visiting the daughter," he said as he walked by leaving the old man still on the deck.

"What in the hell is that supposed to mean?" Jacob asked as he followed Colin into the kitchen.

Placing his hat on the table near the door, Colin took his time responding to his father. Looking in the refrigerator, he pulled out a beer as he took his time answering. "It seems Brian Thompson has found his way here."

Jacob stood there in his five thousand dollar suit and fifteen hundred dollar shoes giving his son an incredulous look. "I don't know any Thompson. What does that have to do with Elliott?"

"You're getting senile old man. You've done so much dirt in your life you can't even remember the names of your victims."

Jacob turned to go to his study. "I don't have to listen to this."

"I'm afraid my father, you do. My guess is Mr. Thompson will be inside shortly and while you may not have to answer to me, I don't think he is going to be easy to avoid."

Angry and tired of hearing the accusatory tone coming from his son, Jacob stopped and turned back. "Who in the hell is Mr. Thompson and what does he have to do with Elliott?"

Smiling as if Satan was about to get his due Colin was happy to answer his question. "Mr. Brian Thompson is an ex-FBI agent who is now the head of Attorney General J.D. Harrison's protection detail. He is here to see about a return visit by Attorney General Harrison. I distinctly remember you asking him to return along with Elliott. See your desire to be one of the elite political figures in this area may very well lead to your demise." Taking another sip from his beer, Colin continued eagerly. "It gets better. Mr. Brian Elliott Thompson also happens to be the father of one Elliott Brian Montgomery-Becker." Colin's grin widened. "That's right father. The man whose son you and Caitlyn's father stole nine years ago is here in Nickelsville. Imagine that." The look of astonishment on his father's face was priceless. There could not have been a more fulfilling moment than this if Colin had planned it himself.

"I don't know that man and I certainly did not steal his son." He took a step towards Colin. "Do I need to remind you which side of the bread your butter is, son?"

Colin waved his father off. "Father, you can take that butter and shove it. In fact, I think you're going to need it. When Mr. Thompson finds out the truth of what took place nine years ago, he's going to screw you raw and you will need that butter. I think I'll stand around and watch." With that, Colin walked out of the kitchen.

Jacob fumed at the way his son had spoken to him. But he'd deal with him later. Right now, he had to make a call.

Elliott continued his walk with his head stilling hanging low and hands in his jeans pocket. Every rock that appeared in his path was kicked with a powerful thump. He needed to be bigger if he was going to protect his mother. The boy never looked up, for he knew the path well. It was the same path he took almost every day to go to the dock and fish. Today he did not have his rod with him and his mother wasn't there either. Why didn't his mother let him stay to protect her? Why did she send him away? His mother had never sent him away. They were always together. Elliott turned to see Colin and his grandfather in the kitchen. Now, his grandfather and Colin were arguing again. Don't they know life is precious? Every moment should be spent loving the people around you. That's what his mommy says.

Elliott reached the dock and saw his grandfather's boat there. Members of the three-man crew waved at him, he waved back then turned to the left and walked further down the path. Near the edge, close to the river was a tree log that Colin said fell across the path when he was a little boy. Colin said he and his mother would come down and sit on the log to fish. He and his mommy began doing the same thing as soon as he could hold and control his fishing pole. Sometimes when he wanted to just think his mommy would let him come down here and sit, as long as she could see him from the window. He looked up, but knew he wouldn't see her there. Something wasn't right, he thought for the third time in the last ten minutes. He picked up a stick, sat down on the log and exhaled.

The area was deserted as the lone figure made plans for his escape. The area was isolated and the route he planned to take would keep him under cover for hours. He had been watching the boy for a few weeks now. Following the school bus, the parents, and yes even the grandfather, Jacob Becker. He knew their routine, studied their habits, and planned accordingly. Another day or two and he would complete his assignment. He froze when he sensed someone was coming in his direction. He eased behind two trees whose trunk was wide and merged together. Watching, he saw the boy was by himself. He waited a few minutes in anticipation that the mother would be there soon. Then he remembered he was there early to map out an escape route. The boy should still be at school and the mother still at work. Looking up, he still did not see the mother approaching. What a perfect opportunity, he thought. "Patience," he whispered, "patience."

"I don't give a damn that he is in court. You get a message to him that Judge Jacob Becker is holding on the telephone." Jacob held the line while he waited. Nine years ago when he received a call from his law school friend Fredrick Montgomery, he thought the plan was the perfect solution to his situation. He'd known something had to be done to control Colin, he was becoming reckless with his behavior. Having lovers from all walks of life was dangerous to his health and his reputation. If blackmail was the only way to protect his son, then so be it—hell he would do it again. It didn't matter that Colin despised him. What mattered was Colin was now a reputable physician, with a thriving practice right there in Nickelsville. If he hadn't resorted to blackmail, Colin would have moved from there years ago. Fredrick's plan gave Colin a wife and a child. What he never asked was why. What was Fredrick's reason for such a plan? He paid fifty thousand for the daughter and if the child she carried was a boy, he paid an additional fifty thousand. No surprise there, Fredrick was always greedy, there was never enough prestige or money for him. But there was something more. There was a reason Fredrick wanted to control his daughter. Some other reason he wanted his daughter to lose contact with the outside world. If he was willing to pay a hundred thousand dollars, to cover his skeletons in the closet, was Fredrick willing to sacrifice his daughter for the same. What was Fredrick hiding?

"Judge Montgomery."

"Freddie this is Jacob. Who in the hell is Brian Thompson and why is he in my town?"

Chapter 6

Elliott heard the man before he reached the log. He could tell it wasn't his mother coming because there was no singing and the steps sounded loud. Why didn't his mommy come to talk to him? When he turned and looked up, then up some more, then up a little more. Now he knew the answer. His mommy sent his daddy to talk to him.

"Hello Elliott," Brian spoke from a distance. Uncertainty consumed him. Not sure how to approach, he could only heed Caitlyn's advice to take it slow. "Your mommy told me I would find you here."

"A man is always supposed to protect the women in his life." Elliott said as he turned around and threw a stone into the lake. "My mommy said you used to always say that. You're a little big, so I can't beat you up. But if you make my mommy cry again I'm sure gonna try."

Pride choked Brian as he tried to speak. "I would never hurt you or your mother Elliott. I was a little upset back there. You may not believe this but I loved your mommy a lot at one time."

"Me too," Elliott smiled, "I mean I still love her a lot."

"You do?"

"Yep. You know some times when she is really mad at me, I feel bad. It hurts me right here," he pointed to his chest. The boy slouched over, "but I guess I'm not supposed to tell you that."

Brian thought, Caitlyn makes me hurt in the exact same spot. He exhaled and took a seat next to his son on the log. A muscle twitched at the nervousness he felt, but he needed to find common ground to continue the conversation that had been eight years in the making. "You can tell me anything Elliott."

Elliott looked behind him, then to each side. Brian followed the boy's action, looking around to see if maybe someone was coming and he didn't hear them. "My mommy told me about you, but we can't tell anybody because mommy told me not to."

Brian smiled at the brown eyes that looked so much like his and that lump, the same one from before, formed in his throat again." Your secret is safe with me." Anxious to hear what his son had to say, Brian held his temper while wondering what Caitlyn told Elliott about him. "What did your mommy tell you about me?"

The boy looked around again. "She said you are an FBI agent, a good one too," the boy nodded his head up and down, reminding Brian just how young his son was. Elliott stopped and looked at his father, "Are you? I mean are you real good?"

Brian raised an eyebrow and gave a half smile, "Yes son. I'm very good."

"That's good. Now you can protect my mommy."

The statement took Brian by surprise. He did not want to startle his son, but he needed to know what the boy was talking about. "Is someone trying to hurt your mommy?"

Elliott looked around again, then he told his father, "My mom said if anything was to happen to her I was supposed to find you. That's why she gave me your name, so I would never forget you are my real dad. And you know what else?"

Caitlyn told Elliott about him and gave him his name. Why would she do that? That damn lump was back in his throat and caused his voice to come out almost as a choke, "No, what?"

"My mommy said you would love me and take real good care of me better than her even, and she takes real good care of me." If Elliott had bothered to look up he would have seen the tears forming in Brian eyes. "Know why I have two last names?" Brian just shook his head no. Excitedly Elliott continued, "Cause my mommy said one day you were going to come looking for me. And when you did she wanted to make sure you could find us. And then you know what's supposed to happen?"

"No, what?" an emotionally flustered Brian asked.

"You're supposed to take us away from here to live with you and then I'm going to have other brothers and sisters. That's what my mommy said." The boy looked at the ground, picked up a rock and threw it in the water. "Now I don't know what's going to happen." He said sadly. "You know what?"

Brian wasn't sure he could take another of Elliott's "you know what's," but he didn't have a choice. He wanted to sit there for as long as he could to listen to his son. "What?"

Elliott looked to the left at the man. "It don't matter if you don't like me, but you should like my mommy and take her away so she can be happy. She's really nice."

Brian picked his son up by his arms and placed him in his lap. "Elliott, look at me son." The boy looked up at his father. Brian could not help but smile at the miniature him. "Damn you're a good looking boy. How could I not love you?" He became serious, "I would never allow anything to happen to you or your mother. Do you hear me son? Now, that I've found you, I will never let either of you out of my sight." He ruffled the boy's hair that was coal black like his mother's.

A Lost Heart

The boy nodded his head enthusiastically then looked out at the river. "Do you have a river for me to fish in at home?"

"No. But I will."

"My mommy and I like to fish. Do you know how to fish?"

"No. But I will."

"Do you know how to ride a horse? My mommy and I like to ride horses."

"No. But I will."

The boy thought again. "Do you like peanut butter and jelly sandwiches?"

"Yep. I sure do," Brian smiled.

"Grape or strawberry jelly?"

"Grape," Brian replied.

Elliott smiled at his father. "I like grape too but mommy likes Strawberry."

"Do you have any children at your house?"

"No."

"But you will, 'cause my mommy said so."

Caitlyn watched out the window in the kitchen. It had been at least a few hours. Brian and Elliott were still sitting on the log near the river talking. She could not believe he was there. Tears still stung her eyes at the thought. How did he find them? He was as shocked to see her as she was to see him. How.....JD! JD told him! He promised he would not tell Brian about Elliott. He promised. Now, she as mad, she trusted JD to keep her secret. Then she stopped and thought, Brian didn't know about Elliott. Why would he have been so shocked if JD had told him? Looking up as she saw a movement in the trees, or she thought she did, but they were still sitting on the log. It dawned on her, JD did not tell him about Elliott, he must have just told Brian about her.

"Caitlyn, your father is on the telephone for you."

Caitlyn turned to Jacob as if he had lost his mind. "My what?"

"Your father," Jacob replied handing the cordless phone to her.

Staring at him in disbelief she took the phone and slowly brought it up to her ears. She swallowed hard. "Hello."

"Didn't I tell you to stay away from Thompson? You called him didn't you? What happens from here on is on you Caitlyn. Keep him away from Elliott you hear me Caitlyn. If you don't I will ruin him." The telephone line went dead.

"What did he say Caitlyn?" She looked at Jacob with the phone still in her hand. It was the first time in nine years she had spoken to her father. Correction, her father had spoken to her, for she did not have an opportunity to say anything to him. Anger and hurt consumed her again. Just like it did when she told him she was pregnant and he disowned her. "Cat, what did he say about this Thompson man?"

"Don't you know Jacob? I'm sure the two of you have talked. How else would he know Brian was here?" She looked out the window and saw Brian and Elliott laughing. Her heart was happy, but her mind told her there was going to be trouble. "I'll tell you this. You and my father better have an army ready. It's going to take that and more to keep Brian away from his son now that he knows."

"I don't know about your father, but I run this town. It may be best if your Mr. Thompson left."

Caitlyn turned to him and gave a chilling laughed. "I'd like to see you try to make Brian do anything he doesn't want too."

Jacob did not like this defiant Caitlyn. Too many things were changing around here for his liking. Enough was enough. "He's no longer a federal agent. He doesn't have the bureau behind him."

"Jacob, you've treated Elliott and me well. I don't want you to make a mistake that could cost you everything. So I'll give you this advice. Don't try to fight my father's battle with Brian. I don't know all that's behind what my father did, but it's his battle not yours. You go after Brian and you will have the force of the Attorney General's Office upon you. You see, Brian is not just head of security. He is also JD Harrison's best friend, has been since childhood. You go after Brian, you are also going up against JD. I don't think you want to do that. Do you?"

Elliott came running in the back door. "Mommy, Mommy, my daddy said I could stay with him at Ms. Margie's place tonight, if it's okay with you. Is it okay Mommy? Is it?"

Caitlyn looked from her excited son to Brian's defiant eyes. "I don't know if that's a good idea."

"I know for a fact it's not." Jacob stated as he took in an assessment of Brian Thompson. "Go upstairs to your room Elliott."

"But Grandfather, this is my daddy. My real daddy. Didn't you tell him Mommy?"

"He knows Elliott," Caitlyn sighed.

"Elliott, come here son," Brian laughed at himself. "I can get used to saying that," he smiled at Caitlyn. Caitlyn smiled back with tears still in her eyes, as Brian bent down to his son's height. "Listen I want you to go upstairs while I talk to your mommy and grandfather. Don't forget what I told you to tell Colin. Okay."

"Okay." Elliott was a little dejected, but he looked back and smiled at his daddy. "You're not going to leave, are you?"

"Not without you."

It was something in the way Brian made the statement that let Caitlyn know he meant what he said. She watched as her son run up the stairs and fear gripped her. He was going to take her child. "Brian please don't take Elliott from me." She pleaded.

The tears and fear were there in her eyes as she turned to Brian. It was as if time had returned them to the UVA campus. The thought of her hurt or afraid turned on the protectiveness in him. From the very first time he confronted her father, she had became his responsibility. It didn't matter that it took him a year and a half after that incident to make her his woman. From that first day, it was his duty to protect her.

"He's not taking Elliott anywhere." Jacob exclaimed. "I don't know what you have in mind, but this is my town. Nothing takes place without my say. I'm thinking it's best for you to leave or I will have you behind bars before you can blink."

Brian raised an eye-brow, remembering that was the same threat Caitlyn's father had given him nine years ago.

"Boy you're in the wrong place at the wrong time. You are in my town. This is not the campus; I'll make your life a living hell. Now, I told you to stay away from my daughter. There is no way in hell I'll let some—some hood rat like you near Caitlyn. You and your high and mighty attitude, doing all you could to turn my daughter against me. You had her doing things she never would have thought of." He advanced on Brian, *"My daughter was raised to advance this family's status, not to end up with the likes of you. Now, I want you to get the hell out of my town. If you show your face around here again, I'll make sure you pay. The FBI can't help you down here boy.*

Brian refused to leave until he knew where Caitlyn was. "You do what you have to do but I'm not leaving until I see Caitlyn."

"Arrest him," Judge Montgomery demanded.

"Judge," The sheriff tried to intervene, "he's just asking about Caitlyn. The boy isn't causing any trouble."

"I said arrest him. Put the handcuffs on him and get him the hell out of my house."

"What charge Judge?"

Montgomery thought for a moment. Then a sly curve of his lips formed. "Kidnapping."

The sheriff frowned. "Of who?"

"Caitlyn."

"Judge you know the boy don't have Caitlyn. She ran away from the doc's office."

"Caitlyn ran off from..." Brian asked confused before he was cut off.

"I said cuff him," the Judge angrily interrupted him.

"What did you do to Caitlyn" Brian jumped towards to the judge's throat.

The sheriff grabbed him back. "Don't do that. You don't want to do that."

Brian was taken out to the patrol car and placed in the back seat. This is where he promised his grandmother he would never be. He slammed his head against the back seat. His whole life was based on what he did at this moment. Everything he ever wanted in life was flashing before him. The academy was in jeopardy. What in the hell was he going to do? He was on his way to jail and he still did not know what had happened to Caitlyn.

The sheriff had gotten into the car. "Son, listen to me. I know this don't seem right and that's just something you are going to have to accept. But you are in a heap of trouble right now and you need to contact your family before we reach the station. Give me a number to call." He pulled out his cell phone.

Brian gave him the number to the only family he knew. When they reached the station he was placed in a cell. Sitting there he wondered what in the hell was going on. Had Caitlyn run away as the sheriff indicated? Why?

A few minutes later he heard the door open and saw Caitlyn's mother. It had been a while since he had seen her at the hearing, but he was sure it was Mrs. Montgomery. The only question was why she was there. She hurried over to the cell and stared at him. "Do you love my daughter?" she asked.

"Why?" he asked angrily.

"I don't have long, please just answer my question," she pleaded.

"Yes, I do."

"Mr. Thompson she is not safe with you here. Leave this town and don't come back. I promise you I will make sure Caitlyn is protected. Leave Mr. Thompson but know Caitlyn loves you just as much as you love her." The woman turned and hurried out the door.

Two hours later Brian sat behind bars explaining to JD's father, Officer James Harrison what led up to this point. "Have you heard from Caitlyn since you left campus?"

"No. I left with the agent representative that Monday. I called her dorm all day and they said she wasn't there. When I got home the next day I found her note." He shook his head. Every time I called the number, I was told she wasn't there. Yesterday Montgomery answered the phone and told me Caitlyn did not want to see or talk to me. He said she did not want anything to do with me. I told him I wanted to hear that from her. That's when he told me Caitlyn was gone and hung up the phone."

"What did he mean by gone?"

"That's just it Mr. H, I don't know. Earlier tonight her mother came here. She seemed frightened. She said Caitlyn was not safe with me in town. I don't know what's going on, but my gut tells me Caitlyn is in trouble. I have to find her. I promised I would protect her. I promised. "He cried. " I promised."

James Harrison looked through the bars at the young man he considered one of his own. The conversation he'd had with Montgomery left no room for negotiation. Either Brian left and gave his word he would not try to contact

Caitlyn or he would press trespassing and kidnapping charges against him. He wasn't worried about the kidnapping that was just a ruse on his part. He knew it and so did the judge. But the charge would sensationalize the situation. As much as he wanted to let Brian at the son-of-a-bitch, he knew it would ruin the boy's chances with the FBI. He couldn't let that happen. "Brian, I know this is difficult and I would be the last person to tell you this. But this man is trying to destroy everything you have worked hard for. Tell him what he wants to hear and let this matter drop. Then look for Caitlyn when you are in a better position."

"That would be the same as giving up on Caitlyn and I can't do that."

"Do you think Caitlyn would want you sitting in this cell when you should be at the academy? Do you think your grandmother would be happy with you not becoming an agent? She worked two jobs until she died to get you into that school. Are you willing to throw her sacrifice back in her face?"

Brian put his head in his hands dejected. How could he let Caitlyn go? He promised to protect her, to be there for her. How could he disappoint his Big Mom? She worked hard keeping him in line all those years. There was no way he could let her down as his mother did. No man should have to make this decision. His only prayer was that Caitlyn's mother would do as she said. He had to trust her with Caitlyn.

After what was a matter of minutes, but what seemed like hours to James, Brian held his head up and stood. What James saw hurt him to his heart. This boy was hurt, probably damaged for life. A moment ago this was a boy sitting on the bunk bed with his head down. The eyes looking at him now were those of a wounded man. His head was held high as he nodded. "I'm ready."

James nodded his head in encouragement, thinking this is what a lost heart looks like. He wondered if Caitlyn was *lost to him forever. "I'm ready," Brian repeated as he stared intently at James. With a swipe of his hand, he wiped the tears from his face. The stone cold expression that appeared indicated it would be a long time before he opened his heart again.*

"Let's go son."

Without hesitation Brian reached out and grabbed Becker by the throat and slammed him against the wall. "Don't ever try to come between me and my son."

Caitlyn rushed over to grab his arm. "Brian," she cried hysterically, "don't Brian. This is what he wants. Don't give it to him Brian. Please don't let him separate us again."

Something in Caitlyn's words reached Brian's brain and his hand opened, allowing Becker to fall to the floor. Brian pulled out his cell phone as he stepped away from the man. This time the Montgomery's and Becker's' of the world were not going to win. Again he called the only family he had. The call was picked up on the second ring. "Déjà vu. A judge is standing between me and my son. I will not turn the other cheek this time. You know what to do." He hung up the telephone, then walked over to Jacob and stood over him. "I don't know you. But if you try to come between me and my son, I will kill you."

"You're a cocky son of a bitch just like Freddie said. You threaten a judge. Not even Harrison can protect you from an attempted murder charge."

"Who's going to testify against him father?" Colin asked from the doorway. "Certainly not me. What about you Cat?"

She looked at Brian. "Never." She shook her head for emphasis, "never."

"I didn't think so." Colin walked over to Brian and directed him away from his father. "Believe me, I feel like killing him myself at times." He looked at Brian trying to do what he could to get the murderous look off the man's face. "I appreciate your words to Elliott. You have a fine son. I will miss him. I hope you allow me to stay a part of his and Caitlyn's life as a friend."

Brian finally looked at Colin. He liked the man. There was a story here, but that would have to wait. "Caitlyn, I believe Elliott needs a hand with packing."

"Cat," Jacob spoke. "I paid your father a lot of money that will have to be returned if you or Elliott leaves. Think about your father."

Brian turned to Caitlyn with a total look of disgust, "You called your father?"

Seeing the look of anger in Brian's eyes, Jacob jumped right in, still holding his hands around his throat trying to ease the discomfort left my Brian. "Of course she spoke to her father."

"Cat hasn't spoken to her father in the nine years she has lived here," Colin tried to clarify.

"I've had about enough of you Colin. Don't forget your place."

"Oh father," Colin waved his hand, "My place was forgotten years ago. I just wish it had been sooner so I wouldn't have ruined Cat's life too."

"My father did call." Caitlyn spoke tentatively. "He's very upset that you are here."

"How did he know I was here?" Brian asked.

All eyes went to Jacob. "That's right. I called him. I don't know who you are or if you plan to bring harm to Elliott. Apparently, Fredrick had reservations about you nine years ago and they haven't changed. He doesn't want you anywhere near the boy. Now, I understand why. You are a dangerous man. In fact, I believe you are a danger to the community."

"So you do know what he said to me," Caitlyn cried as she shook her head. "Haven't you two done enough damage? What else do you want?" She yelled.

Colin and Brian both reached for her. Brian pulled back. "Cat," Colin held her tight, "I told you when the time came I would stand up for you and I will. Don't you worry about my father or yours. Go upstairs and give Elliott a hand."

Caitlyn wiped her eyes and took a deep breath. She looked at Brian, "I'll have Elliott ready in ten minutes." It broke her heart, but she knew Brian would protect Elliott from her father with his life.

Brian looked at Colin, "You too Caitlyn."

Colin smiled as he held Brian's stare. He really liked Caitlyn's FBI agent.

"What?" she said as she reached the door.

"Pack a bag. You're coming with us."

She looked from Brian to Colin. Colin nodded and smiled, "It's time Cat."

"Like hell it is," Jacob yelled. "You're going to let this man go off with your wife."

In that slow lazy drawl of his, Colin exhaled. "Yes father, I am."

With a slight wave of her hand, Caitlyn wiped away the tears that were still flowing down her face as she walked up the staircase. Relieved, at least for today that she would still be with her son. But she had no idea what the future held. The truth was, she had kept Elliott's existence from Brian. The reason she'd done it didn't matter. It had been her decision and she'd done what was best for her and her baby at the time. Her father had proven he would do anything to keep her from Brian. Harming her or her baby was not a far reach for him. Reaching the door, Caitlyn knocked, then walked in. She put her hands on her hips and plastered a reassuring smile on her face. "Well, Mr. Elliott Brian Montgomery-Becker it seems the day we have talked about is here."

"Just like you said it would Mommy. My daddy came to get us."

Er...Caitlyn's mind screeched to a halt. She was going to have to clarify the situation to Elliott at some point in time. His father had come, but he was going to take Elliott, not her. She sat on the side of his bed and looked at the eight year old who could easily pass for ten because of his size. But he wasn't ten, he was still just a little boy. He was her little boy. And after everything she'd had to endure to bring him into this world, she was about to lose him. Her heart was breaking.

"Mommy, do you think I need to take my fishing rod? My daddy said he don't have a river, but he's going to get one."

"Not for one night Elliott." But was this going to be one night Caitlyn wondered. Was she losing her baby for good? The memory of the days of torment she endured during her pregnancy eased into her mind. That first week at home was torture. When she finally confessed to her parents she was pregnant, the fury lashed out by her father would have killed her, if she had not been so determined to protect Brian's child. She'd cried so much, it was a wonder she had not lost the baby.

What was she going to do? The line turned blue. According to the instructions that meant the test was positive. She was pregnant. Not one to over react, Caitlyn took the plastic stick, placed it in a sandwich bag and put it inside her purse. Taking a deep breath, there was one thing for sure. Regardless of Brian's or her parent's feelings about it, she was keeping her baby. Just the thought of having a part of Brian growing inside of her was wonderful. She was elated. How or when it happened, she didn't care. They had used protection every time, she thought. But there were so many times, she just could not swear to it.

She had barely been home a week before she began feeling queasy each morning and was sleeping during the day. That was unusual for her so she searched the internet for the symptoms. The results were a total surprise. Though she was happy, the results did create a bit of a problem. First, Brian had plans for his life. He wanted to become a FBI agent. He made it very clear that he would not let anyone or anything interfere with his plans. A baby would certainly create a bit of a bump—literally. But there was no way she could not let him know. Checking the clock on her nightstand, it was a little after ten in the morning. She could be in Richmond by one o'clock. She picked up her phone and called the telephone number she had for Brian, but she did not get an answer. This was something she could not put off. Her parents were out of the country, but would be returning in a week. She had to let Brian know about the baby before they returned.

The ride wasn't as bad as she thought it would be, especially using the GPS system in the car. It was nice to have the technology at hand, now if she only had a cell phone. She could try to call Brian again, but her father did not see the since in getting something that did not work in their area, it was a waste of money, he would say. So Caitlyn found herself parked in an area of Richmond called Winsor Farms. It did not seem to be an area Brian would live in. The homes were million dollar homes, just like where she lived. For some reason she had the impression that Brian was from a middle class neighborhood, this was anything but. Getting out of her SLK Mercedes, she continued to look around the mansion with the beautiful landscape and circular driveway. Pulling out her address book, she rechecked the address. It was the right address, she sighed. "Ok." The inside of her stomach was not cooperating with the determination to let Brian know about his child. To make matters worse, her nerves were adding to the turmoil. That always happened when she was about to see Brian. Ringing the doorbell, Caitlyn again surveyed the front lawn, it was immaculate. The door opened and Caitlyn was not prepared for what she saw.

"Yes?"

A shocked Caitlyn took a moment before she could speak. "I um...was looking for Brian Thompson. Does he live here?"

"Who wants to know?"

The very beautiful young woman with the hazel eyes looked her up and down. Her expression indicated, she was irritated with the interruption of her day. "Caitlyn. Caitlyn Montgomery," she replied.

"What do you want with him?"

"I would like to talk to him. Is he home?"

"You interrupted my nap looking for Brian. Look, Brian is not interested in any type of long-term relationship with anyone, including you. I'm sure you had a good time while you were together, but believe me, that time is over. I'm sure Brian told you this, because he is usually a very honest guy. It was a fling, girl, get over it."

The emotions of the week were catching up to her. The words from the woman were cutting her deep. The problem was, she knew they were true, but that did not keep the tears from dropping down her cheek.

"Look," The woman, said sarcastically, "I know he made you feel special. That's just who Brian is. He makes all women feel like they are the only woman on earth. He doesn't mean any harm or disrespect, but Brian's concentration is on the academy. In fact, he is there now and from what he told me he will be there for the next twenty weeks. Get over it." The woman slammed the door. Caitlyn wiped away her tears as she turned and walked away.

Once inside the car, she pulled out of the driveway and stopped at the shopping center a few blocks away. What was she thinking? This situation is not good for her or Brian. He was accomplishing his dream and who was she to interfere in that. GOD, what was she going to do now? She put her home address into the GPS and headed for the highway. The three hour ride home filled her with dread. The last thing she wanted to do was be a problem for Brian. He told her, he did not want to get involved with her in the first place, for this very reason. She was inexperienced and could cause him issues later. Well, here it was, the mother of all issues. Laughing and crying at the same time, she almost choked on her tears. How could she tie Brian down with a baby? After all he had told her about his life and why he wanted to become an agent. It was his purpose in life to protect people. Being an agent would bring that purpose to fruition. There was no way she could put this burden on him. He would want to do the right thing and take care of his child. To do that he would have to get a job and leave the academy. She couldn't ask him to do that.

Lord knew she was not capable of taking care of a child on her own. Her parents were going to be so disappointed in her, but she did not have anyone else to turn to. Her mother was an only child, just like her and her father had nothing to do with his family. They were on their own. Doing all she could to think through the situation, one thing was certain, she did not want her father to know who her baby's father was. The fact that she was pregnant was going to send him into a rage and she knew it. Maybe if she got a job before she told her parents, she could show how she would be able to manage without any affect on the family. Yes, she nodded, that could work.

"You whore!" Fredrick Montgomery yelled as he slapped her viciously across her face. "You let that hood rat touch you. Have you no shame? I've worked all my life trying to make something of myself, and you dare to disgrace me with a bastard child. I won't have it. You are not going to have it."

The shock of him striking her and the words he was hurling, shattered her. But the last statement sobered her immediately. "I'm going to have my baby." She stated defiantly.

"Not in my house. You will not bring a bastard into my house." He stormed off.

"Caitlyn," her mother cried out as she came into the room. "Oh Caitlyn, what have you done? Your father had plans for you. He wanted you to marry well—to build onto the legacy he wants for this family. This is not going to help his career. Come with me. I'll put something on your face." Beverly helped her daughter upstairs to the bathroom in her bedroom. Wetting a cloth with cold water, she wiped the tears from her child's face.

"My life is not about his career," Caitlyn cried out.

"Sit down. Let me take a good look at your face." Beverly exhaled, "Of course it is. It has always been about his career. It was your responsibility to meet and marry the son of a senator or a senator himself." She sat beside her daughter, "Your father was determined to marry you off to someone with political connections. That's why he allowed you to go to UVA. It's known that a number of well connected families send their children there. If Howard had not been a Historically Black College, he would have sent you there because of its located in DC. But he did not believe you would make significant connections there.

"You mean I would not meet any white politician's son."

Beverly looked at her daughter, "Was that so wrong? Was it wrong for him to want the best for you?"

"I always thought someone that loved me and treated me well was what was best for me." Tears streamed down her face, "Father wasn't concerned about what is best for me. He was concerned about making the right connections for his career. It never crossed his mind that Brian could be what is best for me."

"Really, if you believe that, where is he? Where is this young man you love so much? If he loved you why is he not here helping you make a decision about this situation?"

"He doesn't know about the baby."

Beverly stared at her. "You didn't tell him? Why?"

"I didn't want to interfere with his future," she cried and fell into her mother's embrace. Beverly just held her daughter. A few hours later, Caitlyn was in her bedroom standing at her open bedroom window. Her parents were on the patio below as their voices carried.

"I can't allow her to disgrace this family. One way or another, this has to be concealed," her father angrily stated.

Then she heard her mother's words. It wasn't just what she said it was the way she said it- it was the chilling tone of her voice that caught Caitlyn's attention. "I've never gone against you Fredrick, for you are my husband and I must honor you in all things. But know this. If you ever put your hands on my daughter again you will pay dearly." The silence that followed sent a chill up Caitlyn's pine. Never in her life had she heard her mother speak to her father in such a hostile tone. She never raised her voice, or cursed. She simply made the statement then walked away.

A few days later, her father came into her room and sat next to her on the bed. "Caitlyn, I handled this poorly. I should have never struck you. Please accept my apology. The situation is not great, but it is also not the end of the world." He turned to his daughter. "You look exhausted."

"I am father," Caitlyn cried. "I'm so tired." She put her arms around her father's neck and he returned the hug.

"I know, Caitlyn. I'll take care of this for you." The housekeeper walked in the room with a cup of tea. "Here," her father reached out and took the cup of tea, "drink this and get some rest." Caitlyn was so relieved to have her father there consoling her. Everything was going to be alright now. Her father had forgiven her and still loved her. She drank the tea, then wrapped her arms around her father. Fredrick sat there and talked to his daughter until she fell asleep.

When Caitlyn awakened, she heard voices. "Fredrick you are crossing the line here." She heard a concerned male voice say. "You drugged your daughter!"

"I don't need a synopsis of what I've done. I need to get rid of that bastard my daughter is carrying." That was her father's voice. What has happened, he sounded angry again or was she dreaming? "Do I need to remind you of the case still pending against you? What do you think your patients' reactions would be if you were found guilty of drunk driving?"

"I don't need a reminder." The man was angry. "I'll do as you've asked, however, you have delayed the process by giving her that sedative. We cannot medicate her further until some time has elapsed. Then we can sedate her for the procedure." Dr. Marcus Green stated as he looked down at Caitlyn. "We will keep her here for another hour or so, then we can proceed. Until then, you can wait in the lobby or you can return later. The choice is yours."

"I want this over with by the time I return." Fredrick walked out of the room, leaving Caitlyn and the doctor alone. The nurse came into the room.

"Dr. Green are we going to do this here? Shouldn't we send her over to County Medical, in case of complications?" Dr. Green, Caitlyn thought. Why was she in a doctor's office? Did something happen to the baby? She almost opened her eyes but something stopped her.

"Not this one Shirley. We have to do this discreetly. I'll need you to stay late to assist me."

"Does she even know what we are about to do?"

Dr. Green turned and looked at Caitlyn, "I'm certain she doesn't," he replied solemnly, "But I don't have a choice. Judge Montgomery will make my life a living hell if I don't do this."

"Your life is going to be a living hell if you do. Suppose she wants her baby—what then?"

Dr. Green sighed, "I can only hope her father is doing what is best for her."

The nurse stared at the doctor then agreed. "I hope you're right. I'll stay and help. But I'll be praying for your soul and mine the whole time. Do you want me to go ahead and start an IV?"

"Yes. And thank you for helping."

The doctor walked out of the room as the nurse proceeded with the IV. Caitlyn lay there as still as she could remembering what her grandmother used to say. All closed eyes aren't sleep. She wasn't sure why she did not let anyone know she was awake. All she knew was her father was in the room and something wasn't right. That's why she did not move or open her eyes as he spoke with the doctor. She was still a little groggy but she knew what she heard. They were going to try to hurt her baby. Brian's baby. Not in this life. They would have to kill her first. It was her responsibility to do what she knew Brian would do if he knew about their baby. He would protect his child with his life. That's what she was going to do. Once the nurse left the room, Caitlyn pulled at the IV in her arm. It hurt, but that was life, things hurt sometimes. Looking around she saw gauze and cotton on the shelf on the other side of the room. Trying to get out of the bed was a little hard; she was not in complete control of her body. Her legs were shaky and she wanted to cry, but that would have to wait. She willed herself to move. Adrenaline began pumping in, she had to move fast or she would not be able to move at all. She used the bed to lean on as she reached for her clothes, then the gauze. With the medical drape still on, she put her dress over her head then picked up her shoes. Slowly she turned the knob to open the door to the hallway of the medical office and looked out. A nurse was standing at the station a few doors down from the room she was in. She looked in the other direction and saw an exit sign. The only question was where did it lead? Did it go out to the lobby? She was sure her father would be there. Or did it lead outside? Either way, she had to take a chance. She could not stay in that room. Looking through the crack of the door, Caitlyn watched everyone's movement. The exit door was literally less than ten feet away, but there was an office between them and the door seemed to be opened.

Hearing voices, she looked in the direction of the nurse's station. The doctor called the nurse into one of the rooms. Caitlyn waited. As soon as the nurse was out of sight, she sneaked out of the room and quietly closed the door behind her. She quickly walked into the office next door. Breathing a sigh of relief, she looked around the empty office. It was a doctor's office with medical books on a shelf lining one wall. The desk was facing the door and a window was behind it. She went to the window, almost losing her balance, but catching herself by grabbing the window sill. Outside the window was a parking lot with several cars there. There were woods on the back end of the building. The door led to the outside. If she could get out of the exit door without being detected, she could escape through the woods. But where was she? There were buildings on the other side of the parking lot, but she did not recognize any of them. They were defiantly not in Cape Colin. Shaking her head, because she was beginning to feel woozy, she knew it was now or never. If she did not leave that place, her father was going to let them kill her baby. It didn't matter where she was, she'd find her way somewhere. Tears began to sting her eyes, as she thought, "where?" She placed her hand on her stomach, "Don't you worry, your mother is going to keep you safe. Don't you worry." With that thought in mind, Caitlyn looked around to see if there was anything she could use to help her cause. She pulled open a desk drawer, nothing notable. Then she pulled open the center drawer, there was a wallet and a set of keys. God, she did not want to steal from anyone, but she did not have a choice. Looking inside the wallet, there were several twenty dollar bills. She took two, leaving three in there and hoping the man in the driver's license picture would not need it right away. She wrote an IOU and placed it inside the wallet with her name on it. Closing the drawer, she hurried back over to the doorway and looked out. The nurse was back at the station talking with someone. She heard the person say, "The file you're talking about is in Dr. Green's office." Caitlyn's head turned back to the desk, the name tag said Dr. Green. Oh God, she was trapped. The nurse turned and began walking in her direction. She wanted to cry out, but she couldn't. Caitlyn stood, hiding behind the open door as the nurse came in, looked at the files on the desk then picked one up. With her back to the door, the nurse scanned through the file. Then with her head still down reading the file, she walked back out of the office, never detecting Caitlyn standing behind the door. Caitlyn's heart rate had increased tenfold. It took a few minutes for Caitlyn's nerves to recover. She listened carefully before coming from behind the door. Peeping back down the hallway, the nurse was not at the station and Caitlyn was not willing to stay there another minute. Taking a moment, she said a short prayer, then rushed out of the door. She held the door, closing it shut softly then ran like hell through the woods.

"Mommy will you make peanut butter and jelly sandwiches for me and my daddy when we get to his house?"

Elliott's question brought her back to the present. Looking at her son, she knew she would do it all again. She smiled, "Now, that he's found you I think your daddy may want to prepare them for you."

The man standing in the woods eased from his hiding spot. The plans may be in jeopardy. Who was the man talking to the little boy? He could not hear the conversation from where he stood, but he did see the man grab Jacob. Actually enjoyed watching the scene, but the man could cause him to lose his target. He had to put his plans in action sooner than he thought.

Chapter 7

"Jeffrey what's going on?" Tracy asked as she watched him hastily begin to pack an overnight bag.

Walking past her to the closet he replied, "Brian has a situation in Nickelsville and he needs me."

"Did Brian shoot someone?"

"Not yet Babe, but I need to be there in case someone tries to shoot him." The thought seem to make him pause. He walked over to the family picture on the wall behind the bed and pushed a button on the corner. The action released the lock and the picture moved to the side revealing the safe. Placing his palm on the screen, the lock clicked open. He reached in and pulled out his fire-arm, bullets and holster.

"Why do you need to take a gun with you?"

JD turned to his wife, "The last time I had to go to a small town for Brian, things got a little rough, but I was too young to help. I want to make sure I'm ready this time."

Watching with a concerned eye Tracy exhaled, "Who's going with you?"

"No one, this has to be low key. I'm driving."

"But you just got home."

"This can't be helped Tracy. Would you rather I leave Brian there alone to handle the situation?"

Tracy frowned, "The town will never be the same."

"You aren't taking Samuel with you for protection?"

"No, Samuel and Magna will stay here with you and the kids."

"Jeffrey with everything that has happened, do you think it's wise for you to be roaming around the country with no protection?"

JD stopped packing hearing the concern in her voice. "Babe I'm going to be fine. No one will know I'm even there. Besides, Samuel needs to be with Cynthia." He kissed her forehead and continued packing.

Too many attempts had been made on her husband's life for Tracy. There was no way she was going to allow him to go to some God forsaken place at the far end of the state without someone having his back. "Alright babe," she calmly replied and walked out of the room.

JD paused for a moment, she gave in a little too easily for his comfort, but he couldn't think about that now. Brian needed him.

Fifteen minutes later JD descended the steps with his overnight bag in hand and his blackberry at his ear. He placed the bag against the bottom of the stairs and walked towards his family room where he heard his son playing with his sister. "Calvin I need you to handle things at the office for a few days." The chiming of the doorbell interrupted his stride as he made a u-turned. He opened the door to Calvin standing there with an overnight bag on his shoulder and his blackberry at his ear. "What in the hell are you doing here?" They both disconnected the call.

"I heard Brian needs some help."

Before JD could question him on how he knew, another vehicle pulled up in front of his house. Douglas got out of the passenger side of the vehicle as a woman stepped out of the driver side. Both men turned to look at the scene. "Is that Karen Holt?" JD asked curiously.

"Yes. I think it is."

"She looks good." JD smiled, "What are you two doing here? He asked as Douglas pulled an overnight bag from the back seat of the vehicle.

Calvin stepped inside the door walking past JD as Douglas joined them in the house. "As I said Brian needs help. So we are here."

Tracy walked into the foyer with Jasmine in her arms and JC running in tow smiling brightly at the two men trying hard to ignore the questioning look on her husband's face. She hugged Calvin and kissed his cheek before turning to Douglas. "Thank you for getting here so quickly. I will feel so much better knowing you guys are going to be with him."

"Uncle Calvin, you going away with daddy?" JC asked as he jumped into his Godfather's arms.

"Yeah little man I'm going with daddy."

Realizing what his wife had done JD sighed inwardly, did she think he could not take care of himself? Noticing the look JD was sending Tracy's way Douglas chimed in. "Look man I would have been pissed if something went down with Brian or you and I wasn't around to help. You know I can take out two people in a split second if need be."

"I know you can Doug, but I'm not sure what the situation may be." JD replied then turned to his wife, "Tracy let's talk in the office for a minute."

"Oh babe we don't have time for that." She knew he was going to share a few choice words with her for calling his boys, but she didn't care how angry he got. Her only concern was that he came home in one piece. "Your ride to the airport will be here any minute."

"What ride to the airport? I told you I was driving."

"That would take hours to get there, this way you will be there in one. Besides all of you are too big to fit comfortably for that long of a ride."

Before he could respond the doorbell chimed again. Opening the door he was not surprised to see James Brooks standing there. "Good afternoon, brother-in-law. Your sister wants to know if I will be home for her next doctor's appointment."

JD closed the door, "What are you doing here?" he asked exasperated.

James was confused looking from JD to Tracy. "I'm your transportation."

JD stared up at the three men that stood before him. He knew without a doubt any one of them would protect his life before thinking of their own, just as Brian would. The problem was they were going to small-town Virginia, population eight hundred and two, ninety percent white, and here stood three African American men ranging from six-two to six-four including himself and Calvin who stood just at six feet. There was no way in hell their presence was not going to be detected. He looked at his wife who seemed very satisfied with herself and realized there was no need in trying to convince her that her concerns were unfounded. The truth of the matter was he did not know what situation he would be walking into once he reached Nickelsville. He exhaled, took his son from Calvin and hugged him. "I'll see you when I get back little man. Will you take care of Mommy and Jazz for me?" His son nodded his head sadly, when he put him down the boy clung to this mother's leg. JD kissed his baby girl who was in her mother's arms and then kissed Tracy. "I'm not sure how long this will take, I'll call."

All three men stood watching the scene and understood how hard it was to leave behind the women they loved but it had been Brian who had protected those women for them and now he was in need.

Calvin picked up his bag he had rested on the floor, "Douglas are you packing?"

"Multiple times. You got a problem with that?"

"Yes, if we have to go through an airport," Calvin replied.

"That shouldn't be an issue gentleman, we are landing at a private airstrip," James replied. "Besides, are you going to try to disarm him? Because I certainly am not?"

JD picked up his bag and looked at Douglas who had an, "I wish you would," look on his face. "I'm not either." He laughed.

"The hell with it," Calvin replied angrily, "Let's roll." He demanded and walked out of the door.

The three men stared at his back. "He is the shortest one here and he has the nerve to be demanding sh----stuff," Douglas changed what he was about to say, seeing the children were still in the room then walked out the door.

"He may be short but I see you moving," JD joked as he and James closed the door behind them.

Pulling up in front of the B&B, Brian wasn't surprised to see the Sheriff's car parked in front with Margie standing in the front. He was surprised the Sheriff wasn't bum rushing his vehicle to put cuffs on him. He parked the car then walked around the passenger side to open the door for Elliott. Colin and Caitlyn pulled up behind him in their vehicle. "Hello Sheriff," Brian said, "I can't say I'm surprised to see you."

"Well Mr. Thompson, I understand we may have a situation here."

"Joe, did my father call you?" Colin asked as he joined them on the porch.

"In fact, he did Colin. Hello there Elliott," Sheriff Wade said as he smiled at the boy.

"Hello Sheriff," Elliott said holding on to his father's hand. "Sheriff, this is my daddy—my real daddy. His name is Brian Elliott Thompson, almost just like mine."

Margie and Sheriff Wade looked from Elliott to Brian then back again. Then Margie looked at Caitlyn, who appeared to be shaken. "Hello Cat." She walked over and hugged her friend then whispered, "Seems like we have a lot to talk about." Caitlyn smiled warily at Margie and just nodded her head unable to speak yet.

Colin took the overnight bag from Caitlyn's shoulder and walked over to Joe. "Sheriff, this is a private situation that my father is not too happy about. Hardly anything that would warrant your being here."

Sheriff Wade looked from Colin to Brian to Elliott. "According to your father Mr. Thompson here assaulted him—tried to choke him to death were his exact words. Now, if that's the case Mr. Thompson I have to take you into custody."

With her arms still around Caitlyn, Margie cleared her throat. "It may be best if we take Elliott inside." She nodded her head towards the boy. "Besides, it seems we are drawing a crowd Joe. She looked down the street at people standing on their store fronts.

Sheriff Wade agreed, "Take Elliott on in while Mr. Thompson and I handle some business."

Brian looked down at Elliott, "I'll be in for you soon."

Elliott smiled up at his father. "Okay Daddy. Come on Mommy. Ms. Margie did you meet my daddy?"

Margie smiled at the beaming child, "Yes, Elliott I did. And you know what?"

"What?"

"Now that I see you two together, you look just like him."

Once the boy was inside, "Sheriff Wade turned to Brian. "Mr. Thompson did you do what Judge Becker accused you of?"

Brian nodded, "I did."

"But there were extenuating circumstances Joe." Colin explained.

"That's for the judge to determine, you know that Colin."

"That hardly seems fair Joe," Colin argued. "You know how my father is an ass at times."

"Judge Becker wants me to leave town without my son." Brian explained. "That's not going to happen. If you have been instructed to arrest me, I will not resist. However, while I'm in your jail I will hold you responsible for Caitlyn and Elliott's safety."

"Do you have reason to suspect they are in danger?" The sheriff asked.

"Of course he does Joe," Colin stated. "From the wrath of my father."

"Sheriff—Sheriff," Becky Sue called from the doorway of the jail which was located across the street from the B&B. The men turned in her direction of the woman as she hurried anxiously towards them. "Sheriff the Attorney General is on the telephone."

Sheriff Wade reached for the cell phone, showing his frustration at being interrupted. "You mean the Commonwealth Attorney."

"No sir. I mean just what I said. The Attorney General of the Commonwealth of Virginia is on the phone requesting to speak with you."

"I think you should take that call Sheriff," Brian suggested.

The Sheriff stared at the woman not believing what she said. He slowly brought the phone to his ear as he turned and intently stared at Brian. "Sheriff Wade here."

"Sheriff Wade, please hold for Attorney General Harrison." His eyes narrowed as he waited. "Sheriff Wade, good afternoon. This is Attorney General Jeffrey Harrison. I understand you have a situation regarding Brian Thompson. I'll be landing there in about an hour. I will consider it a personal favor if you would not take any action until that time."

"I can do that," the Sheriff replied as he stood a little straighter.

"You're a good man Joseph Wade. I'll see you in an hour. May I have a word with Mr. Thompson?"

"Sure thing," Joe passed the phone to Brian.

"Mr. Attorney General," Brian said in a teasing tone.

We are scheduled to land at a private strip in Bristol, about twenty minutes outside of town in an hour. Can you refrain from killing anyone until then?"

"I make no promises." Brian disconnected the call and gave the phone back to the Sheriff. "Let's take this inside where we can talk. However, keep in mind, I'm anxious to spend time with my son."

"We can keep it brief," Sheriff Wade stated, "But I will have to address the complaint from Judge Becker."

As they took a seat in the lounge area, a man walked through the door, looked around then walked towards them. "Oh hell," the Sheriff dropped his head, then looked back up. "Hello Mr. Turner."

The man nodded, then turned to Brian. "Are you the FBI fellow everyone is talking about?"

Brian stood, not knowing what was to come, but being ready for anything. "I am."

"I need your help to find my son," Mr. Turner stated.

That was not what Brian expected to hear. "Your son?"

"Um, Brian Thompson, Nathan Turner. Nate, this is ex-FBI agent Brian Thompson." Sheriff Wade introduced the men with a regretful expression on his face.

Brian noticed the look. He extended his hand to the man. "Mr. Turner, we are in the middle of a personal matter at the moment. Could we meet later to talk about your son?"

"I've waited ten years, another few hours won't hurt none." The man turned and abruptly walked into the restaurant then took a seat in the corner.

Brian watched the man, then turned back to Sheriff Wade. "It's a long story," the Sheriff said as he retook his seat. "Let's settle one case at a time."

"There is no case here to settle," Colin said. "What's happening here with Mr. Thompson and Caitlyn is personal. My father has no say."

"What exactly is happening with you and Caitlyn Mr. Thompson?"

"The gist of it is simple. Caitlyn and I were involved during college. Apparently that involvement resulted in a child, Elliott, whom I am just learning about today. As you may suspect my mind is reeling from this discovery and I am frankly not in the mood to deal rationally with Judge Becker or anyone else attempting to keep me from spending time with my son. Not to forget that I need to have what is sure to be an unpleasant conversation with a woman that disappeared from my life ten years ago carrying my child without telling me." Brian sat forward and glared right at Sheriff Wade face. "I would like to begin that conversation now. Are we through?"

The man sitting across the table from him looked calm, but his eyes let the Sheriff know the question was only put on the table as a polite gesture. "I'll handle Judge Becker. Go spend time with your son. But I will have to take you in."

"I appreciate that Sheriff," Brian stood and looked at Colin. He extended his hand. "You've taken care of my son for years. Not to mention what you've done for me today. I apologize for my rudeness earlier today."

Colin took Brian's hand. "A wrecking ball crashed into your life. Your reaction did not offend me. What you do next will impact your son's life. Keep that in mind when you speak with Caitlyn."

Brian nodded then walked away. He couldn't speak to how he would deal with Caitlyn. There were too many unanswered questions. The fact that she kept the existence of his son away from him was not something he could just let go. There was absolutely no reason for her to have kept that from him. Nine months of pregnancy and eight years of Elliott's life had gone by and she never once picked up a telephone to tell him about his son. What made matters worse, his heart was rejoicing at seeing Caitlyn again and so was his body.

When he reached the top of the steps he could hear Elliott talking to Caitlyn. Hearing the laughter between the two swelled his heart. The sound was like heaven to him. He stood in the doorway of the room next to his and watched as Caitlyn help Elliott unpack for his stay. God she was still beautiful. The stress of the day was showing in her eyes, but she was smiling at her son's excitement. "Our son." Brian thought. Caitlyn and I have a son together. The thought brought a smile to his face. He didn't know when it happened, but just looking at Elliott, it definitely happened. The boy looked just like him. "Damn, he's going to be a heart breaker."

Caitlyn turned at his words then looked back to her son. "Just like his father."

Brian just stared at Caitlyn. There was such sadness in her eyes and it broke his heart to see it. "I'm not going to take him from you."

"Hey Daddy," Elliott said.

"Hey son. Would you do me a favor and go ask Ms. Margie if lunch is ready? I want to talk to your mother for a minute."

"Okay," Elliott ran from the room.

Brian and Caitlyn just stared at each other for what seemed like eternity before either of them spoke. He had to will his feet to stay where they were, for his heart was pushing him forward. She was still his beautiful Caitlyn, standing there in a sundress and sandals, no make-up and her hair loose around her shoulders. "You look good Caitlyn."

Subconsciously, Caitlyn reached up to pat her hair in place. His eyes were smoldering and calling out to her. "Thank you."

"Thank you for giving me a son."

Only this man would take the time to thank her for the biggest joy of her life. "There was never a question for me. From the moment I discovered I was pregnant, I wanted my baby more than life itself."

"It never crossed your mind that it may have been a big moment in my life?"

Caitlyn sat on the edge of the bed, "You were experiencing your big moment at the academy."

Brian stepped away from the door he was leaning against. "The academy was important, but not more important than my son." The statement came out harsh. He stopped. Colin's words came to his mind. He took a deep breath then spoke again. "We have a son together. Where do we go from here?"

I don't know. My dreams never took me this far." She bowed her head, suddenly finding her hands very interesting.

"We have to make decisions."

"Brian I can't lose Elliott. He's my life," she pleaded.

"Now he's my life too. You'll have to learn to share him." He said with a bit of an edge to his voice.

"I agree. I just don't know how."

"Are you so ashamed of what you did that you can't look me in the eye?"

Caitlyn looked up. "I haven't done anything to be ashamed of."

"Haven't you? Elliott is eight years old. It's been nine years since I've seen you. Nine years since you married someone else. Not a word Caitlyn, not one word."

He looked so good standing in the doorway with his arms folded across his chest. It was good to know the shooting did not leave any physical scars. It certainly did not hamper his arrogance—that was still intact. Only his eyes were different. His eyes matched the cool tone of his voice. "I did what I thought was right at the time. You were at the academy and unreachable."

"Caitlyn I had no reason to think I needed to be reached. You knew my plans and what they entailed. I told you everything." He stated a little more angrily than he intended.

"Forgive me. I didn't know I was pregnant until after you had left for the academy. Other than the address in Richmond, I had no way of contacting you. After meeting another of your girlfriends, I was lost, scared. I didn't know what to do."

"I didn't have any girlfriends in Richmond. You were the only one since Cathy. Just you." Taking a deep breath to calm his temper, Brian exhaled. "Going back over the past is not going to get us anywhere. We have a son that we need to put first. What you and I did or didn't do isn't important. Now, he is my number one priority." He shook his head. He still couldn't understand why his body was reacting to her as if the last nine years did not exist. "When does school end?"

"Next week is the end of school," she twisted her hands.

"I would like for Elliott to spend the summer with me."

"The whole summer?" she asked anxiously, looking up at him with those sensuous eyes.

Raising an eyebrow, Brian ignored his thoughts, "Is that a problem?"

"It's just that Elliott has never been away from me. I don't think I could survive a whole summer without him."

"I've been without him his entire life. I don't' think you will die from one summer. And in case you missed the memo, it's not a request. When I go home to Richmond my son will be with me."

Caitlyn's fears had come to light. He wanted Elliott, not her. He was right, he had missed out on so much of Elliott's life. Their son was now at the age where he needed his father to take him into manhood. If she had to let him go, so be it. The last thing she would do was beg Brian to take her with him. Besides, she still had a commitment to Colin.

Caitlyn walked towards the door, then stopped. "Elliott has done very well in school. I'll check with his teachers about an early release. Whenever you are ready to leave, I'll make sure Elliott is prepared to leave with you." Without looking back or waiting for a reply Caitlyn walked out of the room.

There was something about the way she surrendered to him that reminded him of how she used to surrender to her father. That bugged the hell out of him. But she had every right to think he had girlfriends in Richmond. The first year of them being friends, she was surrounded by his girlfriends. There was one for each season. In fact his girlfriends, at one point took over his cause to protect Caitlyn and they were fierce. Hell some of them were so protective of her, that they would turn on him or anyone that bothered Caitlyn. It all started with Wanda.

Back then Brian fought hard against his attraction to Caitlyn. But there was something about the five foot three cutie that stirred him inside. Fortunately, he had an abundance of women waiting in line to get a taste of him. But there was sweetness in Caitlyn that drew him to her. After the night of the step show, whenever he saw her around campus, she was always alone. He had seen girls on campus shun her but after a while, he thought someone would step up to the plate. But no ever gave her a chance. He discovered why on movie night at the student center. He and Wanda, the lucky woman for the moment, were in attendance. The theater was crowded, but not full. They found two seats and Brian went off to get refreshments. When he returned, he saw Caitlyn sitting at the end of a row to his left. A group of girls were sitting next to her. So naturally he thought they were all together. A few minutes into the movie, with Wanda's hand traveling up his thigh and her tongue trailing down his earlobe, Brian was pretty sure they were not going to make it through the movie. Standing to leave he saw Shania, Miss Popularity herself and her entourage approach Caitlyn. Shania stopped and stared at the girls sitting next to Caitlyn until they stood up and moved. The three girls sat in another area, but Caitlyn did not move.

"You're sitting in our seats," Shania said with a threatening tone.

Brian must have moved, because Wanda stopped to see what was distracting her man from the preliminaries she had planned until they got back to his place for the main events.

Shania bent down to Caitlyn, "Are you hard of hearing bitch?"

Brian sat up and that pissed Wanda off. Here she was trying to get her grove on and this little Barbie was interrupting her plans. She patted Brian's thigh, "Excuse me baby while I squash this," Wanda said as she stepped by him. Brian watched as Wanda who played guard on the girls basketball team, standing five ten barefoot and with her stiletto boots, she was an easy six feet. She stood in front of Shania with hands on hips, "Excuse me," she said then took a seat next to Caitlyn. "Hey girl thanks for saving my seat."

Caitlyn looked at the girl that towered over her as they sat next to each other. Then she looked at Shania, and started to stand. "Look I don't want to cause any problems here."

Wanda put her hand on Caitlyn's arm to stop her then glared at Shania. "Let's cut to the chase. You may consider yourself queen of the Barbies on this campus, but we," she pointed to Caitlyn and then around the theater, and every other brown skin sister on this campus have a sisterhood that surpasses your imagined superiority. You mess with her, you mess with all of us. Now sit your little ass down before I really get upset." She stared at Shania with a look that dared her to say anything further.

Shania looked at Wanda, knowing exactly who she was and just how much power she carried on campus and decided she would pass on torturing Caitlyn tonight.

As she walked away Wanda looked over at Brian smiled and winked. "I'm going to wear him out tonight," she said to a stunned Caitlyn.

Caitlyn turned to see Brian in the chair grinning. She waved then turned back to Wanda. "Did he ask you to come over here?"

Wanda shook her head, "No. I did that because there are only a few of us on this campus and we have to have each other's backs. You're new. The Barbies, as we call them, are threatened by you because of your brains, beauty and boldness. So they are trying to intimidate you."

"Thank you. But I'm not any of those things you mentioned."

"Of course you are. Look at you, sitting here by yourself enjoying the movie. Most freshmen would not dare to come out alone. You didn't jump when the brown haired Barbies came over, like the other freshmen did. You stayed and challenged them. That's why I came over, to let you know I got your back." She looked over to see Brian get up. "Girlllll, I'm going to have me a good time tonight. Ummm, um, umm, umm!" Wanda stomped her foot.

"Hello Caitlyn," Brian said as he held his hand out to Wanda.

"Hello Brian,' Caitlyn replied staring up at him.

"You should leave with us," Wanda said. "We'll walk you back to your dorm room."

"I think that's a good idea," Brian said as he held out his hand to Caitlyn.

From that night on, that's the way it was. Any girl that wanted to get with Brian, understood it was a package deal.

His cell phone chimed, pulling him back to the present. He frowned. How in the hell does it work in this room, but not his. What kind of crap is that? He looked at the number, hesitated, then answered. "What?"

"We'll be landing in twenty, bring a van."

"Did you know I have a son?"

JD hesitated then replied, "Yes."

"Be prepared."

JD hung up the cell phone. During the flight JD filled the group on what he knew about the situation. He told them about Caitlyn and Brian during college. Then he told them about the night he went with his father to Cape Charles to get Brian out of jail. Finally, he told them about running into Caitlyn a few weeks ago in Nickelsville. "I'm not sure what he will need or what the reception is going to be when we get there. But whatever it is, I plan to be there for him."

The private plane, belonging to James Brooks, had seats that were arranged the way a conference room would be set up.

Calvin was sitting in the seat across from JD next to the window. "Do you remember that conversation we had at UVA with him about Caitlyn?" He chuckled, "He damn near cut our heads off."

JD smiled, "One thing for sure, he made it clear we were to stay away from Caitlyn or he was going to kick our asses."

Calvin laughed, "Word association." JD laughed at the memory.

"What was word association?" Douglas asked.

"A crazy game we played during college to categorize girls. Here's how it went."

"What happened that night?" James asked.

JD glanced over at Calvin and smiled, then began the story.

"Word association," Calvin suggested.

"Go for it," Brian laughed as he took a swallow from his beer.

"Category–women," JD began.

"Love them," Brian replied and they all laughed.

"That was the category fool. Here's the first name, Wanda."

"Legs – good God that girl had legs." Brian shook his head, "Strong ones too."

"Alright, Gwen."

"Lips. The biggest, sweetest lips this side of Georgia."

"How in the hell would you know that B?" Calvin asked, "Have you ever been to Georgia?"

"No, but I've been on this side and visited quite a few ladies and I'm telling you Gwen had some sweet lips."

Calvin smiled, "What about Cathy."

"That's easy, hands. The things Cathy could do with her hands would drive a sane man crazy." The three friends laughed. "She plans to open a Spa that specializes in massages that make your body move. And I plan on being her first customer."

"I have one," JD said knowing he was about to open a can of worms, "Caitlyn."

Brian stopped with the beer bottle still poised in the air toward his lips. He gave JD a strange look, then finished taking his drink. The atmosphere in the room seemed to have shifted toward dangerous. He placed the empty bottle on the table. "Caitlyn doesn't fit in that category."

"Why not," Calvin asked, "she's a woman–a damn pretty one at that."

"Because I said she doesn't." Brian growled as he stood to get another beer from the refrigerator.

"She's a woman, one of your women according to you. So why not?" Calvin asked.

"Because she's Caitlyn. She's not one of my women. Caitlyn's" he hesitated. "Caitlyn's my friend."

"Like Cynthia," Calvin asked.

"No, no, not like Cynthia. Caitlyn's different."

"Different how B," JD asked as he sat forward to hear his friend's response. "I mean, you said before Caitlyn wasn't open game. So we backed off. Now, you're saying she is not one of yours, she's just a friend. Does that mean she is open game now?" JD, waited for the explosion."

"Hell no," Brian yelled. "I said she was not open game and that's that."

JD held his hands up, "Ok man. That's cool," he laughed. "I really have no intentions of stepping to Caitlyn. I was just messing with you B. But you need to come clean. Caitlyn is special to you. I can see that."

"So can I," Calvin added. "You're the only one that don't see it. Or is it that you see it, but don't want to admit it?"

Brian looked from one friend to another then exhaled. "I've been trying my damnedest to keep my hands off Caitlyn." He shook his head. "It gets harder and harder every day." He sat back down and rested his head on the back of the sofa. "Caitlyn doesn't fit in the category with the rest because she has it all, the legs, the hands, the body and lord, those lips. Those lips. Every time she smiles I want to suck them right off her face."

"What's holding you back B? It's clear Caitlyn is totally into you. So why not make her your woman?" JD asked.

Brian sat up and stared at him. "Caitlyn scares me. You know me. I like women, big ones, small ones, tall ones, short ones." His friends repeated the mantra with him. And they all smiled. Brian became serious again. "I'm not ready to give them up. Being with other women would hurt her, and I don't want to do that."

"At least you know you are not ready, but who knows, you may not want other women once you have Caitlyn," JD said.

Calvin and Brian looked at him as if he had lost his mind. "That coming from a man that has a woman on every campus between Charlottesville and Williamsburg," Calvin interjected.

"Let's see, there's Virginia State, Virginia Union, Virginia Commonwealth University, James Madison University, Norfolk State, Old Dominion University and let's not forget

Hampton and Howard. The only campus you skipped is William and Mary." Brian added. "Come to think of it, is there a campus in Virginia you have not hit?"

JD looked up in thought, "I'm not sure but I am an equal opportunity lover," JD joked.

"Brian, you can't talk. They sent you to Japan for a summit and you went international," Calvin laughed.

"Hey, a woman is a woman. They all need to be loved. And I take my job of spreading my special brand of love around seriously."

"Except when it comes to Caitlyn," JD smirked then sat back.

Brian looked at him, "What is it with you and Caitlyn?" he asked angrily.

"Nothing man. It's just," he hesitated, then continued, "It's just, the last time I was here I watched as Caitlyn stood on the wall at the party as you grinded with every woman there and you didn't give her a second look. She was hurt, man. I'm telling you, that girl is in love with you. And if you can't see that, it's because you don't want to." Brian started to say something, but JD stopped him. "Let me finish. I also witnessed you damn near losing your mind and scholarship when some other dude asked her to dance. The only person you let her dance with was me. How fair is it that, you can have all those women and Caitlyn can't even dance with a guy? Something is not right with that picture B. That's all I'm saying. If you don't want to step to her, you should let someone else."

"Is that someone else you?" Brian narrowed his eyes.

JD shook his head, "No B. we don't roll on each other's turf. If you say Caitlyn is off limits, that's an automatic no no for me, no questions asked."

"Same here B," Calvin said, "But, JD is right man. You have her on lock down, but you're not willing to give her any love. That's not fair."

"Neither of you understand. I'm protecting Caitlyn from brothers like me."

"So there are no good brothers on this campus that you could hook her up with?" JD asked suspiciously.

"Hell no."

JD and Calvin laughed. "Then it's your duty to give Caitlyn some love too. This is your senior year of school. What happens next year when you are gone?" JD raised an eyebrow. "Think about that."

"You can't take her to the academy with you," Calvin stated.

JD stood to get another beer from the refrigerator and hit Brian on the shoulder, "Do you think another woman like Caitlyn exist for you?"

"No. But neither do the kids and the white picket fence."

"Hell, me either," JD said as he retook his seat. Is that what you think of when you think of Caitlyn?"

"Yes."

JD took a drink of his beer. "Then I say you need to lock that down, before this year is out. You can take your time with all the other stuff. But you should at the very least let her know what you're thinking."

Calvin took over the story. "The next week, Brian took Caitlyn to see Frankie Beverly and Maze and the two were inseparable for the rest of the year."

"So he was in love with her then," Douglas stated. "I guess the question is, is he still in love with her?"

James laughed, "They say time can heal all things, except love."

"And love can conquer all," JD smiled.

"So you think Brian still loves Caitlyn?" Calvin asked.

"It is said that love lasts through all times," JD grinned. "We shall find out if that is true."

"We'll know once we get off this plane just how pissed Brian is," Douglas gave JD a wicked smile.

"Brian will be fine," JD said, then turned away praying he was right.

Brian stepped out of the car when the plane landed. The shock of the day's events, then having to deal with Becker when he discovered he was not behind bars, shot his pissedivity level to a whole new high. Anger, the likes of which he had never known, consumed him and he just was not sure how he was going to react once he saw JD. The wait was almost over he thought as JD stepped off the plane, he was going to knock the hell out of him. But then, Douglas stepped off followed by Calvin and then James. He was surprised to see all his friends there, but then as JD stepped off the plane and approached him, he frowned, "Are they here for you or me?"

JD looked over his shoulder at the men then turned back to Brian, "They are here for you."

"Good," was all Brian said before landing a right hook on JD's jaw with so much force he landed on the ground. "You knew! You knew and you didn't say a word, not one damn word. Man how in the hell could you do that?" Brian railed down at him. The friends stood back, it was apparent Brian and JD needed a moment.

JD palmed his jaw with his hand and looked up at Brian. "I owe you that one, but don't think you're going to get away with it again."

Brian took a deep breath then reached down to give JD a hand up. Through the fog of anger, he understood if JD hadn't sent him to Nickelsville he would have never found Caitlyn and Elliott.

JD took the peace offering and stood before his friend. "She begged me not to tell you. So I did the only thing I could think of, make sure you find out on your own. Do you really think I would send you as a good will ambassador anywhere, and especially here, man be real?"

Brian stared at his friend and shook his head, "I could not figure out for the life of me why you were so damn insistent that I come here of all places. Man, they don't even have a stop light." He hesitated then sighed, "But they do have Caitlyn and Elliott." He smiled, "That's his name you know."

JD patted him on the back and nodded, "I know."

Brian turned to the other men. "What are all you supposed to do, scare the town's people with your looks?"

"I'm letting you know up front. You throw a punch at me and I'm going to shoot your ass," Douglass explained as he walked over to the car. The others followed; relieved the tension had been broken. As they piled into the vehicle, Brian looked around to the back seat and laughed at Calvin sitting between James and Douglas, "You alright man?"

"Just drive the damn car so we can get out of here," Calvin replied.

JD, who was sitting in the front seat turned back to the front. "So how is Caitlyn doing?"

Brian stared at him. "How in the hell do you think she is? She is upset just like I am. Now, I have to be an ass to spend time with my son and she has to give up her son. How did you think this shit was going to turn out?"

"Look, I didn't get Caitlyn pregnant, nor did I keep the fact that you have a son from you for eight years. So why in the hell are you mad at me?"

"Because damn it I have to be mad at somebody and you're it."

Calvin laughed, "B, I always wondered what happed at the Maze concert. How did you finally end up with Caitlyn back then. When we talked about her at your apartment, you were dead set against starting anything with her.

"What? Was I the topic of conversation on the plane?"

"With the prospect of you being arrested, what else would we discuss?" James joked.

Brian smirked, "I'll take that. As for Caitlyn and Maze, it was all a set up by Cathy." He looked in the rear-view mirror at Calvin, "Do you remember her?"

"Yeah, she was the masseuse." Calvin replied.

"The girl had skills," Brian smiled. "As for the concert, man, that was a night. I will never forget the look on your father's face when he pulled up next to us." He said to JD. "You know your old man was really cool."

JD smiled, "Yeah, he was. But he never told me what happened."

"You remember the old Maxima I used to drive? Well, we ran out of gas after the concert."

The men in the SUV all yelled, "No, not the run out of gas story." Douglas laughed.

Brian joined in laughing, "Man I'm serious. We literally ran out of gas." His thoughts went back to that time as it had a lot over the last twenty-four hours. He did not realize it then, but it was his girlfriend Cathy that had put the whole incident in motion.

Caitlyn looked up from the kitchen table as Cathy walked in. She smiled and began packing her books up. "Hey Cathy." Of all Brian's girlfriends she liked Cathy the best. It wasn't just that she was beautiful, but she had such a kind spirit. She never made Caitlyn seem like a third wheel even though she knew she was.

"Hello Caitlyn." Cathy replied with a smile. "How have you been?"

"Okay," Caitlyn said as she pulled her sweater on. "Dinner is in the oven."

Cathy sat on the sofa as Brian hung up her jacket. "You're not staying for dinner?"

"No. I have to go to the library to study. I'll see you guys later."

"Hey, don't be at the library late," Brian cautioned.

"Yes father," Caitlyn joked.

"You're not funny," Brian said as the door closed. He watched as Caitlyn walked across the street into the gates of the campus.

"It's a good thing I'm not the jealous type," Cathy said as she walked into the kitchen and opened the oven.

"What would you have to be jealous of?" Brian asked as he wrapped his arms around her.

Cathy turned and smiled as she received the kiss she knew he had waiting. Brian may not be her once in a life time, but he was certainly a nice diversion until the love of her life came along. "Mmmm, now that was worth all the crap I had to take today."

"I try to please," he replied as he closed the oven door, picked her up in his arms and carried her into the bedroom. "Allow me to ease some of that tension from your body."

Cathy sat back on the bed, kicking off her shoes in the process, and held her arms out to him. "Access granted."

Brian pulled his shirt over his head and threw it to the floor, as Cathy did the same with her blouse. He kicked off his shoes and unbuckled his pants allowing them to drop to the floor. There was never a question of brief or boxers when it came to him. The answer was nothing. Cathy smiled at the attention his body was displaying. "Looks like you're the one that needs relief." He pulled the pants she had unzipped down, revealing beautiful long legs, lilac lace panties to match her bra and a butterfly tattoo right above her panty line. Dropping the pants to the floor, he kneeled between her legs and began his trail of kisses at the wings of the butterfly. "I think, I'll start in the valley and work my way up." He pulled her panties off and placed them on his head.

Cathy laughed, "You are a fool and a half."

With her legs bent forward in his arms, he entered her in one powerful thrust. They both sighed as he bent her until his lips reached hers. "Bet I can make you scream."

She cupped his face in her hands. "If I scream you'll scream. I promise you that."

He began to move within her, "Let's see who will scream first. With her lying flat on her back, he placed her legs together, bent in front of him. Slowly he ventured in different directions, watching every expression on her face. He grinned when he saw the one he was waiting for. "Found it," he said and began to pump into her with a little more zeal. "Don't try to hold it in," he smiled, "I know you want to scream. Let it out." Cathy shook her head from side to side. "Okay," Brian unsnapped the front of her bra and immediately took one of her protruding nipples between his lips. The motion of his lips and body were identical. And as much as Cathy wanted to hold back, she couldn't. He was relentless in his determination to make her scream, increasing the rhythm and the power behind each thrust. When she could not hold out any longer she screamed as an orgasm struck her leaving her breathless. Brian released her breast just as she came and placed one leg back so that he was between them again. He closed his eyes and pumped fiercely until he finally moaned his release.

Lying on the bed, both spent from the encounter, Cathy began to laugh. "You are wild."

"I know." He laughed.

"You going somewhere?" he asked with his hand behind his head.

Cathy just smiled as she eased off the bed. "I'm going to jump in the shower, while you put dinner on the table."

Brian watched as she walked into the bathroom. Cathy was going to make some man very lucky one day. She was beautiful, intelligent, ambitious and damn good in bed. No matter what he wanted to try she was there with him. But—and it was a big but, when he closed his eyes it was Caitlyn's face that triggered his release.

A half an hour later they were sitting at the table enjoying the meal Caitlyn had prepared with a glass of wine. "You know Caitlyn's birthday is Friday. I brought two tickets to see Frankie Beverly and Maze, but I can't go now. I'd hate for her to miss out. Can you take her?" Cathy asked.

"You got Caitlyn tickets to see Frankie? Why didn't you get me tickets?"

"It's her birthday, not yours, silly. Now I can't go. Do you remember when she said she had never heard any of Frankie's music? I can't believe anyone hasn't heard Joy and Pain."

"Well Caitlyn has led a pretty sheltered life." Brian said without looking up from his plate.

Cathy watched him. "Have you met her people?"

"Once," he said as he looked up. "It didn't go well."

"What do you mean?" Cathy asked as she sat back and picked up her glass of wine.

Brian put his fork down and did the same. "Her father considered me, what did he say, oh a hood rat and he wanted me to stay away from his daughter."

"Is that why you never thought about dating Caitlyn?"

The question must have struck a core. "Hell no. He nor his type can tell me who I can be with. And what's with the inquisition?"

She held her hand up to stop him. "Hold up. It was just a question. I certainly did not mean to strike a chord. I like Caitlyn a lot. I think she is a great person. But I never see her with anyone or any family visiting. With her birthday coming I thought her family would come to visit, but when I asked her what she had planned she said nothing."

Brian stood from the table and put his plate in the sink. He turned and leaned against the cabinet with his arms folded. "I don't understand her parents. I mean her mother seemed nice enough, but her father is an ass. They drop her off and you don't see them again until the next semester when they bring her back."

"Is that when you met them?"

"No. I met them at a disciplinary hearing for someone else. That's when he called me a hood rat and I called him a pompous jackass."

Cathy laughed and eventually so did Brian. "Well, it's a good thing you stuck by her. You're a good friend."

"Yeah." Ready to change the conversation, he looked up at Cathy. "Am I your good friend too?"

Smiling, she replied, "You're my special friend with benefits. Now tell me you will take Caitlyn to see Frankie and I'll share some of those benefits with you."

Brian retook his seat and grinned. "Let me get this right. You're giving me tickets to take Caitlyn to see Frankie for her birthday and you're going to reward me with special benefits?"

Cathy put her glass on the table, stood and walked over to him with nothing on but his shirt. "Stand up." He complied. She pulled his sweats down then pushed him back into the chair. She straddled him, easing down onto his already erect shaft. "How do you want it? Slow and easy, or hard and fast?"

Brian kissed the valley between of her breasts. "Any kind of way you want to give it to me," he replied.

Cathy threw her head back and closed her eyes. "Slow and easy it is," she said while thinking this would probably be the last time for her. After Friday, she was sure all of this would be exclusively Caitlyn's.

"Well don't leave us hanging," JD probed.

"What happened when you ran out of gas?" Calvin asked.

"Some things you just don't share, not even with your boys." Brian looked at him through the rearview mirror and exhaled. "But I will say this, I damn near lost my mind. For a year and a half, I kept my hands off her, but that night," he shook his head thinking about it, "Frankie Beverly and a damn red sundress did me in. She was just too damn tempting and I fell—I fell hard."

Caitlyn watched from the doorway as Elliott enjoyed his lunch while chatting with Bart. "He is so excited about Brian."

"Is this a good thing Cat? I mean Mr. Thompson being here, is it good or bad?"

"It's a good thing Margie, Caitlyn replied with tears on the verge of flowing from her eyes. "But, I do not want to lose my son." The tears began streaming down her face. "What am I going to do without Elliott?"

Marybeth came running through the door almost out of breath. "My word Caitlyn." she said with her hand covering her heart. "You poor dear. I can't believe that man tried to kill Jacob and take your son. What you must be going through." She hugged Caitlyn, "Is there anything I can do?"

"Marybeth, what are you talking about?" Margie asked frustrated.

"Why everyone in town is talking about how the FBI agent stormed into the judges' place. And how Jacob almost lost his life trying to save little Elliott."

"Marybeth, I swear you are worse than a maggot on a dead mouse. Go get a life and leave Caitlyn alone."

"Well I never."

"Apparently you did once and Earl is regretting the day he rolled in that haystack." Margie took Caitlyn's hand, "Come with me." She led Caitlyn to the back balcony and sat her down. "Take a minute then start talking."

Caitlyn wiped tears away, "Brian is Elliott's father."

"Hell's bells Cat, a blind man can see that," Caitlyn smiled and Margie was happy to see that. She wanted to be there for her friend during this time, but until she knew the whole story it was hard to help. "So—tell me. How did you meet Mr. Thompson?"

"In college," Caitlyn choked out. "He was a senior and I was the lonely freshman. I had the roommate from Hades and she made sure I wasn't liked. Brian literally took me in. For a while he was the only person on campus that talked to me. She smiled at the memory. His girlfriends became my friends. I think I fell in love with him the first time I saw him, and the first time he kissed me, I swear my panties were soaked by the time he let my lips go."

Margie smiled, "Oh my. Can you really get off from just a kiss?"

"Oh yeah." Caitlyn sat back and told Margie the story of their first kiss.

"One of Brian's girlfriends, Cathy, decided we should be together. We did not have real R&B music where I came from, so Brian and some of our friends were a little freaked out when I told them I had never heard of this group. So, for my twentieth birthday she arranged for Brian to take me to a Frankie Beverly and Maze concert."

"Joy and Pain," Margie inserted.

"Yes." Caitlyn smiled and continued. "Well needless to say, I fell in love with the group's music, especially this song called *The Morning After*." Caitlyn lowered her head and just shook it. "Margie I swear to this day, every time I hear that song I melt just thinking about Brian and the way his lips felt against every part of my body. Then I think about Cathy and what true friendship means. She knew how I felt about Brian and I guess she suspected how he felt about me. And even though she was seeing him at the time, she unselfishly stepped aside for us to get together. I would love to take credit for that night, but actually it was all her doing. She came to my dorm room with this dress—a red halter top sundress. I always dressed very professionally and rarely wore anything but business suits. So this red sundress was out of the norm for me. When I put it on, it I felt pretty, you know. I always wore my hair up in a twisted bun but Cathy took it down, gathered it into a clip and allowed it to hang down my back. She started to put make up on me, but she changed her mine. Taking a step back she looked at me and said, "He's not going to know what hit him." You see, Brian was the man on campus. Every girl wanted to go out with him and most of them did. But that night, when I looked in the mirror I looked like I could be with him, like one of his girls. That's when I realized how very much I wanted to be desired as a woman by Brian—not a friend, but a woman." Caitlyn sat back in the rocker reminiscing. "I can still remember the expression on his face even now. He liked what he saw. After a moment of just staring at me, Mr. 'Always in control", Brian Thompson, himself reached his hand out to me and asked "Are you ready?"

Boy was I ever. The concert was wonderful. We—well he danced, I just moved to the rhythm, because I didn't know how to dance. Between the smooth voice of Frankie, the soulful music of Maze and being there with Brian, the night was magical." She laughed, "Before we left, he spent the money he had for gas to buy me the CD. Then on interstate 64, half way between Richmond and Charlottesville, we ran out of gas. Can you believe that—we actually ran out of gas? I didn't have a cell phone, but Brian did. He called his friend J.D.'s father. We sat on the hood of his car and listened to the CD while we waited. When The Morning After came on, he asked me to dance. I told him I didn't know how. So he took my hand and said, I'll show you. He placed my hands around his neck and pulled my body close to his with his hands on my waist and said, just sway to the music and follow my lead. I followed him step by step, thigh to thigh, and chest to chest. His body felt so good next to mine, I instinctively moved closer. His hands moved down my back, pulling me even closer. I remember feeling his muscles tightening around me and I liked it. I felt so safe, so wanted. I closed my eyes and just inhaled. Even his scent was intoxicating. Then he whispered my name and kissed my forehead. His lips were as smooth as his voice I literally became mesmerized and so did he. When I looked up in his eyes they were so soulful it drained all my senses and before I could clear my mind to think what was going to happen, his lips touched mine. Her fingers instinctively went to her lips. Hmm. I had never kissed a man before and my lips were shut tight. Then he used the tip of his tongue to outline my lips, it was so moist, that I stuck my tongue out to get a taste. When the tips of our tongue met one of us moaned, or maybe it was both of us. But the sound made him pull his lips away. I remember feeling abandoned and I opened my eyes to see him staring down at me. Our lips were just a breath away when he said, open your mouth for me Caitlyn and I did. He took total control from that point on. His touch was smooth but demanding, you know. I may not have known what to do at first, but I followed what he did, I was powerless to do anything else. His hold on me tightened and there was no way I was letting go of him. My body began to vibrate all over, I mean everything came alive. It felt like my body was on fire and I didn't want anything between us. I remember him taking the clamp from my hair and his hands holding the back of my head, keeping our lips merged together. The next thing I knew, we were in the backseat of his car with his body covering mine and my body was screaming to get closer. His hands were so hot when he touched my thighs placing my legs around his waist and for the first time in my life I felt a man's desire, his desire for me. Right at the juncture between my legs I could feel him, the feel of a steel rod and I wanted to feel more. Every time he tried to pull away I would hold on tighter with my legs to keep him right there, where I could feel the very essence of him against me. God I never wanted that feeling to stop. He only stopped kissing me long enough once to stare into my eyes and I could see he was just as confused as I was. He said, Caitlyn tell me to stop. I couldn't tell him to stop, I just couldn't. My hands pulled around his neck tighter and all I could say was please don't stop. I begged him not to stop. He was so torn; I could see it in his eyes. But I couldn't tell him." She laughed and crossed her legs. "Just talking about it makes my body tingle."

"I'm with you. But don't stop now," Margie laughed.

Caitlyn smiled and continued. "He didn't stop, if anything his kisses became more intense, his hands seemed to be everywhere at once. I don't know when or how but he pulled the bottom half of the dress up my thighs. The only thing between us was my panties and his jeans. It felt so good as his body moved against mine in the same rhythm of his tongue inside my mouth. The air around us grew hotter and I wanted to remove every barrier between us, but Brian wouldn't let me. All I could do was pull his shirt up his back so I could touch his naked skin, when that happened our bodies went into warp speed. I pushed the core of me up to him and squeezed my legs. His hands were on my bottom holding me right where I wanted to be. I couldn't breathe, didn't want to for fear that the feeling would go away. The faster he moved his body against mine, the more demanding his kisses became. The man took grinding in the back seat of a car to a whole other level. The friction increased, our breathing was coming in gasps and neither of us was coming up for air. I wanted whatever was coming so I did all I could to match what he was doing. The anticipation was driving me crazy and my body responded, moving faster and harder against him until we both screamed. He broke the kiss off and the explosion that followed took my breath away. But our bodies kept moving, pressing against each other, until both our heart beats began to return to normal rhythm. The whole time Brian was staring down into my eyes, with unasked questions. I was scared I had done something wrong and I'm sure he sensed that because he gently kissed the corner of my lips, then my cheek, my neck, then he came back to my lips. I felt his hands between my legs when he unzipped his jeans." She stopped.

"What happened?" Margie asked.

Caitlyn exhaled, "He moved my panties aside and placed his shaft right between my legs. It was hot, thick and throbbing against me. I was wet, so wet and I began vibrating down there from his touch. I could feel his heart racing against my chest. It was like he was having a battle within himself. I wanted him so much that night, but he wouldn't go any further. He laid his head in the crock of my shoulder and just kept calling my name. Caitlyn, and shaking his head. He kissed my neck, then put my panties back in place. I lay there looking at him as he re-zipped his jeans. I was so scared and knew I had done something wrong, but I didn't say anything as he smoothed my dress back down over my legs. He got out of the car and held his hand out to me. When I got out my legs wobbled, and that's when he closed the door, wrapped me in his arms, pulled me close to his chest and said, I'm sorry. He kissed the top of my head. I shouldn't have let things go that far. I want you Brian, I said. He said you have me Caitlyn, you will always have me, but not in that way. I pushed away and asked him why not. He said because you are not that type of girl. I said I could be just tell me how." Caitlyn shook her head. "Then you know what he said?"

"What?" Margie asked breathlessly.

"He looked at me and said, Caitlyn you could never be that type of girl. You are the one that a man loves and spends a lifetime searching for. I'm not ready for that type of commitment. And as much as I want you at this moment, I can't take that away from you. Then he reached out and pulled me back into his arms. He smoothed my hair down and put his chin on my head. We stayed that way until J.D.'s father arrived. I fell for him hook line and sinker and I fell hard."

Minutes ticked by before either woman said anything. "I will miss you when you leave." Margie sighed.

"I'm not going anywhere," Caitlyn sadly replied.

Margie looked at her as if she had lost her mind. "Cat, if I didn't know it before, I do now. That man loves you and has for a very long time. If you think for one moment that Brian Thompson is leaving this town without, you are as crazy as a bedbug in a pig's pen."

Chapter 8

By the time Brian returned to the B&B the dinner crowd was thinning out, but to his surprise the man, Mr. Turner was still sitting in the corner. Elliott came running down the stairs and jumped right into his father's arms. "Daddy, Daddy, you came back." His little arms hung on Brian's neck for dear life.

"Of course I came back," he returned the boy's fierce hug. "I told you I would and a man keeps his word—right."

Nodding his head up and down, Elliott agreed, "Right." Brian set him back on his feet. "Hi Mr. Harrison."

JD stooped down, "Hello Elliott. It's good to see you again," he held out his hand to shake the boy's.

"Well I'll be damned," Douglas said with a smile, "It's a little Brian."

Brian's smile beamed proudly as he took his son's hand. "Elliott, these are some of my friends, you know Mr. Harrison," he pointed to Douglas. This is Douglas Hylton, Calvin Johnson and James Brooks. Everyone," he said with a wide smile, "this is my son Elliott."

"Oh—My—God. I done died and gone to heaven." All the men turned to Redbone who was standing in the doorway to the restaurant. She looked from one to another. "Suzie Mae you better get out here. That Mr. Harrison fella and all the men from the tall dark and handsome club is out chere." She looked around happy as a cat sitting in a bowl of milk. "Damn it's enough of ya'll to last me a good week."

Suzie Mae came out of the kitchen, "Well Mr. Harrison, welcome back. Is Ms. Tracy with you?"

J.D. hugged Suzie Mae, "Hello Suzie Mae. It's nice to see you again. Tracy is home with the children."

"She let you come back here by yourself?"

"No ma'am. As you can see she sent an entourage with me."

"A mighty fine one at that," Redbone grinned.

Suzie Mae turned to her granddaughter, "Gal go in the kitchen and pull out some chicken so I can fix Mr. Harrison some dinner. Go on now."

"Hello J.D., Calvin," everyone turned to the stairs.

"Oh hell," Douglas said as he stared at the woman standing on the stairs.

"Mommy, Mr. Harrison is back. He came in with my daddy."

She smiled at her son holding his father's hand. It was wonderful to see him so happy. "I see him Elliott."

"Hello Caitlyn," J.D. said watching to get some idea of how angry she was at him.

"Is it my imagination or does she remind you of somebody?" James whispered to Calvin.

"It's the eyes," Calvin replied.

"She's the whole package," Douglas whispered. "How in the hell did you get her?" He looked at Brian with a raised eyebrow.

Brian turned and frowned at his friend. "Don't."

Douglas shrugged his shoulders, "I'm just asking."

Caitlyn had reached the bottom of the stairs when Brian turned back around. "Caitlyn you remember J.D. and Calvin. This is James Brooks and Douglas Hylton."

"Hello Mr. Brooks," she smiled and shook his hand. She reached up and hugged Douglas. "Douglas I've heard so much about you. It is really nice to meet you in person."

Douglas returned the hug grinning like a Cheshire cat. Brian gently pried them apart and positioned Caitlyn next to him. "That's enough of that."

J.D. and Calvin looked at each other. "Well it looks like the whole gang is here." Margie said as she entered the foyer. "My, my, my, I have my work cut out for me. Suzie Mae could you give me a hand getting the rooms ready. Mr. Harrison, welcome back. I'll make sure you get the room with the view. Is Tracy with you?"

"Hello Margie, no Tracy's home. As for the rooms, we can double up. That will save you some work."

"Man, I haven't doubled up since college," Calvin said.

"I never doubled up," James stated.

The men all turned and stared at him. "What? I always had my own place."

"We have enough room so everyone can have their own." Margie laughed. "No one has to share with anybody else. Now, Ya'll just come on and follow me. We'll get you all set up."

"I'll be up in a minute," Brian said as the guys followed Margie up the stairs. Once everyone was up-stairs he looked at Caitlyn. Douglas hugging her bothered him. After all these years, she still had a pull on him. He wasn't sure how he felt about that just yet, but he knew he had to figure it out soon. Then he remembered, she's a married woman.

Caitlyn held his eyes. She could see his mind was working, trying to figure out his next move. "We waited for you to have dinner. But I think Mr. Turner has been patient long enough." Brian looked over her shoulder. "Do you have any idea what it's about?"

"According to Jacob, he hasn't accepted his son running off a few years ago. He believes something happened to him."

"Was there an investigation?"

"I think Lil Joe looked into it, but it was before I came."

"Do you think something happened?"

Caitlyn turned and looked at Mr. Turner. "I think someone should talk to him that is not from this town and has not any preconceived notions about his state of mind."

Brian inhaled and nodded. "Okay. Why don't you get us a table and I'll join you in a minute."

"All right." Caitlyn turned with Elliott.

"Caitlyn," Brian called out. She stopped and turned back to him.

"Yes," her eyes shiny from tears he was sure.

"We will work things out."

She smiled, "I know you will."

"Hurry up Daddy," Elliott yelled as they walked away.

Brian walked up the steps to find everyone in the room JD was occupying. He was on the phone talking to Tracy. He turned to James. "Your blackberry works in here?"

"Yeah," James replied.

Brian looked at Calvin. "Yes."

Then he looked at Douglas. "How in the hell did you get that woman?"

"I got it like that." Brian replied. "Or had it."

"From the looks of things, I'd say you still have it." James said as he sat on the end of the desk in the room.

"She's married."

"What?" Douglas raised his voice, "Where's the husband? Is that who you need help with?"

"Douglas, we are not here to take anyone out." Calvin reminded him.

"We will if we have too."

"Hold on. Colin isn't the problem." Brian stated as he watched JD end his call. "The father-in-law is threatening to keep my son from me and I can't have that. I won't have it."

JD sat on the end of the bed and his calm voice of reason brought everyone into the listening mode. "What's the situation?"

Brian explained everything that happened from the time he got into town.

"Why is Judge Montgomery so hell bent on keeping you away from Elliott?" JD asked. "Ten years ago it was because he did not think you had a future. That is certainly not the issue now."

"Where does Judge Becker come in?" Calvin asked.

"I don't have the answer to either of those questions and don't really give a damn. Neither of them will keep my son away from me."

"What's Caitlyn's husband take on all of this?" James asked.

Brian sat forward and rested his elbow on his knees and clasped his hands together. "That's the crazy part. The man walked in on me kissing his wife senseless and his response was "hallelujah, it's about time." He has been clearing the way all day for me. Last night this was the most peaceful place I have ever been in. Today, all hell seems to have broken loose. Nothing is normal about this situation." Brian stood and looked at the men in the room. "When I called, I didn't expect you to come. But I'm glad you are here. It's good to know you have my back."

JD smiled, "It's been an emotional day for you man. Where else would we be?"

Brian held JD's stare. He knew no matter what happened between them JD would always be there for him. "Sorry about earlier."

"What was that?" Calvin put his hands up to his ear. "Did ya'll hear that?"

Douglas laughed. "Yeah we heard it."

"Don't get used to it." Brian frowned.

"You know we love you like a brother man," JD said laughing at his friend's discomfort.

"I think that's as close to a thank you for coming as we are going to get. So you're welcome." James said with a smile.

Brian grinned. "I'm going to have dinner with Caitlyn and Elliott. We have a lot to talk about." He looked at JD. "I need a favor."

"Anything man. What is it?"

"There's a man down-stairs that's been waiting all afternoon to talk to me. I'm not sure what it's about, but will you handle it for me. I really need to have this conversation with Caitlyn."

"We'll take care of him. What's his name?" JD asked.

"Mr. Turner." Brian replied. "From what Caitlyn told me, his son went missing a few years ago. He hasn't let go yet. It may be just a case of someone giving him an ear to listen. I don't know."

"Do they have internet service here?" Calvin asked.

"It depends on where you stand."

A knocked sounded at the door. Douglas opened it since he was the closest. Sheriff Wade stood there with his hat in his hand. "Evening folks, I'm Sheriff Wade. Is Attorney General Harrison here?"

Douglas, who was blocking the door, looked over his shoulder as JD approached extending his hand. "Sheriff Wade," he shook the man's hand. "Thank you for coming." He nudged Douglas, who showed no signs of moving to the side. "I never forget a favor Sheriff," JD turned on the charm. "When you are in need of our assistance, don't hesitate, pick up the phone." He patted the Sheriff on his shoulder. "Please come in, have a seat. I would appreciate your take on the situation at hand. Allow me to make the introductions." JD pointed to Calvin, my Chief of Staff, Calvin Johnson."

Calvin shook the Sheriff's hand. "How do you do Sheriff Wade. I understand you enjoy a little trout fishing from time to time."

"That I do," the Sheriff returned the smile.

"I hope to have the opportunity to get a little fishing in while we are here."

Douglas frowned at Calvin then looked at JD, who shook his head indicating to let it go."

"I'm sure we can arrange that."

JD then pointed to James. "This is my campaign manager James Brooks."

"It's a pleasure Sheriff Wade. My father Avery sends his regards."

Sheriff Wade nodded affirmatively, "Please extend my well wishes to him."

"Douglas Hylton, my security detail." JD held his breath. Douglas did not handle the subtleties well when it came to law enforcement. "Sheriff," he nodded, but kept his stance at the door. JD exhaled, that went better than expected.

"How do," the Sheriff replied as he assessed the man.

JD walked over and stood next to Brian. "Of course you've met my friend and head of my security team, Brian Thompson." He wanted to be very clear on his relationship with Brian.

"We have. I'm sorry to say I'm here to take you into custody Mr. Thompson. Judge Becker chewed me up a month of Sundays for not having you behind bars. He gave me an hour to rectify that or he's taking my badge."

JD put his hands on Brian's shoulder. "I assure you Mr. Thompson is prepared to fully cooperate with you in this matter. However, I was wondering if you would be kind enough to give me your take on this?" JD took a seat indicating it was not a request. The other men around the room followed his lead and took a seat as well, Douglas being the exception as he continued his stance at the door.

Sheriff Wade glanced around the room as the men waited, then took a seat. "Well, as I see it Attorney General Harrison,"

JD put his hand up, "JD Sheriff, we're all friends here."

Douglas raised an eyebrow, but JD ignored him and continued to give the Sheriff his undivided attention.

"It seems to me JD, Judge Becker is hell bent on getting Mr. Thompson out of town. Now, I don't know his reasons, but I can tell you this, since he was told you were on your way here, he's been acting crazier than a rooster in a hen house."

"Why do you think that is?" JD asked.

"Frankly I think the problem he has with you is the same he has with Mr. Thompson here, he's not used to his authority being questioned. You see around these parts Judge Becker's word is law." There was a tiny bit of sarcasm in his response.

"How do you feel about that Sheriff?"

Brian sat there as he had so many times before, observing JD winning the Sheriff over. This is why he admired his friend—his ability to draw people in by listening for their hot spots.

Sheriff Wade adjusted his position, then shrugged his shoulder a little. "At times I feel, that's a little too much power for one man to have. But it's my job to uphold whatever ruling he gives me."

JD let that hang in the air for a moment, then spoke. "Indeed it is Sheriff." He shook his head letting the man know he understood his position. "What do we need to do to clear up this unfortunate situation?"

"Well, I took a statement from Colin and Caitlyn. Now I need to take Mr. Thompson into custody, get his statement, then wait on Judge Becker's return."

"All right Sheriff," JD stood as did Brian. "I'll accompany Brian. Calvin, make sure Caitlyn is made aware of the situation. James put Vernon on notice, his services may be needed." He then looked at Brian. "Let's take this walk."

Walking out of the room, down the hallway, Sheriff Wade turned to see Douglas following behind them. He frowned, "You planning on going to jail today?" He asked Douglas.

"I go where the Attorney General goes. You have a problem with that?"

"Sheriff Wade," JD stepped between the two men. "I'll only be there to ensure Brian's constitutional rights are upheld. Then Mr. Hylton and I will be out of your hair."

"I'm glad to hear that. I like my hair nice, neat and in place," The Sheriff walked ahead with Brian.

"Will you stop trying to intimidate the man?" JD huffed at Douglas.

"As opposed to you kissing his ass?" Douglas asked with a raised eyebrow.

"It's called diplomacy and I'm going to keep on kissing his ass until Brian is cleared of these charges."

Thirty minutes later Brian was behind bars and JD had returned to the B&B to fulfill Brian's request.

"Mr. Tuner," JD said as he walked over to the table in the corner and extended his hand. "I'm Attorney General JD Harrison. Brian Thompson indicated you needed to speak with me regarding your son. May we join you?"

The man stood wearily and took the extended hand. "Thank you for taking the time."

"Mr. Turner, this is Calvin Johnson, my chief of staff. He's going to be taking some notes as we talk. This is James Brooks, my campaign manager. He's going to make sure I don't do or say anything that may jeopardize my campaign. It's a pain at times, but necessary."

Mr. Turner nodded his head, "I understand." Silence ensued for a second or two. Mr. Turner looked at JD, "I've waited so long for someone to listen to me, I'm not sure where to start."

JD nodded his head in understanding, "At times the wheels of justice can be slow. But justice always prevails. Tell me about your son."

"Randy Turner, my youngest son, went missing ten years ago while at the lake. He would go there after school to fish, just like all my sons did. Trudy, that's my wife, Gertrude Turner," he said more to Calvin than JD, Well, we didn't think much of him going there because nothing happens to children around here. Everybody knows everybody. She went out to call him for dinner and he never showed up. My son, Robbie, Robert Turner, spent the afternoon checking with his friends and knocking on doors looking for him until dark. That's when we went to Lil Joe. We found his fishing rod and tackle box, but that was it. There was no sign of the boy. The Sheriff's department dragged the river, but they never found a body. Besides," the man became anxious, "the boy knew how to swim. He was a good swimmer. I told Lil Joe he was wasting time dragging the river. I knew my boy wasn't in there. Someone took my boy, Mr. Harrison. I know with ever breath I take, my boy is still out there, waiting. Waiting for me to come and get him. I know it."

JD looked over at the old man that told the story about his son and realized he really wasn't that old. "How long ago did your son disappear?"

"Ten years ago."

"How old was he at the time?"

Tears welled up in the man's eyes, "Eight. At the age where he expected his father to protect him and I failed. I failed my boy." The man leaned against the table. "Mr. Harrison, I know what folks around here think of me. But I will swear to you on the life of my other five boys, Randy is alive. I'm not telling you something I'm feeling from the sorrow of losing a child. I'm telling what I know. Every month I go to Lil Joe to see if a missing male body has appeared anywhere in this state or in Tennessee, nothing. If that boy was in that river, his hat or sneakers or something would have appeared by now somewhere. It's been ten years and nothing. My other boys are grown now. They have accepted the law's take on what happened to their little brother. But I haven't and until someone can show me a body, I never will. I'm not asking for much here. I just want someone to look into this a little deeper. If you or the FBI comes up with the same conclusion as Lil Joe, then so be it, I'll let it go."

"Harrison. I just heard you were in town. I'll have a word with you," Judge Becker said as he walked towards the table. "What went through your mind sending a renegade like Thompson to this neck of the woods? I'm mighty disappointed to learn you are associated with the likes of him--mighty disappointed."

Calvin and James looked up at the man wondering who in the hell he was and what his problem was. However, it was Douglas that concerned JD more at the moment. "Step back two feet now!" he bellowed as he stood between JD and Judge Becker.

"Boy, get out of my way," Becker demanded.

"Boy!" Douglas exclaimed, "Do I look like a damn boy to you?"

"Douglas," JD stood, "I got this," he said as he positioned himself between Douglas and Judge Becker. "I got it," he said again.

Douglas was slow to return to his position at the doorway. Without Samuel around, he assumed the protection detail. They didn't think it was needed in Nickelsville, but one never knew and Douglas wasn't taking any chances.

"Judge Becker," JD recognized the man from his previous visit to Nickelsville. "I'm in the middle of a conversation here. You and I can speak at another time," JD said as calmly as he could.

Judge Becker, not used to being put off, looked around the table and noticed Nate Turner sitting there. "Don't waste your time on Turner. He's been spreading rumors about his son for years."

"That may be. However, I've given my word that I would speak with Mr. Turner and that's what I'm going to do. If you will excuse us." JD turned to retake his seat but Jacob grabbed his arm. Everyone at the table stood.

"Now wait a minute. You don't dismiss me for the likes of him." Becker sneered. "There is the matter concerning Thompson. Besides, I'm the one that controls the vote in this neck of the woods. It would behoove you to remember that."

Jacob never knew just how close he was to losing his life. Douglas had reached for his gun, but it was Calvin that spoke. "I don't know who you are. But it would be in your best interest to remove your hands from the Attorney General's arm."

JD looked at the man's hands on his arm, then looked into Jacobs eyes. The expression on his face said it all.

Jacob removed his hand and adjusted his suit jacket, then spoke a little more calmly. "Harrison, it is imperative that we speak immediately." He narrowed his eyes as he spoke.

JD just stared at the man for a moment. "It's Attorney General Harrison, Judge Becker. As for Mr. Thompson he is a lifelong friend for whom I would put my life and career on the line. Be careful how you speak of him. At this moment, Mr. Turner will have my undivided attention. You, however will have it soon enough."

"Harrison, I'm not the kind of man you keep waiting."

JD said nothing further to the man as he retook his seat and mentally shut Judge Becker out. "Mr. Turner from what you said you have six children in all."

Nate watched Jacob fuming as he went out the door. "Mr. Harrison you don't want Becker as an enemy around these parts. He not only has the law under his control, but a few unsavory characters as well." He looked around the table. "In case you don't know. You all are black men. The

Tennessee border is just around the corner. It wouldn't take a little of nothing for Becker to get people in these parts all riled up, if you know what I mean."

"Call me JD, Mr. Turner and I know what you mean. Thank you for your concern." JD said as he looked at James. James stepped away from the table and placed a call. "Now, tell me why Judge Becker is so nervous about you and me speaking. The old man frowned, wondering what gave Becker away. "This is a small town. Becker knew we were here within an hour of us landing. We were in the room an hour before coming downstairs. I spent another half hour at the jail. Yet he waited until word got to him that we were talking to you before coming here. His eyes kept shifting to you as we talked. I've been doing this for a while Mr. Turner. I can read people very well."

Mr. Turner nodded then looked around the room uncomfortably. He sat forward and exhaled. "When my son came up missing. Jacob Becker was my number one suspect."

Brian was mildly tickled to see the jail only had two cells and the occupants of one were Bart and Clem. As the deputy closed the cell door behind him, he reminded the brothers to behave. With a slight smile on his face Brian asked from the bars between them, "What are you two doing here?"

"Clem thought it would be a good idea to tip over Becker's cows for the way he's been treating you." Bart said sitting at the edge of the bunk bed.

"Really?" Brian asked with a confused look. "Doesn't a cow weigh like twelve hundred pounds or something? How in the hell do you tip them over?"

"You're not too smart for an FBI agent," Clem said from the bunk he was lying on with his back to Brian.

"I guess I'm not. So enlighten me."

"See," Bart began, "you wait til they go to sleep son. Then you sneak up on them, push with all your might, then run like hell in the opposite direction." He smacked his knee, while laughing as if it was the funniest thing in the world.

Brian couldn't figure out what was funny. "Why?"

Clem turned over and gave him an exasperated look, "Cause you can." He turned back to the wall and settled in again. "Just like snipe hunting," he mumbled.

Brian closed his eyes and shook his head. He knew he shouldn't ask but curiosity got him. "Okay, I'll bite. What is snipe hunting?"

"Now that's a hoot," Bart grinned widely. "We would never pull that on you, being an FBI agent it wouldn't be any fun."

"What is it?"

"It's when we take city slickers like you to the woods at night with a potato sack to catch snipes and leave you out there." Clem said with a chuckle.

"What's funny about that?"

Bart laughed until tears were coming out his eyes. "There ain't no snipes."

"Then why do you take people out in the woods at night to catch something that doesn't exist?"

"Cause we can," Clem replied while Bart fell on the floor laughing.

Brian put his hands up in surrender and flopped down on the bunk. "I have too many things to deal with then to try to figure out what make you people tick."

"Sorry son, we have to find our fun where we can," Bart said as he got up off the floor wiping his eyes. Sobering, he looked at Brian. "What's on your mind son? Cat's a fine woman. It's clear to see she's a bit taken with you. I'll tell you, in the nine years I've known her I ain't never seen her eyes sparkle like they do when she looks at you. Ain't that right Clem?"

"They sho don't sparkle at Colin like that," Clem said, still with his back turned.

"Truth be told, you a little taken with her, now ain't you?"

Brian smiled, then rested his head back against the wall, "More than a little taken. I just don't know how to forgive her for not telling me."

"Forgiveness comes with understanding." Clem said with his back still turned. "Understanding comes from conversations. Conversation consists of listening and talking to each other."

Brian sat up stunned at Clem's words. "That was profound Clem."

"I know. I ain't dumb, I just choose not to speak until I have something worth saying, that's all." He shrugged his shoulder.

The look on Brian's face sobered, "I haven't listened to her reasons," he said to no one in particular. The last twenty-four hours have been like hell and heaven on earth. I found the woman that got away and she has a son—my son."

"How you feel about that?" Bart asked.

Brian thought and exhaled, "Elated." He said almost laughing. "For the last four years I've watched my friends fall in love, get married and have children, all the while thinking something was wrong with me. I now know it had already happened, I just didn't know it."

"Self discovery is a wonderful thing. But only one thing matters." Clem said.

Brian sighed. "What's that Clem?"

Clem sat up and turned facing Brian. "Do you still love her?"

For a few moments Brian sat there staring at Clem, considering the answer to his question. With all the women he had been with over the years, he'd never found the same

feelings he'd had with Caitlyn. No one even came close.
"Yes, I do."

Clem lay back down and turned over. "Everything else is crap."

Bart's eyes shone with pride. "That's my brother."

"He's a fine brother Bart. Brian nodded his head, "a wise man in deed."

Brian stood and walked the six by six cell, pissed at himself. Becker and Montgomery had won again. He was behind bars, separated from Caitlyn and Elliott. He was breaking the first promise he had given his son. He promised he would not let him out of his sight. Calvin was watching over them and he knew they would be fine, but he needed to be with them. Like Clem said, he and Caitlyn needed to talk. But he was in jail. He reached out and punched the wall trying to relieve some of the anger.

"What's ailing you now son," Bart asked.

"I'm behind these damn bars and don't know what's happening with Caitlyn and Elliott. I just need to see that they are safe."

"Well, there's no need to sweat over that son. Go on over there and see them."

Brian looked at Bart exasperated. "I don't think the Sheriff is going to just let me walk out the front door."

"If you can't go out the front door, use the back. Ain't that what Paw always said Bart?" Clem mumbled without moving.

"That's right Clem. One ass don't stop the plowing of the field—you just go get another ass." Brian just stared at the two brothers. He was sure there was a meaning in all they'd just said, but at the moment it escaped him. Bart rolled his eyes. "You a little slow at times son." Bart stood, then pulled the bunk Clem was resting on from the wall. He then began removing the bricks from the wall near the floor, exposing an opening.

A Lost Heart

Curious, Brian walked over to the bars between them to take a closer look. When Bart finished, he stood with a wide grin. "This here leads to the back of Margie's place."

Brian couldn't believe what he saw. He began laughing and didn't stop until tears were coming from his eyes. "Small town USA, GOD bless them." Once he composed himself he stood. "Thanks Bart, I needed that." He sighed. "Unfortunately, the opening is over there, I'm over here."

"Don't need but one." Bart replied confused.

"Bart, I'm over here," he stomped his foot to emphasis his words. "The escape is over there."

"Well," Clem said, getting more comfortable, "bring your dumb ass over here."

"How do you propose I do that from a locked cell?"

Clem jumped up and ran over to the cell door. It was the first time Brian had seen him move so fast. "Lil Joe locked the door?" he asked almost petrified. He pushed the door and it swung open. Clem looked at Brian as if he was the dumbest person on the planet. "Like I said bring your dumb ass over here." He huffed then returned back to his bunk.

Brian could have been bought for a dollar when he pushed the door of his cell and it opened.

Caitlyn sat in the swing on the deck of the B&B with Elliott's head in her lap. He had fallen asleep waiting for his father to come back. Her heart ached for her son and for Brian. She wanted the two to have this day. But it certainly did not go the way she would have liked. Every fiber in her body wanted to go to the jail to see Brian, but JD indicated the last thing Brian wanted was for his son to see him behind bars. And she agreed. But no one seemed to know where Jacob had gone off to and now Colin had disappeared. The morning had a strange start even before Brian appeared as if she had conjured him up from her mind. For whatever reason and now she couldn't remember why, she had decided not to send Elliott to school, thinking it would be a good day to hang out. That in itself was weird, she never kept him home from school. Shaking her head thinking back, the day seemed like a roller coaster from that point on. How she wished Brian were there just to make sure this was not a dream that she was going to wake up from finding he really wasn't in Nickelsville. Turning she heard a sound coming from the other side of the deck. "Brian," she called out and began to stand, but remembered Elliott was in her lap asleep. "Jacob finally returned," relieved the judge released him.

Walking over and sitting next to her, he took the child from her lap and placed him on his. "Not exactly," he gave her a lopsided grin.

"Oh, you discovered Bart's escape route." She smiled.

"Are there any secret's in this town?"

"I'm sure there are. Everybody has some secrets they want to keep."

"What about you Caitlyn?"

She looked out over the river. "The last nine years of my life have been a secret. The ironic part is I'm not sure I even know why."

Brian stretched his long legs out with one arm protectively across his son's waist. Caitlyn sat to their right with her feet curled up under her as she contemplated his questions. This was the time for him to listen not interrogate. "You did a good job with Elliott Caitlyn. He is a wonderful boy. I can never tell you how grateful I am to you for bringing him into this world. There were other options, but you chose to have my son. Tell me about it Caitlyn. Tell me in your own words why you left me."

Closing her eyes, Caitlyn exhaled. "I'm not sure there is enough time in one day to tell you everything," she spoke softly. "The bottom line is I wanted to protect you and our son."

Brian looked over at her, "Protect me? Why?"

"Because I loved you." There was silence for a minute. Caitlyn never looked up at him. She continued to stare out at the water. "When I found out I was pregnant I tried calling the numbers you had given me and didn't receive any answers. So I went to your address in Richmond to find you. Instead I found a woman who in no uncertain terms told me you were not interested in a permanent relationship with anyone and it would be wise of me to move on. I can't explain how much her words hurt. But I knew she was right. You never made a secret of your dreams. When I returned home, I had no idea what to do so I told my parents. To say all hell broke loose would be an understatement. It was the first time in my life my father had struck me." If Caitlyn had looked up she would have seen the warning vein protruding from Brian's neck. "I was black and blue for a few days. Three days later my father came to my room and said he was sorry and we would work things out. He actually took me in his arms and held me. I should have known then something wasn't right." She exhaled. "But at the time I was so desperate to be held I didn't question his motives. He gave me a cup of tea and the next thing I knew I was waking up in a doctor's office. I overheard my father tell the doctor to abort my baby. At first I thought I was hallucinating, but then I heard the doctor and the nurse talking. They did not want to do as my father demanded, but he was blackmailing them. That's when I ran away. I stole money from the doctor's wallet and left an i.o.u. note with my name on it. There were woods outside his office so I took off running and kept running. I ran for hours, through trees, water, mud. It didn't matter. All I knew was I had to get away. Somewhere along the way I must have fallen asleep or blacked out. I'm not sure what. But when I woke up I was in a little town not far from my home called Nassawadox. One of the families there took me in until the day my mother came for me. Caitlyn's thoughts went back to that day as she told the story.

Picking greens as the sun baked down on her, Caitlyn silently thanked God for good people. Satrydra, one of the girls from the small town was kind enough to let her use one of her old dresses and a hat while she worked. These people who opened their home to her were not well off, they were farmers barely making ends meet, yet they were willing to help her. Their food depended on how hard they worked. They didn't ask, but Caitlyn felt it was only fair that she carried her own weight. It had been over a week since she left the doctor's office and ended up in Nassawadox, which was a few miles from her home in Cape Colin. Nassawadox was a small town of a few hundred people where African American's were the majority. The economy had deteriorated over the years and most of the families were members of household staff on the main island. Others worked the farm as Caitlyn was doing now.

It was June and the sun had made its presences known early. She wiped the perspiration from her forehead and continued pulling at the large green leaves, Satrydra told her was salad. Each night she cried for the way she once lived, with house staff to see to her every need. With the sunrise, she thanked God for another day with her baby safe from her father. As she worked, she tried to formulate a plan for her new life with a baby. First she had to decide where she wanted to live. She could not stay here, that was for sure. Her father would cause problems for this family if he knew they were helping them. It was funny, until now, she never realized how manipulative her father could be. Or maybe she knew it but just never wanted to accept it. She shrugged her shoulders and continued pulling. Maybe she could find a place in Richmond. The one time Brian took her there, it seemed large enough to get lost in. It was the Capitol city, she should be able to find a job there, even if she had to work at McDonalds for a while.

A Lost Heart

"Caitlyn."

Turning and looking up sharply, the sun blinded her momentarily. When the blur cleared Caitlyn saw her mother standing before her. She frantically looked around for her father. "He's not here." Her mother said.

Standing Caitlyn began backing up, ready to run if she had to.

"Please don't be afraid Caitlyn. I'm here to help."

"Help? You and father want to kill my baby. Now you're here to help. How could I possibly believe that?"

"Caitlyn," her mother reached out. "I did not know what your father was up to. If I had, I would have stopped him. But, Caitlyn your young man is in trouble. He came to the house and your father had him arrested.

"Brian?" Caitlyn asked. "What are you talking about?"

"He came to the house looking for you. Your father forced him to leave and promise not to look for you. He said he would not try to locate you."

"Brian knows about the baby? "And he left anyway?" Her heart dropped.

Seeing the look in her daughter's eyes, Beverly Montgomery's heart went out to her daughter. "You love him don't you?"

"Yes," Caitlyn cried as she fell back to the ground.

Beverly wiped her daughter's tears away as she bent down beside her. "Don't you cry. Don't you dare cry. You have a precious child to take care of." She cupped Caitlyn's face in the hands, "That young man loves you. If he knew about the baby I have no doubt he would kill to find you." Caitlyn was so confused and upset, she wasn't paying attention. "Listen to me. Your father has threatened to ruin your young man's career if he contacts you. So if you care about this young man, you do all you can to keep his baby safe and healthy. Your father's reasons for wanting to keep him away from you are based on greed. He wants' what your child is due to inherit. He doesn't want your Brian around, because he can't control him. When the time is right you will be told all you need to know, but for now Caitlyn, you make sure you do whatever it takes to keep your child safe. I believe in my heart Brian Thompson will find you." She pulled Caitlyn up and began to brush the dirt off her. "Your father has made arrangements for you." Caitlyn tried to pull away. "No, listen to me Caitlyn. This is one time we are going to beat him at his own game. Let him think he has won, for now. I need to know you are safe and away from him. I can't stand the thought of you alone out there trying to have a child on your own. Please Caitlyn do what he says. Tell your child about his father and when the time comes, and it will, he will find you. God help your father when he does."

Brian listened and his heart hurt for all that Caitlyn endured because of him. But the investigator in him wanted to know more. "What was your father afraid of losing control over?"

"I have no idea and I don't care. My only concern was Elliott's well being. When I returned to the house, I was told of his plan to marry me off to Colin."

"So this is an arranged marriage?"

"Yes."

"So what did Colin get out of agreeing to this?" Caitlyn looked around to make sure no one was around. Colin told her to tell Brian the whole truth and that's what she intended to do. Brian saw her hesitation as she looked around, "Caitlyn?"

"This is a small town Brian. What I'm about to say could ruin Colin's practice."

"I don't give a damn Caitlyn. I want to know the truth. Everything."

Caitlyn exhaled, "Colin's sexual preference is not of the opposite sex."

Brian frowned trying to figure out what she meant. When he did not say anything, Caitlyn tried to explain further, "he likes being with the same sex." She sighed exasperated because he was still not getting it. "He doesn't like—you know women."

"He likes some women. You're a woman, so is his nurse. If he didn't like women why does he keep you two around?" Brian asked now teasing just to see her squirm.

"Not like that," she sighed. "He doesn't like—you know having sex with women.

Damn if she did not remind him of Tracy. "He's gay."

"Yes," she said relieved to have it out.

Brian almost shouted with relief. "So you and he never..."

"No. Of course not." Caitlyn replied also insulted that he would ask.

"Don't tell me the people around here are so small minded that they cannot accept people's different sexual preference." He reached up and touched the smooth skin behind her ear. "I mean, think about it. What would they say if they knew how kinky you were?" He raised his eyebrow with the question.

Caitlyn turned to face him wondering how the conversation turned to this. "They would think what I already know—you're a freak."

Brian smiled, "In bed and out."

Caitlyn gasped. "Brian," she said looking around.

Brian ignored her. "Do you remember when we broke the bed? Whew, that was a night. Oh wait that was during the day wasn't it." The core of Caitlyn begin contracting at the memory. Brian ran his free hand down his face stopping at his chin. "If I remember correctly you came to my apartment from class."

"Brian please don't."

"Oh I was. I was very pleased with all you did that day. It was the last time we were together." He held her eyes captive. "From the moment you walked in the door and pulled my shirt off it was on." The tone of his voice changed from normal conversation to smooth and luring. "You had started wearing more sundresses. I think you enjoyed the easy access they granted." He grinned at her. "On this day I don't think we ever got that dress completely off of you. You unbuttoned my jeans and ran your hands behind and grabbed my butt while I tried to pull that damn dress over your head. Remember?" he sighed, "I remember I had to stop removing your clothes because that little hot mouth of yours was playing havoc on my nipple." He smiled, "You know, I think you liked the fact that I didn't wear underwear. I still don't," He heard Caitlyn gasp, but he was in the moment now and there was no stopping him. "Yep I remember you taking special care when you unzipped my jeans, pushed them down, then you took me in your hands as soon as I sprung free. Do you remember what you asked me Cait? Do you?" Caitlyn was unable to answer. Her mind was on that day. She nodded. Brian smiled, "You asked if you could taste me and before I could answer your little tongue glided across the length of me." He closed his eyes at the memory. Hell, he was supposed to be turning her on, not himself—he tried to tell his body that, but it had a mind of its own. He sighed then continued his story. "I remember reaching down and trying to stop you, but you wouldn't let go. You took me inside your hot little mouth so fast you almost gagged, I had to pull back. When I looked down and your lips were around me, with your hair hanging lose around your shoulders I almost died in that moment. I told you to go slow and you did—damn near killed me going slow. Then just when I was on the verge of coming you pulled away and pulled me down to you. Do you remember that Cait. I do. I remember not being able to wait, not even long enough to pull your panties down. All I could do was push them aside. Then I just slid right inside of you. Cait you were so wet and hot. Both of us lost our breath in that moment. We didn't move, we just stared at each other and that's when I knew I would never be free of you. Your muscles contracted around me and you pulled Elliot's life from me. Nothing every felt so right in my life as your legs wrapping around my waist holding me there, as if our very lives depended on it. And I was content right there in your arms. Do you remember what you said when I began to move inside of you?"

Caitlyn was still being held captive by his eyes, he had not moved once doing his detailed description of their love making. "No one will ever love me like I do." She mumbled along with him.

He smiled, "And we weren't finished were we?" she shook her head. "No, our bodies started moving slowly together. I didn't want to miss a beat as you raised your body to mine and I met you stroke for stroke watching your eyes the whole time as they showed me all the love you had for me. That was the hardest and sweetest orgasm I have ever had and you gave it to me Cait. Only you. I've thought about this all day today. From the moment I set eyes on Elliott, I thought about that day, when you took the one thing I never gave any woman. You took my seed inside of you. We did not use protection, not once that day." Brian stopped talking and just enjoyed looking into her eyes.

"Why did you do that? Why did you bring those memories back up?"

Brian grinned, "I know you Caitlyn. If your husband is gay, that tells me that you haven't been with a man since that day—since me. Are you hot and bothered now?

Caitlyn just sighed, not mentally able or prepared to answer his questions.

"Good, that's just the way I want you. Do you have any idea how it makes me feel to know that I'm the only man you have ever been with? From the moment I realized that I've been as hard as cement thinking about when we make love again. And have no doubt about it Cait, we will make love again. But not as long as you are married, real or not, to another man." Brian stood, put Elliott over his shoulder and reached out his hand to her. "We are going to work through whatever comes for us. But for him," he looked down at

Elliott, "we are going to be a family." He sighed, "It's been a long day. You need to get him to bed and I need to go back to jail."

"I'm sorry about all of this."

"It's not your fault. I lost my temper. I let him get the best of me, but it won't happen again. I have too much to lose." He placed Elliott in her arms.

Taking her son, Caitlyn hesitated, why she didn't know. Could things be this simple? That's not what history in her life had dictated. But then again, Brian wasn't in her life. Slowly she took his hand. "This is not going to be easy Brian. Whatever my father wants he will not stop until he gets it."

"Then I'm sorry to say we have something in common. I'm just as determined to make sure he doesn't get it—whatever it may be."

"Just like I'm determined," Caitlyn smiled.

"Determined to do what?"

"Make you suffer for the stunt you just pulled with a trip down memory lane. Two can play that game you know."

Brian stared at her wondering as she walked by, "You don't know how to tell a story like that. You don't have it in you." Caitlyn looked over her shoulder and smiled, then just walked away. All he could do was watch the sway of her hips as she walked away. "She wouldn't," he said then followed her upstairs.

"Attorney General JD Harrison is in Nickelsville and he is not alone. Stop all visits until further notice."

"The plan for replacement is already in motion and cannot be stopped."

"Well you damn well better find a way."

Chapter 9

The more he was in the presence of Judge Becker, the more JD disliked the man. Becker was the kind of man that abused the power granted to him as a public figure. He was a replica of Munford, the police chief that killed his father. He silently wondered how many public figures he was going to run into with the same mentality. "You know Harrison, I can guarantee the vote in Southwest Virginia goes your way. Do you have any idea how difficult that would be for an African-American in these parts? All I require is that you pack up, get Thompson away from my daughter-in-law and this town by morning. Now, I've done my part, dropped the charges and had Sheriff Wade release him. Now I want him out of my town."

Without letting his true thoughts be known JD continued the conversation with the despicable man. "You can guarantee the vote across the Southwest? How can you accomplish that?"

Becker smiled, thinking Harrison is just like any other politician. "I control the electorate here and all the surrounding counties. The vote goes the way I say it goes." He chuckled boastfully. "Hell, I can guarantee you sixty percent of the Tea Party vote from this area. Think about the power you'll take to the capitol with their support in addition to your core democratic base. You could literally write your own ticket to the White House. It's that simple."

JD looked around to ensure he was not being overheard, "Judge Becker, an African-American man could use a little help in this region of the state. But here's my problem. If I have to go through you to get the vote here, I wouldn't want it." JD stood, pulled his wallet out and placed a few bills on the table. He put his hands in his pocket while glaring at the man who could possibly be abusing voter's rights to choose with intimidation. "There are going to be two investigations. The first—voter tampering in the Southwest region and the other—the disappearance of Randy Turner." He leaned on the table coming eye to eye with Judge Becker. "It would give me great pleasure to find you involved in one or both of those cases. Rest assured, if you are involved in either, I'll do my best to ensure you spend your time in the worst Federal Prison I can find." He stood and smirked at the Judge. "But just in case I don't, I might be inclined to convince Mr. Thompson to hang around for awhile. He has quite an imagination when it comes to dealing with his enemies." He turned to walk away.

"Harrison," Jacob called out angrily. He stood and walked over to JD. "Now you listen to me. I don't give a damn who you are, this is my territory. You don't threaten me! I'll have your hide strung up before the night is out." Becker stomped out of the room.

Douglas stood in the doorway, "He didn't take too kindly to your words, I take it."

JD watched as the man walked out to his car. "No, he didn't," he said slowly as he thought. "You know, it takes a lot of balls to threaten the Attorney General of the State. He either has a hell of an underground network in this neck of the woods or he has some powerful connections in Washington. Where is everyone?"

A Lost Heart

Brian walked through the door, his black shirt and pants covered with dirt.

"What in the hell happened to you?" Douglas asked with a laugh about to explode from him.

"I've been exploring underground tunnels. I'll catch up with you as soon as I shower and check in on Caitlyn."

JD smiled, "You're going to work things out with her?"

"That's my plan," Brian said taking the steps two at a time.

JD knocked on Calvin's door, then James door. As the doors opened, JD pointed at his door. "Conference time."

Calvin stood in his pajamas as he looked from JD to Douglas. "I'll change."

"No don't change, I like your pjs," Douglas tried to smother a laugh.

Calvin frowned and looked at James. "You didn't say anything about James pajamas."

"He's bare chested and has on a pair of sweats. I will bet money he sleeps in the buff. You on the other hand have on a two piece set."

JD, who had walked into his room leaving his door open, looked back out, "Now gentlemen."

"It's going to take a minute," Douglas laughed, "Calvin has to change out of his pjs."

James walked out of his room with a tee shirt in his hand and his chest out. Suzie Mae was coming up the stairs, with the salve for Brian's back in her hand, just as he closed his door. "My lord in heaven, two in one week," she gasped.

James began putting the shirt over his head. "Why ya'll always want to cover up your body. My goodness you are a tall, fine specimen of a man. My, my, my what I wouldn't give to touch that body."

Douglas and JD looked up at James. He pulled the tee shirt over his head and down his chest. "Thank you Ms. Suzie Mae, but I'm a happily married man with a very jealous wife. She would not understand me allowing another woman to touch her merchandise."

"I damn sure don't blame her with prime merchandise like you. Hmm, hmm, hmm. And a deep sexy voice." She shook her head "I don't know if I'm going to make it through all ya'll hanging around here." She laughed. "I was looking for Mr. Thompson for his rub down."

"Brian?" JD and Douglas asked simultaneously.

"That's right." She noticed the surprised looks on their face. "Don't knock it until you've tried it. Made his back like new." Suzie Mae smiled proudly as she knocked on Brian's door. The men looked at each other, shook their heads and walked into JD's room.

"We have something brewing here James and it may get sticky. Judge Becker just offered me the Tea Party's vote from this area if I get Brian out of town."

James raised an eyebrow. "Forgive me, if I'm wrong but isn't Becker black?"

"The Tea Party has a few African American followers amongst them," Calvin said as he walked through the door. "How you can support people that despise the fact that the current President of the United States is a black man, I don't know, but they do."

"There are always a few misguided souls around us. But, it's their right to support whatever party they choose." JD said, "That's the beauty of living in America. I take that right to choose seriously, that's why Becker's claim is making my skin crawl." JD was sitting at the writing desk in the room. Calvin sat on the bed, James in the chair near the window and Douglas stood at the door. "Calvin what did you find on any cases involving missing children in the area?"

Calvin exhaled, "More than you are going to like. During the last ten years a total of eleven children have gone missing. Three were determined to be run aways. Eight are unaccounted for."

"How did that many children go missing and no one noticed?" James asked.

"Yeah, it's not like we're talking about a big city. This town has what, two hundred people in it?" Douglas stated.

"Eight hundred and fifty-two," Calvin corrected. "The missing children were not noticed because no two were taken from the same locality." He turned his lap-top around, "Take a look at this map. The counties in red signify a child missing in the last ten years. Goose bumps appeared when I saw this map. So I placed a call to Rossie. He went into the office and sent me the case files on each of the missing children. And you know Rossie Brown, he did a wider search and this is what he found." He hit the enter button on the computer. More dots appeared on the screen." The men gathered around to get a closer look.

"What timeframe are we looking at here?" A concerned JD asked.

"Here's where things get very interesting. Each child in each area was taken almost exactly ten years apart. There's another interesting similarity."

The men all looked over at Calvin. He looked up, "All of them were boys and all were seven or eight years old."

"What, you think there's a pattern going on here?" Douglas asked.

"I won't know for sure until I talk with Rossie in the morning and check a few more facts. But, it's a hell of a coincidence.

"We need to talk to Mr. Turner again," James stated.

"Definitely," JD and Calvin said in unison.

"Calvin." JD said looking at the map on the computer. "Does this remind you of anything?"

"I was wondering if you remembered that case we worked in Roanoke a few years back. We never found the little boy."

Suzie Mae knocked on Brian's door, then waited. After waiting a minute, Suzie Mae smiled, then knocked on the door next to his. As she suspected, Brian opened the door. "Hello you caramel sugar daddy. I could just lick you until you melt in my mouth."

Brian smiled. "Suzie Mae, you certainly know how to make a man feel good."

"I do my best. I see you made it back through the tunnel, the Sheriff was a little concerned about that."

"He knew I was out?"

"Oh yeah, we watched you and Caitlyn from the lounge downstairs."

"Why all the cloak and dagger, he could have just let me walk through out the door."

"Oh no he couldn't do that, he gotta keep face, you know. Besides he's just as curious as the rest of us--we all want to know what's going to happen with you and Cat."

"Speaking of which, will I be applying your salve tonight or will Cat be handling things from here on out?"

Brian reached out and took the jar. "I'll see if I can convince Caitlyn to do that."

Suzie Mae looked around him into the room. "Where's Cat?" she whispered.

"Getting Elliott ready for bed. Why?"

"Now, I don't know your story and I know you've been through a lot today, but I do know Cat is a fine woman. She has nothing but a kind word for everyone she comes in contact with. Now, I don't know what your plans are, but if they are anything less than taking her away from this place, you are not the man you appear to be. You can leave her right here with Colin and the rest of us cause we love her. That's just my say about the situation."

"You realize Caitlyn is a married woman."

"We know that. But she's married to a man that ain't never touched her like a man should touch a woman—you know what I mean." She looked him up and down, "I don't suspect you have a problem in that area." She laughed and walked away.

Brian grinned and closed the door, just as a sleepy Elliott climbed into bed trying to keep his eyes on his father. Brian walked over and tucked his son in. "Hello son."

"You came back Daddy." Elliott smiled then rubbed his sleepy eyes. "Will you be here when I wake up daddy?"

Brian ran his hand down his son's face closing his eyelids. Then he kissed his forehead. "I'll be right here waiting for you. We'll spend the day together, okay."

"K, Daddy." The child smiled and fell asleep within minutes. Caitlyn stood in the doorway between the bathroom and the bedroom watching father and son. The sight tugged at her heart. This was something she prayed for, but never really knew when or if it was going to happen.

Brian stood and stretched, his back was about to flare up again. He was sure crawling through the dirt tunnel didn't help matters, but spending time talking with Caitlyn was worth it. He sighed, he arrived in this town a little over twenty-four hours ago and his life had been turned upside down. This morning Caitlyn was on his mind and now she was here. He looked down at Elliott, he definitely did not think about him, but damn if he didn't like the outcome. Twisting to ease the discomfort beginning in his back he turned. Caitlyn was standing in the doorway watching him. Their eyes met and held. The little prank he pulled on her earlier probably affected him more than it did her, but he couldn't resist seeing her blush.

"Your back brothering you?" she asked, not moving from where she stood.

The sight of her still mesmerized him. It was as if time had stood still. Caitlyn was still a beautiful woman that he was finding hard to resist. Who's stupid decision was it not to touch her until she was a free woman—oh yeah, his. *She was yours first,* the little devil on his left shoulder told him. *Legally she belongs to Colin Becker,* the angel on his right shoulder persisted. *The hell with that,* the devil to the left declared, *it's in name only, her heart belongs to you.* The angel on the right snickered, *Remember what happened when you kissed JD's wife? He knocked you on your you know what. These are country folks. They like guns.*

Standing in the doorway, Caitlyn watched the play of emotions on Brian's face and could only speculate on what he was thinking. She stepped away from the doorway, "Your mind is working overtime. History has proven that can only mean trouble." She walked over to the dresser. "Did Marybeth send this for you?"

"Yes," he replied as he continued to contemplate his decision. The angel was right. The last time he kissed another man's wife it almost cost him a friendship. He turned, walked towards the door and told the little devil on his shoulder to shut the hell up.

"Where are you going?" Caitlyn asked.

"Back to my room to shower."

"You can shower after I put this cream on. Lay across the foot of the bed. I'll rub your back down," Caitlyn said as she opened the jar.

Brian looked at her as if she had lost her mind. As soon as she touched his body all his will power would be lost.

Caitlyn turned back to look at him, "Something wrong?"

"No." he said a little too harshly.

"Ok," she said slowly, "Then take off your shirt."

Hesitating for a moment, he exhaled then pulled his shirt over his head.

There was slow release of air that escaped between Caitlyn's lips as she thought, *oh my, what have I gotten myself into.* Brian kicked off his shoes and placed his long, lean, muscle toned body across the foot of the bed. His feet hung over the side of the bed. Placing his folded hands under his head he relaxed. Caitlyn took slow deep breaths the same as she did when she gave birth to Elliott, trying to settle her raging hormones. She took a quick look at the top of the bed to make sure Elliott was still asleep. The peaceful look on his face made her smile. Then she looked over at his father and sighed, *God that man looked good.* Taking steps toward the bed, Caitlyn smiled. It was payback time. Kicking off her shoes, she pulled up the hem of her sundress and made herself comfortable straddling him. His behind was solid muscle, his waist slim, his back toned with smooth caramel skin. She didn't know why, but the urge to kiss the scars on his back from the bullets that invaded his body was strong. Tentatively she ran her fingers over the four distinctive marks. Then she bent over and kissed each one. She sat back up, settled comfortably on his butt and reveled in having his body between her legs, the core of her responded to the familiar body beneath it. She could tell by the moisture that was beginning to form there. Reaching into the jar, she took a generous amount of the cream out and slowly rubbed it evenly over his back. She put the lid back on the jar and dropped it to the foot of the bed. Now it was her turn to share memories.

She began massaging the cream into his skin, one small section at a time, starting at his shoulders. "Brian," she called out in that low seductive voice she hadn't used in ten years.

He tried like hell to stay still, not to reach around, grab her and put her beneath him where she belonged. From the moment she sat on his butt his anatomy acknowledged who she was by coming to attention. He was surprised it didn't push her up for he was as hard as a steel bar. Then her finger brushed across his scars, his breath caught, ashamed that she was seeing his defects. But then, she kissed each of them. *Hell why did she have to go and do that?* His body began to hum. Closing his eyes the phrase, *fighting destiny*, was all that came to his mind. She called out his name. The only response he could manage was a grunt.

"Do you remember The Morning After," she asked while kneading into his shoulder muscles with slow deliberate strokes. "The dance by the car—the first time you kissed me—my first orgasm." She glided her hands to his other shoulder, methodically massaging his hard muscles, relieving the tension in his upper body, while doing the exact opposite in his lower regions. "I do. I remember like it was yesterday." She slowly moved her hands over his back. "Do you remember the drive back to your apartment? We missed curfew at the dorm so you told me to sleep in your bed, while you slept on the sofa." Her hand moved to the first scar where she applied more pressure as she continued to reminisce about that night. "My body wouldn't let me sleep. It kept yearning…for what I didn't know, but you showed me. Do you remember?"

"Caitlyn don't."

Moving to the next scar, she smiled. "That' exactly the same warning you gave me that night. I paid you about as much mind that night as I'm paying you tonight. Remember when I stood before you on the sofa with nothing on but your old tee shirt. You said, Caitlyn don't." she shifted her body.

"Caitlyn," Brian moaned out a warning.

She smiled, "I pulled the shirt you gave me off and begged you to please make love to me. I wanted to know what it felt like to be one of your women. I didn't care what happened the morning after. You didn't say anything, so I straddled you, kind of like I'm doing now. I leaned in and used my tongue like this," she leaned down and ran the tip of her tongue across his neck. "Do you remember my tongue tracing your lips from one end to the next?" she sighed, "I do. I remember as if it was just yesterday. I remember the taste of your bottom lip when I sucked on it when you wouldn't open your mouth. You know what else I remember? Just when I was about to lose all hope, your arms," she moved her hands to the muscles in his triceps and squeezed, "these same arms wrapped around my waist as if they were the jaws of life. Then your lips took mine." Her hands moved slowly down the center of his back. "I wrapped my arms around your neck and held on for dear life. Nothing—nothing could have pulled me away from you. You stood and my legs wrapped around your waist." She leaned forward and whispered in his ear. "Then you carried me to your bed, where I wanted to be with you. That was when I realized I was feeling all skin, you had on absolutely nothing and I loved it." Sitting back up, she squeezed her thighs with his butt between them. "I loved feeling your hard body between my legs." She exhaled, "But nothing could have prepared me for the feeling that jerked my body when your lips touched my breast." She sighed. "My goodness I thought I had died and gone to heaven. Your tongue was so wet exploring, sucking until I was delirious. All I wanted was for you to never stop. My body was vibrating from the inside out, wanting whatever you were willing to give." Her legs began to tighten against his thighs.

"Cait," Brian shifted beneath her barely whispering her name.

Sliding her hands down to his waist she applied more pressure and moved her body against him. "You taught me to let go that night Brian. You showed me the pleasures of being a woman. At first I was afraid of the unknown, but I wanted you too much to let fear stop me." She was now becoming a victim of her own memories, as her hands slowed on his body. "Then I felt the tip of you at my center, the fear disappeared. The moment you entered my body I knew, it was right. I loved the silky smooth feel of you inside of me. I remember squeezing every inch of you." Her body continued to rotate against his, "Do you remember Brian? Do you remember the moment you made me your woman. You broke through my barrier, you slid in and out slowly at first, but then it was like your body needed mine as much as I needed yours. The rhythm increased. Do you remember?

I do. I remember the power behind every stroke. But you know what I remember most? The love you poured into me like a sweet wine that had bottled up for ages and was now freely flowing. I didn't care about the morning after; I only cared about that moment and the unbelievable feelings that washed over me that last time it felt your powerful thrust. I long to feel that again Brian." Her hands stopped. "You are the only man I've ever been with. You are the only man I will ever be with." Her hands and her body stretched up his back. "I love you Brian. I always have and I always will."

The tears touched his neck as she spoke. Damn, damn, damn, damn----damn. He was going to break his own rule to never kiss another man's wife. Hard—steel would be softer than he was at that moment. He reached behind him, pulled her beneath him then ravished her lips. The hell with his decision, this was his woman and he was taking her. His hands moved under her sundress, pulling it up until he reach the smooth curve of her behind. His hand squeezing her softness—pressing her firmly against his erection. "Cait," he moaned kissing her without mercy, claiming all that he had dreamed of and missed for years. Reaching down between their bodies, Brian unzipped his pants allowing his rod to spring free, landing right at her core. It didn't need guidance, it knew where it belonged. Moving the thin material of her panties aside the tip of him aimed right for home plate.

"Brian," Caitlyn gasped, "Brian," she pulled him closer and shifted her body for better entry.

"Cait," Brian entered her in one powerful thrust, then froze.

"Daddy, why you wrestling with mommy?"

Brian and Caitlyn's faces turned towards their son. Neither spoke for a moment. Their hearts were racing, and their eyes couldn't believe things went that far with Elliott not only in the room, but in the same bed. Brian pushed Caitlyn leg and dress down hoping to cover any exposed body parts from his son.

"We were wrestling sweetheart," Caitlyn said as she blushed with embarrassment.

"Ok Mommy," Elliott turned over and closed his eyes, "Have fun, but don't hurt Daddy." And that quick, the boy was asleep again.

Brian looked down at Caitlyn, his forehead touching hers, perspiration dripping, both trying to control their breathing. He was vibrating inside her as her inner muscles squeezed him uncontrollably. His body and mind fighting against each other as to what he should do. God it felt so good inside of her, but his son was there. He brushed her hair from her face. "I'm sorry Caitlyn," he kissed her lips, with his breath coming out harshly. He could see the disappointment in her eyes and feel the contractions as her body protested against his withdrawal. He un-wrapped her legs from around him and pulled her dress down. Falling to her side he pulled her into his arms and just held her until they were both in control. "As soon as my body will allow it, I'm going to my room to take a shower." He placed a kiss on top of her head. "I want you Caitlyn. As mad and confused as I am, my body knows who you are. It felt like the first time all over again."

Kissing his neck she nestled in close. "I missed you so much Brian. There are so many things I want to tell you, but right now my body needed your touch. If that's all it can be for now, I'll take it, with no complaints." She closed her eyes. "It felt so good to have you inside me again." Tears dropped, "It's been so long since I've felt your touch."

All Brian could do was close his eyes and hold her. "A very cold shower is in order for you too. When Elliott leaves for school in the morning, we'll talk to Colin together. I have to tell him what just happened."

Caitlyn moved her leg across his, "Then we should make it worth our confession—don't you think?"

Brian looked down at her as she looked up at him. He couldn't help but smile. "Once you got started, I never could get you to stop. Hell, I didn't want to. Remember the gym on the weight bench."

"Oh my goodness, yes. That was the first time I was on top." Caitlyn laughed remembering how they almost got caught by his coach. "You were so long I had to press against your chest to come up. Then I would ease back down."

"It felt like you were doing bench presses. That felt so good." They were both silent as they each remembered the moment. "Where is Colin now?"

Caitlyn laughed against his chest. Being there, holding her in his arms as they fell asleep, was the most natural thing he had done in years. It felt right, even if it was wrong.

Chapter 10

The only thing on Brian's mind after he and Caitlyn dropped Elliott off at school was to find Colin. But as soon as he stepped out of the room, JD, Calvin, James and Douglas pulled him into the lounge and filled him in on the conversation with Nate Turner and Judge Becker.

"Let me get this straight, Mr. Turner's son went missing ten years ago. He thought Becker was connected, but no investigation was done. Now, you think this missing child case is connected to the one out of Roanoke a few years ago and possibly others."

"You got it," Calvin stated, "To compound things, Becker threatened JD."

"I think it was an idle threat," JD responded.

"A threat is a threat. What did he say?" Brian's radar came to attention.

JD waved it off, "It wasn't important."

"Did you call Samuel?"

"Yes. Cynthia is having pre-mature labor so he is sending back-up." JD replied.

"That would be me." The men turned to see Joshua Lassiter leaning against the fireplace behind them.

"Oh hell," Brian exclaimed. "Don't you have a country to blow up somewhere?"

"It's a slow day," Joshua shrugged as he walked towards them in one of his signature Armani suits, with Michel Perry shoes.

Joshua Lassiter was a CIA Operative and Samuel Lassiter's younger brother. He was as well known for his suits as he was for the number of bodies he left whenever he was in a town. His orders generally came straight from the President of the United States and in most cases involved terrorist cells inside the country. The great thing about Joshua was he was damn good at his job. He always caught the bad guys. The bad thing about Joshua was he was damn good at his job. The bad guys never lived to tell their side of the story. Joshua's motto was simple, shoot first—ask questions later. He shook hands around the table then took a seat. "Your judge went out on his boat late last night while you guys were meeting in JD's room. Nate Turner is at his home with his wife. Caitlyn Montgomery-Becker is at the house packing, it appears. Colin Becker is not in this town. And Elliott is in school enjoying the attention regarding his father." He turned to Brian, "Congratulations man, I mean that."

The men stared at him astonished at the information he's acquired. "When did you get here?" JD asked.

"Last night."

"Where did you stay?" Brian asked.

He sat forward, "I met this redbone when I got in last night. We kind of hung out."

"She's eighteen," Brian stated.

"Is that right," Joshua shook his head, "Damn if they don't learn young these days. I believe the legal age of consent in the state of Virginia is sixteen." He looked at JD, who nodded.

The men looked at each and laughed. "Leave it to you," Brian said.

"Yeah, well a brother has to do what a brother has to do. Hell, somebody has to help the sisters, all of you are tied down."

Brian and Calvin looked at each other and fell out laughing. "I've heard that before," Calvin laughed.

Joshua liked the men in the room. He believed, as others did, that JD is going to be President one day. Meaning he would have to answer to him. There is no time like the present to get use to the way he operates. "Someone is staking out Becker's place."

Brian sa up, as the other men came to attention. "What are you talking about?"

"Cigarette stubs behind a tree that gives a clear view of the back of the house. It could be nothing, but from the number of stubs it appears someone has been spending a lot of time there." Joshua sat forward, "Another thing, as we speak Becker is meeting a Robert Canter across the border in Tennessee."

"Which Becker?" Brian asked.

"Funny you should ask that. Last night while you were with Mrs. Becker, Dr. Colin Becker was with Canter. This morning it appears he was on his way to Washington."

"How do you know he's going to Washington?" James asked.

Joshua just raised an eyebrow, "I just know. Canter left young Becker and met this morning with Judge Becker at which time he received an envelope." The men looked at each other wondering what all of this was leading to. "There's more. Canter leaves the judge and meets up with a foreign unknown and deliver's that envelope. How you like me now?" Joshua said as he sat back in his chair.

"Caitlyn is at Becker's place. I want to see the area?" Brian said as he stood.

"I don't think any of us will be welcome there," Douglas said.

JD nodded, "I have to agree Brian. Becker isn't going to be happy to see you."

Brian walked pass him, "My woman is there, welcome or not I'm going."

The look in Brian's eyes let JD know there was no talking him out of going. "Be careful Brian." He turned to Calvin. "I think it's time we take a closer look at Becker. Something isn't kosher with him."

"Take this," Joshua gave Calvin a small handheld computer. "There's a picture of Canter and the other man he met with. Do a face recognition. See if we get a hit."

Calvin looked at the device. "How does this work?"

Joshua took the device, snapped a picture of Calvin, then pushed a button. A few seconds later the device beeped. Joshua turned the device around and showed it to Calvin. "Like that."

Calvin took the device that now had a picture of him with all his pertinent information. "I have got to get me one of these," he beamed and walked away examining the device.

"Does his security clearance level allow him access to that?" JD asked as Joshua walked away.

"Probably not. I'm not telling—are you?"

JD just shook his head and grinned. "Working with you is going to be interesting isn't it?"

Joshua smiled, "Never a dull moment. I try to keep it that way."

JD pulled him aside, "I need you to have Brian's back. He's preoccupied with Caitlyn. I don't want anything to happen to him or his family."

"He's covered." Joshua stated and walked away. Brian and Douglas began walking towards the front door of the B&B. "Where are ya'll going?" Joshua asked walking towards the back.

"To the Becker's," Brian replied as turned the handle to open the door.

"My transportation is out back."

A Lost Heart

"Out back?" Brian and Douglas stared at each other then followed Joshua out to the patio.

Sitting in the field as pretty as it can be was a military issued chopper. Brian and Douglas stopped, stared at it, then grinned from ear to ear.

Margie and Sheriff Wade watched from her bedroom window as the three men boarded the chopper. She turned and laughed, "Boys will be boys, I don't care how old they are."

Lil Joe smiled, but it didn't reach his eyes. "What's wrong Joe?" Margie asked as she watched a frown appear on her friend's face.

He looked down at the woman he had been in love with for years. He just hadn't had the nerve to tell her. Hell, he reckoned she knew. Everybody else in town knew. "I got a feeling before those fellas leave, this town is going to be turned upside down."

"Why do you say that?"

"Sometimes, to clean up the past you have to stir up a lot of dirt."

Judge Becker docked his boat knowing he would be leaving out again soon. Walking up the path leading to the house he went over the plans in his head. According to his contact, the cargo would be moved out tonight. If they waited any longer they ran the risk of being discovered by Harrison and his crew. Hell, it might be best to let Caitlyn and the boy leave here, just to get Thompson out of town. Montgomery's problems be damned, he had his own issues to deal with. All this unwanted activity and visitors were threatening to eliminate a million dollar a year enterprise. Not to mention his own private source of enjoyment.

Thinking about it brought him joy. Not just from the financial stand point, but knowing a venture he created for his personal needs grew into an international merger. Who knew, when his wife clamped down on his extracurricular activities in the house, his new set up would lead to years of enjoyment and profit. Little did he know at the time, that there were other men that shared a taste for his type of satisfaction. When the room he had in the basement of the house no longer sufficed, he had to search for a place where no one would discover his secret desires, unless he wanted them to. His wife pissed him off when Colin ventured down to the basement and witnessed his special brand of entertainment, insisting he take his pleasures elsewhere. Hell she knew the deal when they married. All he wanted from her was one child to sustain the image of a family. It's not like he promised her a rose garden. Doing what relaxed him after her constant nagging, he took the boat over to the island and did some fishing. It was on one of those fishing trips that he took a stroll to the other side to discover a perfect sight to build a sanctuary. And that's exactly what he did.

To ensure his privacy, he used a construction crew out of Tennessee, to build a house on a clearing nestled behind a growth of trees. The house had a lounge area downstairs, kitchen, dining area and upstairs, five bedroom suites, complete with a sitting room, which could be closed off from the bedroom, private balcony and bath. At the time he was going to use it for whenever he wanted to watch others enjoying their pleasures. Mounting a two-way mirror in each bedroom made it simple. It allowed for comfortable viewing from the sitting room.

The clientele really just fell in his lap. He would invite a friend over to enjoying the viewing, then another friend invited another and then another. The charge was cash only, $1,000.00 a night—not expensive at all. The entertainment was easy enough, for the right price. But he was careful, he only used entertainment from across the river—never anyone out of Virginia.

A Lost Heart

His personal enjoyment varied. Sometimes he just watched, but other time he would partake in a session or two. On one particular night, his partner for the evening introduced him to a group of business men from another country. They explained they were a part of a cartel and were so impressed with his operation, that they were interested in forming a partnership. The offer was one he simply couldn't refuse. He would remain the sole owner of the property, but they would own and conduct the business, providing entertainment and the clientele, paying him five million a year for the use of the house.

That's when the business changed. The foreigners were to supply their own entertainment, most of them young boys. Some, becoming in-house slaves, so to speak. They were cared for, fed well, given a daily exercise regimen and a clean comfortable home. What more could a young boy want?

With the change in ownership, Jacob did not partake in the activities upstairs and didn't really care what was going on, as long as he was getting paid, and had his private room whenever he wanted his special brand of entertainment.

Now, because of Montgomery, Thompson and Harrison were in town and could create a problem, especially if the cartel didn't control that fool Canter. He did not like the man and Becker had no problem making sure he knew. When all of this mess with Thompson blows over, he was getting rid of Canter once and for all.

Robert Canter stood behind his tree and watched as Jacob walked up to the house. A cynical smile touched his lips as he thought of his meeting last night with Colin Becker. To say the man was shocked at seeing pictures of his father's extracurricular activities would be an understatement. He wasn't sure what the man was going to do with the information and didn't care. He had two projects and both were going to be completed today. After that, he would have no more dealings with Becker. He hated the pompous man, always walking around flaunting his money and power instead of using it to help the less fortunate. The members of the Cartel did not want to waste time dealing with the *Coloured*, so they hired him to be the middle man. And they paid well for it. But Becker did not like his way of doing things once the boys' usefulness had expired. Becker's greed for more money took precedence, vying to ship the boys overseas to be auctioned, lining his pockets more. Now, Canter believed in the more traditional way of disposing of useless trash. His motto being, "dead boys tell no tales." Simple, hands clean—nothing left behind. Unlike his old partner, Charles Melvin who had to keep souvenirs, and look where that got him—jerking from a needle JD Harrison put in his arm with a conviction. He was not going out that way. With Harrison in the area, it was time to move on.

With the cargo being shipped out tonight, he no longer had to secure the house. Leaving the area would not be an issued. Now, the side job was a bit of both, personal and business. He would be making a little extra money and getting back at Becker at the same time. Who could ask for anything more? Canter dropped his cigarette to the ground stomped it out, then followed his escape route off the grounds, the same as he had done so many times before.

"Get out of my house." Becker demanded as he picked up the telephone to call the Sheriff. "I'll have all of you behind bars."

"You're not referring to that little building in town are you?" Joshua asked.

"Who in the hell are you?"

"You really don't want to know Becker." Brian said really meaning it.

"Well I know this, I want you out of here."

"Jacob, Brian is here for me. It is still my home isn't it?" Caitlyn stated.

"Is it your intention to leave Colin for this man?" Becker asked bitterly.

"That's a discussion for Colin and I. Speaking of which, have you seen him since yesterday?"

"No. But I'm sure he is distraught over this man being here."

"Well it's not like him to just disappear."

"It's not like you to stay out with another man either."

"Now look, I've had about enough of you." Brian took a step towards the man.

"Brian it's not worth it." Caitlyn said as she stood between the two. "Will you two help?" she asked desperate not to have a repeat of yesterday.

"Sure," Joshua walked over taking a hand towel along the way, caught Becker by the throat and shoved the towel into his mouth. Still holding Becker by the throat as he began to gag, Joshua turned back to Caitlyn, "Is that better?"

Brian and Douglas laughed as Caitlyn looked shocked, "You are worse than he is. Please release him."

"Okay," Joshua released his hand and walked away as Becker slid to the floor.

Caitlyn ran over and pulled the dish cloth from Becker's mouth. "I think it would be safer for everyone if you wait out on the patio for Elliott to come home?"

Brian looked down at Becker. "Look, I know you think you got us by the balls here, because this is your town. But it only appears that way. My suggestion is that you stay out of our sight until arrangements can be made for Caitlyn and Elliott to leave this town. It may save your life."

Brian, Douglas and Joshua walked out to the patio. "I don't think the man likes you Brian," Douglas stated the obvious. They walked out the door and looked around. "It looks so peaceful out here." Douglas said.

"It a façade," Joshua said. "Something is not right in this town." He walked off the deck as the others followed him.

"This is Elliott's tree stump, he fishes from here." Brian said proudly. "Hey," he hit Douglas on the shoulder, "I'm going to have to buy a house, near a river, so Elliott can still go fishing." They continued walking, "Hey, you know what else?"

Douglas stopped and just stared at Brian. This was the first time in all the years he had been Brian's friend that he had expressed his thoughts out loud. Douglas' plan was to tell him just that but he caught himself.

"What?" Brian asked when he saw the expression on Douglas face.

Not one for sentiments, Douglas held his glare for a moment then smiled. "You are going to be a good father."

Brian grinned from ear to ear. "Thanks man."

"Is this sentimental shit going to last much longer?" Joshua, who had bent down to examine the ground, asked looking exasperated at the two men. "First Samuel and now you."

"Don't worry yours is coming," Brian said as he bent down. "What you got?"

"Look at this," Joshua pointed to the dirt in the area, "Those foot prints weren't there this morning. Someone's been here since I left."

Brian stood where the foot-prints were and looked up. "Following the line of view, anyone standing here would have been looking into the kitchen or," he looked up to the second level of the house and saw Caitlyn through the window, "watching Caitlyn."

Douglas came to stand next to him. He came to the same conclusion. They looked around and Joshua was nowhere to be found. "Where in the hell did he go?"

"He'll show up when we need him," Brian said with a voice laced with concern. "Why would anyone be watching Caitlyn?"

They began walking back up the path, when Joshua joined them while placing a plastic bag in his suit pocket. "These cigarette butts are still warm. I need to check the DNA. We need to get back to the B&B."

"You two go back," Brian said, "I'm going to stay here with Caitlyn and wait for Elliott. Call me if you have anything."

"I think that's a good idea. Keep your eyes open," Joshua said as he walked towards the chopper he landed in the front of the house.

"Your friend certainly knows how to make an exit," Caitlyn smiled as Brian reached the patio.

At three o'clock as always the bus pulled up in front of the house. This time Caitlyn and Brian was there waiting for Elliott as he ran from the bus.

"Hello my Elliott." She hugged her son, happier than she'd been in years.

"Hi Mommy. Hey Daddy. You know what?" He said to his father.

"What?" Brian smiled down at his son.

"Everybody at school was talking about you today. Even Jim Bob came over and talked to me about you and Jim Bob don't talk to no little kids. And you know what else happened, I told my teacher about you and Mommy playing wrestling." Brian and Caitlyn froze as Elliott walked up the steps of the porch. "And you know what my teacher said?" Brian and Caitlyn both shook their heads no, holding their breath to hear the response. "She said mommies and daddies do that all the time. Why she and her husband did a little wrestling themselves last night." The boy turned to see his parents who had stopped at the bottom of the steps. "Ya'll coming in the house?" the boy asked as he opened the door.

Brian was the first to recover, "Yes son, we're coming."

A few minutes later the family was sitting at the breakfast bar having their afternoon snack. Elliott had a peanut butter and grape jelly sandwich like his father, as Caitlyn had peanut butter and strawberry jam. They washed the sandwiches down with a glass of milk. "Mommy, can I get my fishing rod and take Daddy fishing?"

"If that's what your father wants to do," Caitlyn replied smiling up at Brian.

"I don't know a lot about fishing, son."

"I can teach you Daddy," Elliott went running up the stairs.

"Don't forget to change your clothes," Caitlyn yelled after him.

"Okay."

Brian couldn't help but smile as he looked at Caitlyn. He exhaled and looked away. "I don't have all of this Caitlyn. I have a condo with three bedrooms with furniture in only one. I can buy us a house, but it won't be on the scale of this and definitely not like the one you grew up in. I'm doing okay, but I'm not balling like this. Can you leave all this behind Caitlyn?"

She smiled at him, "I would live with you in a cardboard box and be happy. As for Elliott, it would be an adventure. You don't have to give us anything but you."

"Careful, you wouldn't want Elliott to catch us wrestling on the kitchen floor."

The sweet laughter that came from Caitlyn was music to his ears. He sat there just taking his fill of her. She was still an exquisite woman in his eyes. Yes, she was older, but she still had that killer body, that she always tried to hide under those business suits. Her eyes, were shining with happiness rather than the tears of yesterday, her hair hung just past her shoulder blades, it was no longer at her waist and her lips were still full and tempting. He closed his eyes. He had to get his mind off her or he was going to take her on the floor, the sink, the breakfast bar, whatever was available.

Elliott came running down the stairs with his fishing rod. "I'm ready Daddy."

Brian smiled, thankful for the interruption. "Okay son. You go set up and I'll be right there as soon as I finish talking to your mother."

"Okay Daddy." The boy ran out the back door.

Brian and Caitlyn held each other's eyes until a sound from one of the other rooms interrupted them. Brian looked out the window behind Caitlyn to see Elliott setting up at his spot on the tree branch. Then he saw Becker walking towards his boat. "How much do you know about Becker?"

"Not much. He treats Elliott and me well, but Colin is another story. It's like he has something against him. I don't know. It's hard to explain."

"Have you ever met any of Colin's male friends?"

"No. Why do you ask?"

"JD met with Mr. Turner last night. He indicated when his son was missing his main suspect was Becker."

"Colin?" Caitlyn asked curiously.

"No. Judge Becker." Brian looked out the window over Caitlyn's shoulder again. This time he noticed the boat was gone and he did not see Elliott. He blinked, and then started walking towards the door.

Caitlyn looked out the window, "What is it Brian?"

He didn't respond, he kept walking out the door. She followed behind him. "Elliott," he called out. When he did not hear a reply, Brian walked faster, "Elliott." He called again with his heart rate increasing.

"Elliott," Caitlyn called out with a little nervousness to her voice.

"Elliott, answer me. Elliott." She called out again.

Brian took off running towards the tree branch. "Elliott! Elliott!" Still no answer. The blood started rushing through his veins. As he saw the fishing rod on the ground

"Elliott," Caitlyn called out in a panic. "Elliott—answer me Elliott." Silence.

Brian ran over to the area they were at earlier in the day and searched through the woods. He came back out to Caitlyn who was now working herself into a panic. "Caitlyn does Elliott have a hiding place or anywhere he plays?"

"No," she cried out. The branch is the only place he would be. Brian, where's my baby? Elliott—Elliott!"

Brian reached out to her, but she pulled away and ran over to the trees. Brian pulled out his cell, "Elliott's missing. My son is gone."

"Where are you?" JD asked as he stood and motioned to Calvin.

"Becker's place. Get Joshua out here now."

Brian disconnected the call. A chill went up his back. This was not anyone else's child, this was his son. For years he had spent his life protecting others, now he needed to focus to find his own. Trying to shut down the feeling of loss, he went to get Caitlyn who was roaming through the woods, calling out her child's name. "Elliott. Where are you Elliott?" The fear he heard in her voice cut him so deep, he wanted to scream. Not even the pain he experienced during the shooting could compare to what he was feeling now.

"Caitlyn," Brian reached out, but she pulled away.

"We have to find him Brian. Help me find our son."

"We'll find him Caitlyn," Brian said as he pulled her into his arms.

"Elliott, Elliott, Elliott," Caitlyn cried as she fell to her knees in Brian's arms.

Chapter 11

When the chopper landed, Brian was sitting in the back near the branch with Caitlyn in his arms rocking her as she cried. Douglas took Caitlyn from Brian's arms and carried her into the house. Joshua went to the area they were at earlier, while JD and Calvin began questioning Brian. "Brian, where did you last see Elliott?"

A distraught Brian stood and ran his hand down his face to wipe away the tears. He couldn't explain why, but he felt empty, where not even an hour ago his heart was full. "Brian focus, your son's life depends on this." JD demanded. "Where was the last place you saw Elliott?"

"At the tree branch."

"How long ago?" JD continued to ask questions

"Twenty minutes at the most. He came out to set up the fishing pole." Brian stopped then looked at JD. "The last time I looked out the window, Becker was walking towards his boat and Elliott was standing right there at the tree branch. I turned away talking to Caitlyn and when I looked back up Becker and Elliott were gone."

"What direction did the boat go?"

"I didn't see the boat leave."

"Think Brian," JD yelled. "Think."

"I didn't see the damn boat leave." He yelled back at JD as he walked around in circles. "I didn't see it."

"Okay." JD needed to keep Brian focused. "What did Elliott have on?"

"I don't know. He changed clothes after school. All I remember is his blue NY Yankees baseball cap. I remember because I thought it would be good to take him to a game. You know."

"Yeah, I know Brian." JD replied. "What else?" JD asked as the Sheriff's vehicle pulled up with a few cars behind him.

Brian shook his head, "I don't know! I don't know."

JD put his hands on Brian's shoulder. "Yes you do B. You see everything," he said calmly. "Now think. Where were you?"

Brian closed his eyes and exhaled, then began talking. "I was in the kitchen with Caitlyn. I looked out the window. Becker walked out in a blue suit with a pinstripe tie. Elliott watched as Becker walked towards him. He had on a white tee shirt, blue jean shorts and a blue baseball cap."

JD motioned for the crowd of people forming to be quiet. "Okay Brian. Now think, what direction did the boat go. "I didn't see the boat. I looked straight out to the log, but I didn't see the boat. So it had to go off to the north. My line of vision from the kitchen would have seen it if it had gone south."

"Alright Brian, you did good. We're going to find him."

"We need a boat," Brian yelled. He turned to the sheriff, "Get a boat out here."

"We need somebody that knows this river." JD said to the Sheriff. "Who knows this river?"

"Nate Turner." Sheriff Wade said. He traveled this river up and down when his son went missing. "I'll get him and his boat here."

"Where's Caitlyn?" Brian asked.

"Douglas took her in the house." Calvin said. Brian turned and walked back into the house.

The lawn was covered with people at this point. One group was organizing town people to begin a search by foot. It was a huge estate and it would take hours to cover all of it. However, JD knew the boy was not on the property. During their research Calvin discovered a connection not only between Canter and a Russian Cartel, but Charles Melvin as well. Melvin was a sexual predator that took children for his pleasures, then killed them, but he always kept a piece of their clothing. That was his downfall. They convicted the man a few years ago and he died of a lethal injection last year. That in itself was bad news, but when they discovered the Cartel's newest venture, his blood ran cold. To make matters worse, a ship belonging to the Cartel left Senegal, Africa for America and was docked in the Chesapeake Bay, near Norfolk. "Joshua, could Becker have taken the boy by boat?"

"It's possible, but I don't think so. Somebody else has been here since earlier. There are more foot-prints that weren't there before. I also picked up a fresh butt of a cigarette. Still wet. The DNA came back as Canter." Joshua shook his head, not liking what he was about to say. "The DNA also hit a match from another case."

JD knew before Joshua said it. "Melvin. Canter was the missing link."

"The report on Canter indicates, he was one of fourteen children. The family was from a rural area and couldn't afford to feed all of them. Canter's solution was to kill his brother and sisters to survive. He was found to be unstable and placed in a mental institution until he turned eighteen. At that time they ruled him no longer a threat to society. "

"You think Canter has the boy?" JD asked knowing the answer. JD swore under his breath. "Two search areas." JD yelled. "If there was a person on foot, he had to have an escape route and a vehicle waiting somewhere near." JD surmised.

"I'll take the foot," Joshua said and disappeared into the woods.

"We need a map of this area including the river." JD turned as one of the Sheriff's officers approached with a map. He stretched it out on the table on the patio.

"We're here," the man pointed to an area on the map.

"Is it possible to get to Norfolk from here by river?" JD asked.

"Sure," Sheriff Wade pointed to the map. "Going north he could hit the Potomac then turn into the Chesapeake at Point Lookout which would take him directly into Norfolk.

"It would take too long to search that area. We need more to go on." JD said. He walked in the house to find Margie and Suzie Mae with Caitlyn talking to her. "Brian."

Brian and Caitlyn looked up at JD expectantly. "I need to talk to Caitlyn."

"What is it JD?" Caitlyn sat up anxiously with tears in her eyes.

JD took a seat in front of Caitlyn. "We are going to find Elliott. I give you my word. We are going to find him. But I need your help. When your father-in-law goes out on his boat, how long is he gone?"

"It varies," she sniffed. "Sometimes he's gone for hours. But a lot of times maybe an hour or less."

"That's good Caitlyn. Now, have you ever noticed what direction he goes in or comes from?"

"Due north, coming and going. Do you think Jacob has Elliott?"

"I don't know, but that was the last person near him before he disappeared."

"Has Elliott ever gone with him on the boat?"

"No, never. Colin forbids it."

"Why?" Brian asked.

"I don't know" Caitlyn replied. "I don't know." Tears began to fall again.

"It's okay Caitlyn," Margie said with a smile. "It's okay."

JD squeezed Caitlyn's hand. "You did good Caitlyn." He stood and motioned for Brian to follow.

Brian took Caitlyn by her hand pulling her from the sofa, then walked her over to an empty corner of the room. Pulling her into his arms, her head rested on his chest and she quietly allowed the tears to flow. Brian spoke softly into her ear. "Caitlyn if you never believed in anything before in your life, believe this. I'm going to bring our son home alive and well. She wrapped her arms around his waist to draw on his strength. He held her head close to his heart. "God did not bring you and Elliott back into my life for me to lose either of you. I truly believe that and you have to believe as well. Do you believe Caitlyn?" He looked down into her eyes. The tears shinning up at him cut straight through to his heart. Whoever was responsible for those tears was going to pay with their life.

"I believe," Caitlyn whimpered.

A brief smile of encouragement was difficult but he knew she needed it. "I'm going with JD. When I return, I'll have Elliott with me." He kissed her, pulled her tight, then walked out the door with JD.

When Brian walked out onto the patio his game face was on. A knowing look passed between James and Calvin. Douglas gave Brian an encouraging pat on the back. JD began reviewing the information and instructing the search party. The Sheriff gave each group a walkie-talkie to report back to the house. Redbone had arrived with food and drinks for those that were searching. The entire town was there with their support.

Brian looked at his watch. "It's five-twenty. I want my son back in his mother's arms before nine o'clock. Anybody here has any doubts it can be done, I don't need you here." He looked around at the crowd that had gathered to help with the search. No one moved. Looking around he saw Bart and Clem with their dogs ready to search. He acknowledged the town's people he had only met two days ago. "Thank you." He said as the crowd disbursed.

Joshua walked out of the woods to the deck where they stood. "This wasn't random. I followed an escape route to the road outside the entrance to the property."

"Becker would have no need for an escape route." JD replied.

"Somebody did," Joshua said as he stared at JD, both silently agreeing Brian did not need to know about Canter.

JD turned to the group remaining on the deck. "Mr. Turner and a few of his friends are here with their boats. We'll split, half taking the river north the other half going south."

"You're not going anywhere," James stated. "You will remain here directing the flow of information. Calvin, man the computer while the rest of us help with the search."

"Like hell," JD exclaimed.

"Brian and Douglas will go north with Mr. Turner." James stated ignoring JD's protest. "I'll join Sheriff Wade going south."

"I'm joining the search."

"Bart and Clem," Sheriff Wade spoke, "take the dogs through the woods and follow that trail to the road."

"I'll be in the chopper," Joshua stated as he turned to Brian. "Time is on our side, we'll find him."

"We're checking in every fifteen minutes?" James shouted as the group walked away.

No words could express what Brian was feeling at that moment. The man he had vowed to sacrifice his life for was willing to do the same for him.

JD could see the fear in Brian's eyes. He remembered the feeling a few months ago when he was searching for his family and felt helpless to do anything. Brian had been there for him, he'd saved his son's life. JD only hoped he could return the act. But he needed Brian mad, not sentimental. "We're going to take out whoever has your son."

"You can't take anybody out. You're the Attorney General. I can't let you do it. I'm going to handle this like I always have—kick ass and ask questions later." Brian could see JD was angry with the outcome. "Look man, I'm still responsible for your safety. If you are out there in danger, I'll have to make a choice between you and my son. I need you here, so I can concentrate on Elliott."

JD stared at him for a moment then looked away. "Go find your son."

Brian touched his shoulder, "I know you're with me, but James right, you can't go." Brian turned and walked away. "Let's roll out."

Ten minutes after Brian, Douglas and Mr. Turner pulled out of the dock they received a call from Joshua. "Northwest from your location there's an island. Pull in quietly on your side I'll meet you there. Come loaded."

Brian ended the call. "There's an island northwest of here. That's where we are heading."

"I know the place." Mr. Turner stated. "Me and my boys used to fish there until Becker put a stop to it."

"Can you cut the motor?" Brian asked as he checked his weapon.

"As we get closer we can coast in."

"What's going on Brian?" Douglas asked.

"There may be hostiles on the island ahead. Load and lock."

Douglas pulled out his weapon, checked the ammunition. "How many?"

"Doesn't matter. If they have my son, they're all going down."

"We're coming up on the island boys." Mr. Turner said as he silenced the motor. He docked the boat at the pier as Brian and Douglas jumped off with their weapons in their hands looking around.

"Mr. Turner, what do you know about this place?" Brian asked.

"I don't reckon I know much. Used to fish over yonder near the pier. Land used to belong to the Nickel's a little ways back. I guess Becker owns it now."

"What's through the woods?" Brian asked.

"I can't rightly say, never been on the other side."

Brian and Douglas looked at each other. "Let's go discover America," Douglas shrugged. The sound of Mr. Tuner cocking his shot gun caused both men to turn around. Just as Brian was about to tell him to stay behind, the man spoke. "Don't even think about it." He walked pass them, "Ya'll coming?"

The men began walking through the dense wooded area, with no clearing anywhere in sight. It was as if it was truly an uncharted area. The deeper in they walked, the darker the area became. The only sign of daylight was when you looked up through the trees that seemed to go on forever. Brian kept walking, leading the way. No one spoke, they just kept moving forward while surveying the area. Brian's phone vibrated. "Yeah."

"Look straight ahead." Joshua said. Brian put up a hand stopping their progress and looked in front of him. On a tree he could see the laser beam.

"I got it," he said and disconnected the call. "This way," He moved quickly with Douglas and Mr. Turner following him.

"Where is he?" Douglas asked while looking around.

"Who?" The men jumped and turned to find Joshua standing right behind them.

"Shit," Douglas exclaimed with his heart racing, "Will you stop doing that?"

Joshua shrugged, "Doing what?" then turned to Brian. "There's a house about twenty feet past these trees." He pulled an instrument that looked like a calculator, flipped it open then touched it with his forefinger. A screen appeared showing red dots. The men gathered around. "There are five rooms upstairs—four with a single occupant, one empty." He pointed to the dots at the top. "Five rooms on the lower level. Becker is one of the three bodies in this room. There's two here, one stationary and one moving." Pointing to one of the stationary dots he said, "Because of the size, I think that's Elliott." He paused then continued. "On the other side of the house there are three boats docked. I've checked them out, no one is aboard. Everyone is inside." There's eight maybe nine, all could be hostiles. Brian you go to Elliott. I'll take the upstairs. Douglas that leaves you and Turner with the three here." He put the device back into his suit jacket pocket. We shoot to kill and ask questions later. Stay low."

Brian looked at Douglas and nodded, when they turned back Joshua was gone. Turner looked around searching. "That boy sure knows how to make an exit."

"That he does," Brian said. "We ready?"

Douglas nodded, "Stay low." They moved in the direction Joshua indicated and sure enough the back of the house appeared. The deck was wide, almost circled the house. On the lower level, windows were visible on both sides of the house, with a sliding door in the middle. Moving across the grassy area, low to the ground, they each stayed away from the windows until they reached the deck. Loud voices could be heard coming from inside. One of them clearly Becker. "What in the hell is he doing here?"

"He's shipping out with the rest of them tonight, just in a different direction," Canter snickered.

"The hell he is, I'm taking him home."

While the men continued to argue Brian peeked through the window and saw Becker, with two other men. He motioned to Douglas indicating where the men were standing. Once Douglas and Turner were in positions on both sides of the window, Brian walked down to the next window. Staying close to the outer wall of the house, Brian peeked inside the room Joshua indicated. Elliott was laying on a bed still. There was no sign of blood, or injury. But, something inside of him snapped. Without giving it a second thought, Brian stepped back and fired three rounds nonstop through the window hitting the man that stood over his son.

Gun fire broke out in the house. "Oh shit," Douglas kicked in the back door and hit the floor. Before he could get off a round, Mr. Turner walked straight in and fired taking one man out. Douglas held the gun on the other who was reaching for his weapon. "Don't do it."

The man spoke in a language Douglas did not understand, but he saw his hand grab his weapon. Three shots rang out, from different directions, dropping the man to the floor. Douglas looked over his shoulder and smiled, Turner's shot gun was still smoking and Joshua was at the bottom of the steps with his gun pointing at Becker, who had hit the floor ducking from the gun fire. Brian emerged from the back room with Elliott in his arms.

All was silent for a minute. Joshua walked over to Brian to check out Elliott. He touched the boy's head then sniffed, "They used chloroform he should be okay." Joshua nodded at Brian then looked at the other men in the room. "That's the way you back up a man," Joshua smiled.

"Judge Becker, it seems you've been a naughtily boy." Brian said adjusting Elliott on his shoulder.

"Judge Becker, you're about to be all over the news. Or you are going to be the star witness against the cartel. Take your time to think about what you are going to do." Joshua turned to the other men in the room. "You are not going to believe what we have stumbled onto. Here I thought hanging out with JD Harrison's boys would be dull. Hell, I could hang with ya'll. Let me tell you what you have here." He pointed to the man Douglas shot, "This man and the one in the room back there are a part of an international criminal cartel out of Africa, which transports children into sexual slavery." He pointed to the man Mr. Turner took out, "This man is Robert Canter. He was a partner of Charles Melvin and enjoyed killing children. JD will be glad to know he's a done deal." Joshua stood and stared at Brian, "You might want to see what's upstairs. Turner, if the judge moves, shoot him."

Turner smiled at the thought, then cocked his gun.

Brian froze in his tracks when he approached the first room. "What the hell?" He put Elliott in a surprised Douglas arms, then walked over to the two-way mirror in the room. He turned back and looked at Joshua

Joshua walked over to the door leading to an adjoining room, removed the key that was on a hook and unlocked the door. Standing in the open doorway, Joshua and Brian stared at a rather fit young man. "What's your name son?" Brian asked.

The boy stood and removed his shirt, "John."

"Don't," Brian said. The boy looked at him with a blank expression. "How old are you?"

"Seventeen."

"How long you been here?"

"I don't know."

Joshua stared at Brian's shocked expression. "There's more." He looked at the boy. "We'll be right back to take you home." He then relocked the door. Brian looked through the mirror at the boy with a stunned expression on his face.

As they reached the next rooms, they found the same, with each of the boys stating their name was John. When they reached room number five, which was at the end of the hallway, the door leading to the room behind the mirror had an additional lock. "This one is interesting."

They opened the door and asked the same questions as before. "What's your name son?" Brian asked.

"Randy Clifford Turner," the boy defiantly replied.

Brian and Joshua looked at each other. "Come with me son." Brian said.

"I ain't going nowhere with you," the boy drew back his fist.

Brian and Joshua raised an eye brow. "You going to take him down or should I." Joshua laughed.

"Neither. Let's go." Brian and Joshua turned and walked away without locking the door. As they walked back down the hallway, they could hear other's had arrived at the house. Joshua, nor Brian bothered to turn back to see if the boy was coming, for both knew the minute he stepped outside the room. At the end of the hallway, Brian took Elliott from Douglas.

"Who's your friend?" Douglas asked nodding towards the boy.

"Randy Clifford Turner," Brian replied and walked down the stairs. When he reached the bottom he smiled at Turner with the shot-gun pointed at Judge Becker. Sheriff Wade, James, Bart and Clem were standing in the entrance. Sheriff, you're going to need another boat. "Clem, would you take over watch on Judge Becker while the Sheriff goes upstairs. Brian asked.

"So the skunk's finally out of the cage—bout time," Clem said as he pointed his rifle at Becker.

Tuner turned around just as Joshua took the last step into the room to see a boy standing at the top of the stairs. He squinted at the boy, then took a tentative step towards him. "Randy." He whispered. He looked closer, "Randy!"

"Pop. I knew you was going to come," the boy ran to his father and hugged him. Turner held the boy at arm's length and just stared at him as tears filled his eyes. "Randy," was all he could say as he pulled his son to him and cried.

The chopper landed on the front lawn a little before nine, to a crowd that had gathered to welcome the boy home. When Brian stepped out of the chopper with Elliott in his arms, the crowd roared with cheers for the boys safe return. Walking up on the porch, Brian saw Caitlyn standing in the doorway with tears in her eyes. "I brought our son home."

She fell into his arms and hugged both her man and her son. "I knew you would. I knew you would."

Chapter 12

There was no way in hell Brian was going to let Becker get off without a scratch, he didn't give a damn what his position in life was. He endangered the life of his son because of his extra-curricular activities. The more he thought about it the angrier he became. If he agrees to become a federal witness against the Cartel, and he would, Becker was going to get a clean walk. Brian respected the law more than the average man. Witnesses were needed to take the bad guys down. But the thought of the Becker's of the world continuously getting away with breaking the law gnawed at him. Looking down at his son, who was safe and sound asleep in his mother's arms, a cynical smile creased his lips. Brian pulled out his blackberry and dialed a number. "Interested in a little action?"

"When and where," Joshua replied.

"JD's room, ten minutes." He disconnected the call. Walking to the side of the bed, he bent over Caitlyn to kiss Elliott's, forehead. He then gently kissed her lips.

Caitlyn eyes opened perplexed. "Where are you going?"

"To see a man about a dog," he whispered against her lips.

Caitlyn closed her eyes and hugged her son a little tighter. Brian opened the door to walk out and heard her say, "Make sure the dog doesn't wag his tail around any more children."

Brian did not turn around, he just smiled. *That woman knew him too damn well.* He gently closed the door behind him. Walking down the hallway he stopped at JD's room and knocked. When he opened the door, he motioned for JD to step into the hallway. "You got a minute?" JD grabbed his robe then closed the door behind him. He then knocked on James door, then walked away. Before he could knock, Douglas opened the door. "What's up man," he asked as Brian stepped inside the room, followed by JD, James and Calvin.

Brian looked at Calvin, "I don't want any righteous speeches from you tonight."

Calvin stared at the man he loved like a brother. "My job has always been to try to get you to see reason; it's not going to change now. So what are you up too?"

All the men took a seat in Douglas room and turned to Brian. "I can't let Becker walk without a scratch. He has to pay a price, if only financial."

"What do you have in mind?" JD asked.

"I'm going to blow up the island." Calvin and James looked at him as if he had lost his mind.

"You can't blow up the island B." Calvin said with a low chuckle.

"We can blow up the island," Joshua announced from the doorway, as if it was the most natural thing in the world.

"Do you have access to the equipment we need?" Brian turned to him and asked.

"Brian," Calvin exclaimed, "you cannot be serious." Brian only stared at him, not saying a word. Calvin looked at Joshua and let out a nervous laugh then turned to JD. Calvin's expression froze as he realized JD was not laughing. "JD?"

Sitting forward, resting his elbows on his legs JD stared thoughtfully at Brian. The man had been through hell in the last 36 hours. There was no guarantee that the person who caused that hell was going to pay. He believed in the justice system, but just like his wife told him a few years ago, everyone has the propensity for violence when protecting someone you love. Besides, this incident could have international implications. "Any area that is used to harbor criminals that harm our children and put our country on the brink of war should be eliminated in my book." He let the statement float in the air for a moment, then he continued. "However, it's against the law and I'm not sure the President will be too happy with us. Let's get legal advice before we proceed."

JD looked at James and nodded. James pulled out his blackberry and dialed a number.

"Who's in trouble Little Brother?" Vernon asked on the other end of the line.

"With his eyes still honed in on JD, he asked, "We need you to look at statutes surrounding demolition of enemy territory under the Patriot's Act."

Vernon stop scanning the document in his hand, sat back in his seat and gave James his full attention. "What and who?"

"A remote property, located on the Virginia –Tennessee border. AG."

"He can't. It would be political suicide. Once he is President we can work around it, but not now. Give me details."

James told Vernon the situation and what they suspected was going on at the location. "Do you know for a fact the boys were held on the property?"

"Four other boys including Randy Turner we found there. According to the Turner boy that is where he has been for eight years."

"Unbelievable. I've dealt with some sick puppies in my day, but to do this to children, it's just un-freaking believable. Are they selling the boys overseas and if so, what country?"
"We believe so and we're not sure what country."
"If it's one we are at war with we can blow the place up, but your man should have nothing to do with the act if it's on American soil. It would be too damaging. Absolute, on the other hand, could and will be protected. Proceed with caution here. We don't want to pay the price of a million dollar heist for a ten cent crime."
"I'll keep you posted."
"Don't. The less I know the better, if you need my services later."
The call ended and James gave JD what he needed when he nodded towards Joshua.
"Let's go," Brian stood ready for action.
"No." JD stated, "you and I have to sit this one out."
"You can't deny me the right to revenge my son."
"Your son is the reason I'm sitting you down on this."
Joshua stood, "I got you on this." Everyone turned to Brian, when they looked back Joshua was gone.
"How in the hell does he do that?" James asked.
"Damned if I know," JD said then turned to Calvin. "Calvin, we are not going to blow up the island, just the house. We are going to eliminate the threat against the children and this country." He held Calvin's stare until he was sure they were on the same page. "Ok, now that we are all in agreement, Calvin, get the US Attorney General on the line, I'll call the Governor. Let's make sure everyone knows what is about to go down. Then he turned to James. "You shouldn't be in this conversation. It's a state issue, not a campaign issue. Besides, it's better if you don't know how this is going down.
"James, check in on Caitlyn and Elliott, will you." JD added.

"That goes without saying." James nodded. "They are a part of the family now." The sentiment was echoed by everyone in the group. It was easy to see that Brian was touched by the statement. "I like that woman of yours Brian," James said as he walked out the door.

"After all these years, she is still in love with him." Calvin said to JD in disbelief. "I hope he recognizes just how fortunate he is to have a second chance with her."

"I don't know," Douglas stated, "he can be damn right stubborn at times."

"An ass is a more accurate term, wouldn't you say JD," Calvin interjected.

"I wouldn't say he's an ass, but he would be stupid to let this chance at happiness slip away."

"You all do realize I'm sitting right here," Brian stated.

"Yeah we know you're here. Hell, we haven't talked behind your back before, no sense starting now." Douglas laughed tapping Brian on the leg. "They're going to be at it for a while." He motioned towards JD and Calvin, who had already turned away making calls. "I'll walk you back to your room."

Brian frowned at him thinking, *since when do I need to be walked back to my room.* Once outside the door, Douglas stopped. "I'll keep an eye on your family. You go do what you have to do."

"So you said that walking back to my room shit for Calvin's sake?"

"You and I know Calvin and JD are by the book. They are going to follow the law. But there is a law of the street that over-rules here. Never leave a man standing to attack your family again. Protect what's yours."

Five minutes later Brian walked out on the patio. "The chopper is waiting." Joshua stepped out of the shadows.

Brian smiled, "You have everything we will need?" he asked as they climbed into the AH-6J Little Bird chopper as they called it.

"A few missiles, Hellfire anti-tank missiles, Air to Air missiles, two miniguns, two grenade launchers." Joshua frowned, "Hold up. " He reached around the back of the chopper and placed something in his suit jacket pocket. "You can never have too many hand grenades."

Brian grinned at Joshua, "I like the way you think."

"I don't want to leave anything that might give them the idea of rebuilding."

"You get no arguments from me."

The helicopter landed quietly behind the house that looked just as menacing at night as it did earlier that day. Every time the house came to Brian's mind, the thought of his son being in there and what could have happened pissed him off. Walking up the steps to the front porch of the house Joshua and Brian both froze in their tracks. They saw movement. The two hit the ground rolling in opposite directions, neither standing until they reach the opposite sides of the porch, with weapons drawn. Joshua pointed indicating he was going around the back. Brian advanced taking a look inside the first window he reached wondering, *who in the hell could be in the house. They cleared all the boys out that afternoon. The creep working with Becker was dead, so who was in the house?*

Then he heard voices coming from the inside. One man spoke with a heavy French accent and Brian could barely make out what was being said. The other voice sent a chill up Brian's spine. *It can't be*, he thought. He listened a little more intensely. "Only a portion of the plan worked. Becker is being held responsible, but I still don't have the boy." The man replied, but Brian was only able to get a portion of what he said, something about replacing cargo. "I don't give a damn about your cargo. What you do with those young boys is sick in my opinion. I paid you well for my request. Now what are you going to do to see it through?"

"It was my cartel activities that allowed you access to the boy. Don't be so quick to judge us. As long as the boy's father is alive, you will never get to him." The man with the accent replied.

"Then kill him!"

"That could very well cause an international war with your country, all for your greed. What do you American's say—I don't think so."

"If you are not going to finish the job, then return my payment."

The man laughed, "You are under the misconception that you are in control here. You are not, The Cartel is. In fact they believe your cause has cost them dearly. We were looking to relocate, not to dismantle the operation. You brought in your government when you hired one of our people to take the boy. You knew who the boy's father was and his connections."

Brian knew what was coming, he had to make a move. But for a moment—a long moment he was considering allowing it to happen. But how would he explain it to Caitlyn. "Damn, damn, damn," he cursed in a whisper. In that moment he knew without a doubt he still loved Caitlyn and would never allow anyone to hurt her. Which meant only one thing, he had to save the SOB. Brian peeked through the window again. He only heard two voices, but he was sure there were more men inside. Ducking under the windows he made his way to the door. Using his shoulders, he knocked the door in and hit the floor firing two shoots into the corner. He then heard shots from the back of the house and knew Absolute was indeed in the house. The man with the accent now had none other than Fredrick T. Montgomery by the throat with a gun pointed to his head. Brian was still on the floor with his weapon pointed right at the man's heart. "We seem to be at an impasse here," Brian said.

"It only appears that way Mr. Thompson." The man replied with a heavy accent.

Brian smiled, "Now, see that's not right. You know who I am, but I have no idea who you are. I do know this," he said, never taking his eyes from the man's, "I can't allow you to take that man's life."

The man grinned, "Mr. Thompson, do you even know why Montgomery wants your son?"

That got Brian's attention, in addition to Joshua leaning against the wall behind the two men as if he didn't have a care in the world. "Don't know," the man flinched at a sound from behind him, Brian pulled his trigger, taking the man out with a gunshot to the center of his head, "Don't care." He said as he stood.

"Now that's what I'm talking about. Just take his ass out. Man I could work for you." Joshua boasted as he examined the body.

Judge Montgomery was so shocked, he actually pissed in his pants. Brian stared down at the man who had made Caitlyn's life a living hell for ten years. Montgomery turned to look at him. "You have been a thorn in my side since the day you met Caitlyn. Why didn't you die like any normal man would that was shot four times?"

"I'm not normal. I died the day you hid Caitlyn from me." Brian turned to Joshua, "Who are they?"

"Members of the cartel from South Africa, from what I gathered. I'll know more by morning." Joshua pulled out a blade, a plastic baggie and cut a finger from the man on the floor. Blood splatter on his suit. "Awe man, I ruined my suit."

Brian grinned, "I'll buy you another one."

"Okay," Joshua dropped the finger in the bag just as Judge Montgomery began to hurl.

Joshua looked at Brian, "He's riding in the back with you."

Brian looked disgusted at the judge. "Is everything set?"

"Just waiting for your exit," Joshua replied.

Brian grabbed Montgomery by his jacket, "Let's go." He dragged the man out with him.

Once outside the house, Brian and Joshua turned and threw a grenade each through a window. They turned and walked away just as the house burst into flames behind them. Brian literally threw Montgomery into the back of the chopper, as Joshua lifted off. The chopper silently rose and perched over the dwelling. Joshua pushed a button releasing one of the missiles, turned the chopper and headed in the opposite direction. The area that was once a nice sized island was now reduced to small strips of land.

The sunrise came a little early for the residents of Nickelsville, and the surrounding counties from an explosion that lit up the sky. News stations were reporting a brush fire that hit a gas line causing the explosion that was heard in Virginia and Tennessee. The small town was now inundated with FBI agents, ATF agents, and some believed to be CIA operatives, but they weren't sure.

Margie's B&B was running at full capacity and it wasn't six a.m. She had called in as many favors as she could to handle the multitude of people. Fortunately, Margie had to spend most of her time trying to keep the town folks away from the conversations taking place in the lounge area. Sheriff Wade, was in one corner busy controlling the onslaught of law enforcement and government authorities, all asking the same question, *How could this cartel have infiltrated the area without law enforcement's knowledge.* Judge Becker had been taken into custody by federal agents. Judge Montgomery was being sequestered in a room upstairs with Douglas. He wasn't officially guarding him, but it was clearly understood that force of any type was to be taken if the judge attempted to leave that room or alert anyone of his presence. For extra measure, Douglas was instructed to kick

A Lost Heart

Montgomery's ass if he tried to sleep. Sleep deprivation is a form of torture, Douglas explained to Brian. "I know," Brian grinned, "Enjoy." He said as he left the room.

"Damn it, Absolute, I said the building, the house not the east coast," the director of the CIA yelled as he stood in Margie's office with Joshua, JD and Calvin. "How in the hell am I supposed to explain this to the President?"

"It slipped," Joshua said calmly. "I hit the wrong button."

He could see the unspoken expletives through the facial expression of his boss. If he didn't think the President would have to listen to another lecture from his boss on how he was out of control, he would have laughed. But Joshua figured the President was catching enough hell from the Tea Party assholes and didn't need him adding to it, so he sat there calmly wondering when he could be putting on a clean suit. "Did you leave any dead bodies?" His boss hissed through clinched teeth.

"One or two," Joshua replied, "maybe five."

JD listened to the conversation as Brian entered the room. He motioned his head for JD and Calvin to step out. They followed. "Douglas has Montgomery stashed away upstairs."

"Have you decided how you want to handle him?" JD asked. Brian gave him a knowing look. "Other than killing him," JD clarified.

"If I can't kill him, then I want him to have to face the court system."

Calvin just shook his head, "Talk about an abuse of power. The very people we put in place to judge those that break the law have surpassed the crimes committed by the people they've put away tenfold."

JD leaned against the wall. "The first night I met Tracy we were in the old condo talking about justice."

"Stimulating conversation," Brian smirked.

JD grinned, "It was. She asked me, if the people running the system are corrupted, is justice being served. At the time

I told her, I believed in time, those who are corrupt would be brought to justice. Well that time is here. This unthinkable crime was brought against you. You have to decide what the punishment will be. Whatever you decide, I am sworn by the state of Virginia to take action against Judge Montgomery and I will. He will never sit on a bench again. How deep that punishment will reach is on you. I suggest you talk with Caitlyn before you make a decision."

"Brian, I believe in turning the other cheek, you know that. But you have to ask yourself, how many times will you allow this man to interfere in your life. There was a time the only person you had to look out for was yourself. Those days are gone. Your job as a father is to protect your son. To do that you need to know what you are protecting him from. Whatever Montgomery is after, he has been willing to sacrifice his own daughter. He's already shown you, how far he will go with your son." Calvin stepped closer to Brian and punched him in the chest. "You need to squash his ass now, before you can move on and be happy with Caitlyn."

Staring at his friend, Brian was a little surprised Calvin took this position on the matter. This was the one that was always against violence of any kind for any reason. A smile creased Brian lips. "You're alright Calvin. I never told you, but you know I love you like a brother." The smile disappeared, "Don't ever punch me again." He hit him on the shoulder. "But you're right. I need to talk to Caitlyn and Montgomery. We need to know what all the cloak and dagger is about. You think you can sit in on the conversation with us. You know, just in case I forget I'm not supposed to kill him?" JD smiled inwardly. It was good to see Brian acknowledge he needed Calvin around.

"Yeah, I can do that." Calvin replied smiling as if he had accomplished something monumental.

"You can take that shit eating grin off your face. In the end I'm still going to kick his ass. Let's go."

A Lost Heart

Calvin stared at his friends back as he walked away and sighed. "I'm going to make him civilized if it kills me." He heard JD laugh as he walked away.

Caitlyn stood at the counter waiting for Sallie Mae to fill the order she had taken from one of the FBI agents when Brian walked through the door. With all that was going on around them, to her, he was the only man in the room. He was her personal hero in more ways than one.

"Good morning tall, dark and handsome. Three days and you done turned the town upside down." Suzie Mae laughed. "I knew this town had never seen the likes of you and will never see it again. Just blew everybody away. And where is the Joshua fellow that everybody is talking bout. I think he could bring Redbone down a notch or two."

Brian smiled at Suzie Mae. He was going to miss her cheerfulness. "Good Morning Suzie Mae. Joshua is a little busy at the moment, but I'll send him your way when he is finished. Can I borrow Caitlyn for minute?"

"Boy, that's your woman. I've declared it such. You can take her anytime you like."

Brian smiled as he took Caitlyn's hand and walked away. "Thank you Suzie Mae, I appreciate that." They reached the stairs before he began talking. "Caitlyn we have to talk," he said as they climbed the stairs. "I don't think it's going to be pleasant." He stopped when he reached Douglas' door, where Calvin was waiting. "But we have to do this if we are going to have any chance at being happy. Please trust me and don't interfere, just listen."

Caitlyn looked at him, then at Calvin, then turned back to Brian. "I do trust you, I always have."

With that said Brian opened the door then stepped back for her to enter. Caitlyn walked in, looked up and saw her father standing in a corner on one leg. At first she couldn't believe he was there, but then she wondered why he was in a corner as if he was on punishment. She turned as she heard Brian snicker behind her. He cleared his throat. "Take a seat Montgomery."

Judge Montgomery put his foot down and turned to see his daughter standing in the room. "It isn't legal to hold me against my will. I'll have you arrested and thrown in jail for this." He said to Brian.

Douglas grabbed him by his jacket and forcefully sat him down in the chair near the window. "He doesn't smell too great," Douglas said to Brian.

"I'll be sure to keep my distance." Brian took Caitlyn's hand, sat on the side of the bed and faced Montgomery. "In the few times I've been in your presences one thing has been consistent—you are a pompous ass. You consort with a foreign criminal Cartel, try to have your grandson kidnapped and you have the audacity to threaten to have me arrested. That's the thanks I get for saving your sorry ass. No hello for your daughter, no thank you for me. Judge I'm beginning to think you don't like us very much."

"You don't scare me Thompson. If you were going to harm me you would have done it by now. So what do you want?"

Brian grabbed Montgomery out of the chair. "The only reason you are still alive is because of Caitlyn. Now say hello to your daughter—nicely." He dropped him roughly back into the chair.

Judge Montgomery grunted, "Hello Caitlyn."

"Man you said that as if it left a bad taste in your mouth," Calvin said as he stepped away from the door he was leaning against. "I'm Deputy Attorney General Calvin Johnson, Judge Montgomery. Oh, wait that would now be Mr. Montgomery, as of ten minutes ago you were removed from the bench and disbarred."

"You can't do that," Montgomery sneered.

"Oh, I can and I did." Calvin smiled. "What other remedies are forthcoming depends on you. Let's take a moment and contemplate that." Calvin simply stared at the man. "Now, that we understand the consequences of your actions let's determine if all that will happen to you will be the disbarment or will there be more. Is this woman your daughter Judge Montgomery?"

"Yes."

"How long has it been since you've seen her?"

Montgomery flinched. "Nine years or so," he answered gruffly.

"Hum, the greeting you gave her earlier wasn't one of a parent that had not seen his child in years. It seemed more like a greeting you would give your worst enemy."

"Is there a point to this line of questioning?"

"I'm glad you asked." Calvin smiled. "Yes there is. I'm trying to establish a pattern of malicious acts you have done against Caitlyn in the ten years I've known her. Oh, did I forget to mention I met Caitlyn back at college years ago. When she befriended Mr. Thompson here, she also became my friend. So now in addition to acting on behalf of the state, I'm also here as her friend. Your daughter has powerful friends. You had no way of knowing that because you abandoned her—oh pardon me, I have that wrong—you sold her out." I'm still a little bothered by that, but we'll get to that later. Right now, if you would be so kind, I would like for you to explain to Brian and Caitlyn why you attempted to abort their child, why you blackmailed Caitlyn into keeping Elliot's birth from Brian and finally, why are you so hell bent on getting custody of Elliott."

Montgomery's eyes narrowed as he glared at Calvin. "I don't have to answer any of your questions. If I'm under arrest, then I get a phone call. I choose to call my attorney."

"Mr. Montgomery, you are thinking we are working under state law," Calvin laughed. "We're not," he sobered. "Because you involved another country's criminal cartel, we are operating under the Patriot's Act. You are familiar with that aren't you? Just in case you are not, let me explain the fundamental element of it—you have no rights."

Caitlyn watched and listened as the conversation went on. All she could think was this is the man that she admired. She wanted to make him proud. Then he wanted to kill her child. "Father?"

Montgomery snatched his head around. "Don't call me that." He growled.

It was incredulous to think it could happen, but his words cut deep and tears formed in Caitlyn's eyes. Brian squeezed her hands for comfort. Turning to him she realized, he was there to be her strength, so she leaned into him. "I don't want to know," she said.

Brian kissed her forehead. "We have to know."

"Then I'll ask my mother."

"No!" Montgomery yelled and came out of the chair.

Douglas who was leaning casually against the wall came to attention. Caitlyn's head shot up. Brian and Calvin stared questioningly at each other. Douglas pushed Montgomery, "Sit down and don't get back up until I tell you to."

"Caitlyn," Calvin called out while he watched Montgomery's reaction. "Do you know how to reach your mother?"

"Don't you dare call your mother. Haven't you hurt her enough, bringing a bastard child into our life?"

Brian pulled out his cell phone, "Caitlyn call your mother."

Still unsure of what was happening, Caitlyn took the phone, then turned it on. "You don't have any service in this room."

Brian swore under his breath. "Here stand by the window."

Nodding her head, "It's working," she said, then began to dial the number to her home. Before she completed dialing, her father stood and slapped her across the face knocking the phone from her hand. In a flash Brian had the man in a head lock and was applying pressure. Douglas and Calvin were pulling at his arms to get him to release the man with no success. The man's face was turning white as a sheet. "Brian he's losing consciousness, let him go," Calvin begged.

Caitlyn looked up and saw what was happening. She jumped up, reached out and touched Brian's face. "Let him go Brian," she said calmly. She pulled Brian's face until his eyes were looking into hers. "Let him go, please let him go. Don't let him separate us again."

Douglas and Calvin looked stunned as they watched this soft spoken woman talk Brian into slowly releasing Montgomery. Montgomery fell to the floor gasping for air as Caitlyn eased into Brian's arms.

She could feel the anger in his heartbeat. "Don't ever touch her," Brian growled as he held her tight. JD and Joshua burst through the room as Brian was pushing Caitlyn's hair from her face searching for the mark he knew was there. Finding it, he gently held her face in his large hands and softly kissed the spot of impact. "I'm sorry Caitlyn," he whispered, "I'm sorry I wasn't there when he hurt you before. I'm sorry I wasn't there when you were running to protect our child." A tear dropped from his eyes to her cheek, "I'm sorry I wasn't there when you gave our son life. I'm sorry Caitlyn."

Caitlyn kissed him with tears in her eyes, "I'm sorry I allowed him to do this to us."

"Don't move," Douglas put his foot on Montgomery when he attempted to move.

"Brian," JD walked over to his friend. "Let's go to your room." Brian didn't move.

Margie walked over and touched Brian's other arm. "Brian, will you let me take care of Caitlyn?"

He looked at Margie then reluctantly began to release his hold on Caitlyn. Everyone breathed a sigh of relief as the couple walked towards the door. Brian stopped and turned to Montgomery. "She saved your life. If you ever touch her again, I will kill you." He glared at the man to ensure he got his meaning, then walked out with Caitlyn.

"Caitlyn before you go, what is your mother's full name?" Calvin asked.

"Beverly Cheyenne Montgomery."

"Thank you." Calvin pulled out his black berry, then stepped over Montgomery to reach the window. "One acts irrationally when love or money is involved in an equation. Which is it for you Mr. Montgomery? "Rossie," he said into his phone as he looked down into the eyes of Fredrick T. Montgomery, "Find everything you can on a Beverly Cheyenne Montgomery. Start with finances then work your way back." Calvin bent down next to Montgomery. "Why are you so afraid of your wife?"

It was close to ten in the morning when Colin strolled into the B&B. "My lord Margie, what's going on? It looks as if we have been invaded by a foreign country."

"Colin, where have you been for the last two days? Things have been crazier than a bed bug in dirty laundry around here and you were nowhere to be found. Do you know they have arrested your father on child abduction, child endangerment and a few other ungodly things I haven't heard of? "She was trying her best to whisper but her voice kept escalating. "And where were you when Caitlyn needed you. Did you know one of your father's associates kidnapped Elliott? Did you know the FBI was searching for you? Shame on you for just up and disappearing like that."

Colin was trying to follow every question and did you know statement, but Margie was beginning to lose him. "Margie darling, slow down." He grabbed her by the shoulders. "Now take a deep breath and tell me what happened to Elliott and Caitlyn?"

"Dr. Becker," JD called out from the doorway of the lounge area.

"Attorney General Harrison, welcome back to Nickelsville. There really wasn't any need for the fanfare of escorts." He extended his hand.

JD accepted it. "I'm afraid that was not my doing. "May we have a word with you?"

"Certainly," Colin replied just as Marybeth came running through the front doors.

"Colin," she cried almost out of breath. "I did my best to keep them away from you and the office. But they all just barged in and started searching through everything. I tried to stop them, I swear I did."

"Marybeth, calm down. What are you talking about?"

"I believe we can explain Dr. Becker," JD said as he pointed into the lounge area.

Marybeth stepped closer to Colin and whispered, "I think he's one of the uppity ones that got a little power."

Colin looked at Marybeth. "I think you better go back to the office before they rub off on you."

Margie tried not to laugh, but she had to let out a little smirk as Colin walked into the lounge. "Well," he said as he placed his hat on the ledge over the fireplace and sat his briefcase on the floor. "Seems like the gangs all here. Margie mentioned something about Elliott and where is Cat?"

"We have a few questions for you Dr. Becker," the director of the CIA stated.

"I'll be happy to answer all of your questions once I see Cat and Elliott. Now where are they?"

"They're upstairs Dr. Becker." JD replied.

"Thank you Mr. Harrison. I'll return as soon as I'm sure they are fine." Colin climbed the stairs two at a time until he saw a rather menacing looking man leaning against the door at the end of the hallway. He started to take a step towards Brian's room then thought better of it. Staring at the man,

Colin decided to chance it. "You wouldn't happen to be standing guard over Cat and Elliott now would you?"

Douglas stood where he was. "And you are?"

Colin smiled. He knew no harm would come to Caitlyn or Elliott with Brian Thompson in their life. "I'm just the husband, no one special," he replied in his slow southern drawl.

Douglas knocked. "There's a husband out here to see you. Should I let him in?"

The door swung wider and revealed Brian's angry face. "Where in the hell have you been?"

Colin walked forward almost laughing. "Why Mr. Thompson, it's a pleasure to see you again too." He stopped when he reached the door, then raised an curious eyebrow at Douglas. "May I come in?"

"Colin," Caitlyn called out. "Where have you been?"

Seeing the concerned look on her face, Colin walked over to her. "What's wrong Cat?"

"Everything Colin, everything."

"Where's Elliott?"

"I'm right here, Daddy Colin," Elliott said as he came out of the bathroom.

The boy had a way of bringing life into a room. Colin smiled as he bent down, taking the boy into his arms for a strong hug. "Did anyone touch you Elliott in the way we talked about?" The boy shook his head no. "And you would tell me if they had, right?"

"Yes." Elliott replied.

Colin rubbed the top of his head and smiled, with visible relief. "Well now, they tell me you had a bit of an adventure yesterday." He said as he causally examined the child.

"I did," Elliott proclaimed excitedly, "I just don't remember everything. But my Daddy found me and brought me home to my mommy."

"Sounds like you have a good daddy there," Colin smiled. He lifted the child and sat him on the edge of the

A Lost Heart 211

bed. He checked his pulse first, then his eyes. "Looks like you survived alright."

"I did, and you know what?"

"No, what," Colin couldn't help but smile.

"Me and Mommy going to Richmond to live with my daddy."

"And you know what else?"

"No." Colin said as he stood.

"You can come too. My Daddy said so."

Colin looked at Brian and Caitlyn who were standing to the side as he discreetly examined Elliott. "That's mighty nice of your daddy. But if I go to Richmond with you, who's going to take care of the sick people here in Nickelsville?" Elliott held his head down thinking.

"Maybe Colin could come and visit us in Richmond," Caitlyn offered.

Colin nodded and took it for what it was—an open invitation to continue to be a part of their life. "I think I'd like that." He looked back down at Elliott. "Why don't you go to see Suzie Mae. I'm sure she has some chocolate cake down there somewhere."

Elliott's eyes grew as big and around as a circle, "Can I Mommy?"

At first Caitlyn was hesitant to have the boy out of her sight, but Brian opened the door. "Doug, would you take Elliott downstairs to Suzie Mae?"

"I think I can do that. You ready Elliott?"

Elliott jumped down from the bed and ran to the tall man. "Oh boy, chocolate cake for breakfast." He took Douglas' outstretched hand. "Do you have a little boy Mr. Doug?"

"Not yet."

"You know what Mr. Doug?"

"No, what?"

"You will one day."

"You think so huh?"

"Yep."

Caitlyn smiled as she watched the two walk down the hallway. "That boy has never met a stranger." Colin said with a slow laugh. "So, how are you two doing?"

"It's been a rough two days," Caitlyn replied as she took a seat next to Colin who was now sitting on the bed. Brian listened and observed the body language between the two as Caitlyn told Colin all that had taken place. It was clear they cared about each other, as friends. The conversation flowed easily between them, even the parts about his father. It appeared Colin was not surprised about his father's activities, but he was stunned when Caitlyn told him, her father was behind Elliott's kidnapping.

"But why? He could have had Elliott all to himself if he hadn't married you off to me. It just doesn't make sense Cat."

"We don't' know why," Caitlyn replied, "But he is still very angry."

Colin shook his head, "Cat, after what I've learned about my father, nothing surprises me. We're all raised to believe our father's responsibility is to care and protect his children. But your father and my father are from a different breed. Here my father has condemned me all my life for my sexual preference, while he was engaged in something like this. How hypocritical is that? Then your father literally sells you to me. God only knows why. Yet they both proclaim to be the righteous arm of justice. I know this is cruel, but I honestly hope they both rot in hell, together. That would certainly be poetic justice." He looked at Brian, "You're not going to give him another shot at Elliott are you?"

"Hell will freeze over before Montgomery gets anywhere near Caitlyn or my son," Brian replied forcefully.

That statement made Colin smile, "Well then. My job is over. You asked me earlier where I had been for the last day or two. I was in Washington visiting with my attorneys. According to them, since our marriage was never consummated a divorce wasn't necessary. Therefore, we took steps to simply have it annulled."

Caitlyn gasped, "Can we do that?"

"It's done darling. All you have to do is sign the paperwork." Colin stood then walked over to the door. "That, Mr. Thompson puts the ball in your court." He opened the door to walk out, "With that done, I believe the authorities may have a question or two for me. I'll be downstairs with the paperwork when you're ready."

The door closed behind him. You could hear a pin drop in the carpeted room. Could life be that simple after nine years of wanting and wondering—could it really be that simple? If anyone had told him he was about to do this, Brian would have told them to go straight to hell. But the last thirty-six hours had given him something he never thought he would have again—a family. The question was, whether he was man enough to take what he so desperately wanted. "Will you marry me Caitlyn?" The surprised expression on his face encouraged him as he took a step towards her. "In good times and bad," he took another step. "In sickness and in health," he took her hand as he watched tears stream down her face. "To love and cherish," he bent down on one knee. "To have and to hold from this day forward," he held her eyes, and then held his breath.

Bending down on her knees, Caitlyn kissed his fingers and replied, "Yes." She cupped his face with her hands and then kissed his lips, "A thousand times yes."

Pulling Caitlyn into his arms, for Brian there was no rush, no urgency, and no desperation in the kiss. It was a final acceptance of this woman becoming his. Finally believing their lives were now as tangled as their tongues, as full as their hearts and as unending as their love for each other.

Downstairs, Colin had just completed his conversation with the Director, where he turned over documents Robert

Canter had given him implicating his father in a number of crimes. When told about the accident on the island, he simply shrugged it off. "A little more dramatic than I would have done, but the outcome would have been the same. Justice would be served if my father and Caitlyn's father remain in the same cell until one of them kills the other." With that he stood, "I think I'll go join Elliott in what I'm sure will be our last meal together."

JD was pleased, another situation Joshua had escaped unscathed. But he knew the day would come when one of Joshua's antics was going to bite him in the butt. JD watched as the Director and Joshua boarded the chopper and lifted off. "Thank God he is on our side," JD laughed.

"You are not going to believe what we found." Calvin said as he entered the room with James in tow."

JD turned to Calvin and the computer. "We just recovered from the last time you found something on that computer. Can't we just go home?"

"Not until we've decided what we are going to do with Montgomery."

"Just turn him over to the feds," JD said as he slumped in the chair.

Calvin grinned, "We have a better idea." James sat on the chair opposite JD and could not contain his laughter.

Caught up in the excitement, JD smiled and sat forward. "I'm going to regret this aren't I?"

"Actually, I think it's justice." Calvin offered.

"As do I," James added.

"Okay, I give. What do you have?"

"The reason Montgomery is afraid of his wife finding out about his antics is because of the law of her people."

"Her people?" JD asked.

"Beverly Cheyenne Montgomery is an African Native American and a member of the Cherokee Nation. Any crimes committed against them will be heard before the

Tribal Council. They have their own version of crime and punishment."

"Interesting." JD nodded, "Has a call been placed to Mrs. Montgomery?"

James smiled, "She is in the air as we speak. With any luck, I will be home in bed with my wife tonight."

"Does the punishment involve tar and feathers?" JD laughed.

James and Calvin stared at each other then laughed. "How does the word castration sound to you?"

JD reached down between his legs to console his crown jewels, "Ouch."

"B," Calvin called out as he saw Brian and Caitlyn coming down the stairs.

"Give me a minute Calvin," Brian said. "Where is Colin?"

"In the restaurant with Elliott."

Colin watched as the couple walked into the restaurant. A slow knowing smile appeared on his face. "Shall I be the first to say congratulations?"

"None of that until the papers are signed." Brian replied, anxious to have this legality handled.

"I totally understand." Colin stood and walked into the lounge area where his briefcase still rested next to the fireplace. Picking up the briefcase, he opened it and pulled out a folder, handing it to Caitlyn. "There are two copies. I'll fax this over to my attorney who's waiting to file it with the courts today. You two have been apart long enough."

After signing, Caitlyn gave the documents to Brian, then pulled Colin into a loving embrace, "Thank you Colin. Thank you for everything."

Accepting the goodbye embrace, Colin kissed her cheek. "I will miss you and Elliott, but I'm thrilled for you. The reverend is free at three this afternoon."

After reviewing the document, Brian took it over to JD. "Take a look at this and tell me if it's legal."

A curious JD, glanced at him, then reviewed the document. With each sentence his smile widened. He passed it to Calvin to review. Grinning up at Brian, Calvin passed the document to James and stood. "Did you ask the question?"

"I did," Brian replied.

"And?" JD asked.

Wise men say if you want to know what your woman is going to look like in twenty years, take a good look at her mother. Although he had seen Mrs. Montgomery ten years ago, Brian did not remember her looking like this. Beverly Montgomery was a tall slim, sophisticated woman dressed in a teal form fitting dress and heels. Her hair was shiny black like Caitlyn's only her mother's hung down to her waist. There was little or no makeup, but none was needed. When she stepped inside the B&B, he stepped away from the window. Caitlyn was the spitting image of her mother, he was a very lucky man. "Caitlyn, your mother is here."

"You must be Caitlyn's mother," Margie said. "Now I know where her looks come from. Both of you are just beautiful. Welcome to Nickelsville. I'm Margie Nickels. How was your flight?"

It was clear it took Beverly a moment to understand all that Margie said, so JD took mercy on her. "I have to agree Mrs. Montgomery, you are a beautiful woman. My name is Attorney General JD Harrison. Thank you for coming on such short notice." He extended his hand.

"Hello Ms. Nickels. My flight was fine, thank you for asking. Mr. Attorney General. An introduction is not necessary. I know who you are and why I'm here. Where is Caitlyn?"

"I'm here mother."

Beverly turned to see the daughter that left her home as a young girl and now stood before her as a beautiful young woman. Tears came to the tips of her long lashes then spilled over. Holding out her arms she cried, "Caitlyn." Her daughter eased into her embrace.

Other than Brian, no one had ever held her, out of love, like her mother. "I missed you so much mother."

Beverly held her daughter at arm's length, pushed her hair from her face and smiled. "You cut your hair."

Caitlyn self consciously touched her hair, "Yes ma'am."

"I like it. It looks sassy. Your father would have a fit."

"He did." Caitlyn took her mother's hand, then turned back to Brian and proudly took his. "Brian this is my mother, Beverly Montgomery. Mother this is Brian Thompson."

"Mr. Thompson. I told my husband that you were going to be the death of him ten years ago. I'm so sorry you did not fulfill the prophecy." She turned back to Caitlyn, "Where's Elliott? Is he here?"

"Yes, he's with Colin."

"First, I'm going to take care of you, then I want to meet that grandson of mine."

"Why don't y'all take a seat in the lounge. I'll have Suzie Mae bring in some refreshments." Margie offered.

"This way mother," Caitlyn said.

When Brian reached her, Beverly kissed him on the cheek. "I'm glad you came back into my daughter's life."

Brian smiled. "Thank you for keeping my unborn child safe."

Stopping suddenly she turned to Brian. "Please know I had no idea what Fredrick was up to until Caitlyn ran away. I would have never agreed with what he tried to do to you."

"Let's take a seat," JD suggested. Brian and Caitlyn took seats in front of Beverly, while JD stood. "Mrs. Montgomery, your husband is being held in connection to your grandson's disappearance. Earlier Judge Montgomery became violent when Caitlyn attempted to call you, prompting us to believe there is more to this investigation than we know. We are hoping you can shed some light on things."

"Father has done some awful things mother. Do you know why? Why does father hate me so much?"

"You weren't born a boy," Beverly said. "Our heritage is deep and rich. We are a proud people that believe our leaders are all wise and brave. Unfortunately, my father was not wise when he married me off to Fredrick. The land in Northampton County was owned by our ancestors who were African-Native Americans, or what some called Freemen. The stretch of land known as the Eastern Shore is owned by our ancestors. As laws changed, our ancestors began to lose large portions of their property. To stop this from happening, generations ago, one of our wise leaders put in a legal clause stating that the land can only be inherited by direct male descendants. Since that time, the last male was my father. For most of my life, my grandfather was the richest man in the county. Farming was our main source of income and our main clientele were inhabitants on the mainland. As the economy grew and chain grocery stores came into play, the desire for fresh farm goods began to diminish and the clientele all but disappeared. Most of the island suffered, but our family held pretty firm. My father, in an attempt to help the economy, began boycotting the development of more chain stores. After several arrests, for trespassing or disturbing the peace, he was accused of arson. Everyone knew he did not start the fire, but the establishment wanted to get rid of him. He came before Fredrick who offered him a deal he could not refuse—prison or his daughter's hand in marriage. Needless to say, I lost out and was promptly married to your father. All was well as the economy turned around, somewhat. Developers took an interest in turning the eastern shore into a resort area for the wealthy. This brought the area to the point it is now—a multibillion dollar industry. Then my father died and the terms of the will were read. Once Fredrick learned he would never control the land, he became obsessed with preparing you to marry someone he could control. Of course you defied him when you met Mr. Thompson. Fredrick was not used to a man like your Brian standing up to him. Fredrick was used to having the power to control people. Around our parts no one dared to stand up to him—until you came along." She smiled at Brian. "From the moment you confronted him at the board hearing with Senator McClintock's son, you became his enemy. When Caitlyn told us she was pregnant, his hatred for you only intensified. When Dr. Green called and told me about the incident with you. I told Fredrick if he ever harmed you in anyway, I would go to the council. That's when he decided to send you here to marry Jacob's son. When he found out you had a boy, his mission became two-fold. Never let Mr. Thompson find out about Elliott, which meant keeping you away from him, until Elliott turns ten."

"What happens when Elliott turns ten?" Brian asked.

"He officially becomes the owner of Northampton County."

Brian and Caitlyn turned to each other shocked. "Elliott?" Caitlyn asked shaking her head.

Beverly smiled, "Yes, your Elliott will be a multi-billionaire at the age of ten." She laughed, "Frankly, I don't think he could be in better hands, Mr. Thompson. I know you will guide him well."

"A ten year old will own the county?" Brian asked still not believing.

"Not just any ten-year-old, your ten-year-old." Beverly could not have enjoyed the moment more, if she had planned it herself. "As for your father Caitlyn, tradition forbids my ever divorcing him unless he has disgraced the marriage. I'm not sure but being imprisoned just might satisfy the requirement. But his crimes were against you, not me. It's your decision what his punishment will be. Before you make your decision, understand, a man like your father never sees his own faults. He will always see that you wronged him by not being a boy and then by marrying Mr. Thompson. I assume you will be marrying my daughter." She looked expectantly at Brian.

Unfortunately, his mind was still trying to wrap around the fact that his son owns a county. "Who controls the inheritance until he turns twenty-one?

"I do, until Caitlyn turns thirty, then she will control it on his behalf."

"How will you live?" he asked out of concern.

"My family has provided well for me and for Caitlyn." The confusion was clearly on Brian's face. Beverly felt it was time for her to explain. "Mr. Thompson, you are what my people would call a warrior—a proud protector of others. The Gods did well when they picked you to be Elliott's father. A mother can nurture and love, but only a father can teach a boy how to be a man. It's time for you to fulfill the prophecy."

Colin walked into the room, "JD with your assistance, the papers are filed. The way is clear."

Brian and Caitlyn turned to Colin, confused by his words. Brian turned to JD. James walked in. "Do you have the application?" JD asked.

"Better," James stepped aside and a short woman with a laptop appeared.

"Olivia, what are you doing here?" Caitlyn walked over and hugged the woman.

"I received a fax of Brian Thompson's and Caitlyn Montgomery's birth certificates. Then I received a call from the Attorney General's office stating a car would be waiting to bring me here. Now, I just need to see your driver's licenses, then gather ya'lls signatures and ya'll will be good to go by three." She looked around, "Where can I set up?"

"Over here will be just fine," Colin stated as he carried Olivia's laptop to a table.

Caitlyn looked at Brian who just sat there as if this was a normal day. "I'm sorry. I don't understand."

"Why, I'm here to process your marriage license. You'll need that if you are going to be married at three, silly."

A shocked Caitlyn turned to Brian. He stood and took her hand, "The Reverend should be here by the time we complete the application. I've waited nine years. When we go home tonight it will be as husband and wife."

Through tears and laughter, Brian and Caitlyn completed the application then were whisked off quickly. Caitlyn with her mother, Suzie Mae and Margie upstairs in Margie's quarters. Brian, with JD, James, Calvin and Douglas in Brian's room while Colin and Elliott waited patiently downstairs as the towns folks prepared for the impromptu wedding.

"You know life is going to be a little different in the big city," Colin said to Elliott.

"It won't matter as long as I have my Mommy and Daddy with me." Elliott replied grinning.

At precisely three o'clock Brian and JD walked into the lounge that was decorated with pink paper bells and streamers hanging from the ceiling. An arch decorated in pink and white flowers stood in front of the fire place. Standing in front of the arch in a minister's outfit, was Clem with a bible in his hand. "You have got to be kidding me," a shocked Brian smiled. "The people in this town will never cease to amaze me."

"Yeah son, we do have a lot of talents around here," Bart grinned.

JD hit Brian on the shoulder, "You sure you are ready for this?"

Brian smiled at his friend, "This is the first thing I've been sure of in ten years."

JD smiled, "Then let's do it."

At three-thirty in the afternoon, on June sixteenth, surrounded by the town of Nickelsville, Virginia, with JD as the best man, Margie as the maid of honor, Elliott as the ring bearer and Colin giving away the bride, Brian Elliott Thompson took Caitlyn Cheyenne Montgomery as his wife.

Chapter 13

Be careful what you ask for was an understatement for Brian. The adventure of the last three days began with him begging for excitement. Well, he got it and much more. He looked over at Caitlyn who sat next to him in the limo James had provided for him and his family, then he looked down at Elliott who was asleep from the trip. He would not have changed any of it. Even during the time when Elliott was missing had merit. It led them to Nate Turner's son and other missing children. Those cases would have gone unsolved if JD had not sent him to Nickelsville. He sighed. The sound caused Caitlyn to turn to him. The soft smile caused a stirring in him. He knew was partially due to want, the other part was due to need. He wanted and needed this woman in his life. Reaching out he moved a strand of hair from her face. He was looking forward to a few days of peace and quiet to get to know her all over again, in more ways than one. The driver pulled in front of his condo and stopped. Brian stepped out of the car with Elliott draped across his shoulder. A boy his size would have looked strange on any other man's shoulder, but on Brian, it looked and felt just right. Walking around the other side of the vehicle to open Caitlyn's door, Brian turned at the sound of his front door opening. "Oh hell," he murmured as a very angry Pearl stood in the doorway. "Where in the hell have you been and why haven't you called in three days?"

A stunned Caitlyn stared at the very attractive angry young woman who apparently had keys to Brian's home. Brian who seemed unfazed by the woman's emotional outburst, simply walked by her and into the house. Caitlyn turned to the driver and thanked him. It had been a while, but Caitlyn was used to being sized up by Brian's women. The woman standing in the doorway did not faze her in the least bit. She just wished Brian had prepared her for what was to come. "Who are you?" Pearl asked, still frowning from Brian's action.

"Caitlyn."

With arms folded, Pearl replied. "That tells me nothing except your name. Why are you here?"

Caitlyn exhaled then took a step to walk inside. Pearl blocked her by placing her arm across the doorway. Caitlyn stopped then turned to the woman. "I believe this is now my home." She pushed the stunned woman's arm out of the way and walked inside. The entrance was open, allowing a view of the great room, dining room and kitchen, with a set of French doors at the back. There was a room off to the left that looked like it could be an office. A staircase was on the left between the office and an area that had to be the family room or the man room from the look of the furniture or lack thereof. Caitlyn smiled, it felt like home. She turned as she heard the slamming of the door behind her.

Brian came down the steps frowning. "I see you are still upset with me." Pearl started to say something but Brian put up his hand and stopped her. "However, whatever I did or did not do will have to wait. As you can see we have company."

"Company!" Pearl exclaimed. Which were Caitlyn's sentiments exactly, as her eyebrows rose at his comments,

A Lost Heart

only for a different reason. "She indicated this was now home."

So much for peace and quiet, Brian thought. "Pearl, Caitlyn. He pulled Caitlyn to him, Caitlyn this is Pearl, my nurse-maid and royal pain in the butt. Pearl this is Caitlyn" he hesitated a moment and then said, "my wife."

Pearl looked from Brian to Caitlyn still frowning. "Wife? It appears a lot has happened in three days."

Pearl glared at both of them curiously. "Hum-hum. He is not up for any strenuous activities including that of the sexual nature," she said to Caitlyn then turned back to Brian. "Have you been taking your meds?"

Brian sighed, "Don't need them" He moved away from Caitlyn, picked up Pearl's purse which was on the stand near the door, took Pearl by the arm, opened the door and set Pearl outside. "Thank you and good bye." Closing the door, he smiled at Caitlyn, Welcome to my life." Taking her hand he gestured around. "Allow me to show you your new home."

Brian and Caitlyn had taken a tour of the house. The tour ended at the door of the master bedroom. They both stood there watching Elliott sleep. "Come in, I'll quietly show you around."

Caitlyn pulled back. "I don't think that's a good idea. Remember what happened the last time we were in a bedroom together?"

Brian thought back to the night he found Caitlyn. "Yeah, and the problem is?" The alarm system sounded indicating someone had entered the front door.

"Brian! Brian!" Brian released a silent curse. He kissed Caitlyn's parted lips. "To be continued." He walked down the stairs to find a very pregnant Cynthia standing at the bottom of his stairs. "Tell me you did not put all of that behind the wheel of a car." He laughed.

"What took you so long to get home? I can't believe you left me here all alone and I'm to give birth any moment. You promised you would be here for me and you are off gallivanting around God only knows where. And then you don't call. Do you know how worried I've been? No you don't because you don't care...." Brian stood with his arms folded allowing Cynthia to get all her frustration out. He knew she was just afraid of the changes taking place in her life. When her tantrum suddenly stopped, he turned to see Caitlyn on the stairs staring down at Cynthia—and she didn't look too happy. Looking back at Cynthia he realized what she could be thinking. "Who in the hell are you?" Cynthia asked.

"His wife," Caitlyn replied a tad bit pissed.

"Brian doesn't have a wife," Cynthia replied in a voice that was a bit testy. "You want to try again?"

Sensing this scene was going real wrong real fast, it was time for him to step in. "Hello Cynthia. It's good to be home. Thanks for asking." The looks passing between the two women in his life were not welcoming at all. In fact it looked like two women about to fight over a man—him. "Caitlyn, this is Cynthia. Cynthia this is my wife. While I'm used to your less then welcoming moods, she is not. Let's play nice."

"She started it with that if looks could kill stare." Cynthia exclaimed. "And what do you mean wife. I'm about to explode and you are running around getting married."

Cynthia's mouth stopped moving and literally dropped open. Brian turned to see what caused her to stop just as Elliott grabbed his leg. "Daddy does she have a beach ball under her shirt?"

Brian couldn't help but laugh as he glanced down at his son.

"Daddy?" Cynthia yelled gasping at Brian.

"Yes," Caitlyn responded coolly as she walked down the steps into the foyer, "Daddy as in father." The front door opened and Caitlyn took a few steps back to get closer to

Brian just as the door slammed closed. A giant stood in the foyer and he did not look happy.

"Wow," Elliott said as his mother took his hand and casually stepped behind Brian.

"Brian."

"Samuel."

Samuel looked at Caitlyn, then extended his hand as he noticed Cynthia move closer to Brian. "Samuel Lassiter," he said sweetly.

"Caitlyn Montgomery," she replied cautiously as she took his hand.

"Thompson," Brian corrected.

Samuel then turned his full attention on his wife. "I can't imagine what possessed you to leave the house after I told you not to come here."

"I'm a grown woman Samuel, you don't tell me what to do. Right, Brian?" Cynthia stepped closer to him.

"Oh no you don't," Brian said as he took Caitlyn's hand and moved her and Elliott out of the line of fire.

Samuel stood with his arms folded across his chest. "Woman I swear you are treading on thin ice here.

"I told you I was coming to see Brian."

"When Cynthia Antoinette?"

That wasn't a good sign, she thought, he used her given name. She held her chin high, "When you were in the shower."

Brian began to laugh until Samuel threw him a very evil look.

Cynthia stomped on the floor. "I had to come, Sammy and it's a good thing I did." She threw evil eyes on Caitlyn. This woman is claiming to be his wife and this little boy is calling him Daddy."

"It's not a claim Cynthia," Brian chimed in. "You know who Caitlyn is to me. Elliot is our son."

"Brian you have so many women, how am I supposed to know one from the other. And how do you know he is your son? Did you do a DNA test?"
"DNA test! Sweetheart, look at that boy. He is DAMN NEAR ANOTHER Brian. There's your DNA test."
"Sweetheart?" Caitlyn exclaimed looking from Brian to Samuel. "That's not your baby she is carrying?"
"Hell no!" Brian and Samuel said simultaneously.
Samuel reached out and pulled Cynthia into his arms. "This spitfire is my wife even though she tends to forget it at times."
"I only forget it when you are over bearing." She kissed his cheek and hugged him.
"Why in the hell did you think that was my baby?" Brian asked Caitlyn.
"Well I don't know Brian, maybe the fact that she has a key to your home. Or it could be the evil eye she gave me when I came down the stairs. Or it could be the way she fussed about you getting married. Or the way she questioned Elliott's paternity."
"Well what do you expect walking in here with a boy this old claiming Brian was the father? Hell he would have had the child while he was in college and we all know...." Her eyes grew big and roamed up and down Caitlyn, then turned to Brian. "Did you say her name is Caitlyn?"
"I did." He waited as the clouds in Cynthia's mind began to clear.
"It takes her a minute," Samuel joked as he winked at his wife.
"The Caitlyn?" Cynthia asked, ignoring her husband.
"Yes," Brian replied.
"Oh."
"And I'm the Elliott."
Cynthia walked over to the boy. "Well, The Elliott, where have you been all this time?"

Caitlyn pulled Elliot closer to her. "With me," she responded coldly. "If you will excuse us, I'll show Elliott around his new home." Caitlyn gave Cynthia a stern stare, then turned to Samuel. "It was nice to meet you Mr. Lassiter," she said then turned and walked out of the room.

Brian shook his head and turned to Cynthia. "Open mouth-insert foot."

"What? How was I supposed to know who she was? It's not like you called anyone while you were gone. I'll go talk to her and explain my position in your life." Cynthia took a step towards the kitchen, just as Samuel reached out and grabbed her.

"Oh no you don't. If anyone is going to explain it would be Brian. We're going home and give Brian time to handle his business."

"Cynthia, go home with your husband and let me handle my wife."

"Stop saying that." Cynthia pouted.

Brian could not understand what Cynthia's problem was. "Get used to it."

"It's time to go Cynthia." The always cool Samuel said. "Leave your car, I'm driving." Cynthia opened her mouth to say something but Samuel looked a little bit upset, so she decided now was not the time. She just turned and stomped out of the door.

Samuel looked at Brian and laughed. "You got a problem."

"What?"

"A while back I asked you if there was something between you and Cynthia?

"Yeah, I remember and I told you no. I'm like a big brother to her."

"Well, that would make her your little sister. Since you are an only child you missed all the pranks they pull on girlfriends you brought home."

"Cynthia is your wife. She doesn't live here with me. I don't foresee any problems in that area."

Samuel raised an expressive eyebrow, "You don't?"

"No, I don't," Brian confidently replied. "I know how to handle my women."

Samuel smiled, "More power to you my brother." He turned and walked out of the door laughing.

When Samuel reached the car, he could still see Cynthia was fuming. "What makes her think she can just come up in here and take over?" she huffed as Samuel slid in behind the wheel and closed his door. "You should have heard the way that woman said, "I'm his wife." How dare her."

"Cynthia, Caitlyn is the woman in Brian's life now. You and the other ladies are going to accept it and welcome her into the fold."

"I don't have to do anything but be black and die. I don't even have to pay taxes unless I want too." Cynthia huffed.

Samuel smiled at his very emotional wife. God she was beautiful. He wished everyone could see the woman he knew. "Did you take a good look at Brian?"

"Of course I looked at him."

"No, Cynthia, I don't think you did. If you had, you would have seen just how much he loves that woman. Now, Brian has always supported you, even when he knew you were doing things to hurt yourself. When you were with Gavin, he didn't like it and he told you so, but he never criticized or interfered in your life, did he?"

Cynthia stared at her husband blankly, then shook her head, "No."

"Don't you think he deserves the same from you?"

"Yes, but."

"But what Cynthia?" Samuel asked. "Brian has had everyone's back for years now. Then we almost lost him a few months ago, it's time we think about him and not ourselves. It's time for him to be happy."

"How do you know that woman can make him happy? She broke his heart years ago."

"Apparently he has forgiven her. Why can't you?"

"Because Samuel, it's Brian, he's my Brian," she cried.

Samuel sat up, "Really?"

"Not like that," Cynthia waved his look off. "No matter how many women he's had in his life, he's always been my Brian. We've gone through everything together. Even when I was in love with you and committed to LaVere', it was Brian that listened and held me when my parents moved to California leaving me behind. And it was Brian that helped me to pick up the pieces after Gavin married Carolyn. He's just always been there."

"He's still is going to be there for you."

Carolyn shook her head as tears came down her face, "No Samuel. You didn't see the way that woman looked at me. She is not going to let Brian be there for me."

Samuel put a finger under her chin and turned her tear-streaked face to him. "I think Brian will have a say in that. But you know, you really don't need Brian the way you used to because I'm here." He wiped the tears from her face with the back of his hand. "Now I want you to really think about this. Since you and I have been married how often did you really need Brian for anything?"

Cynthia thought and thought. She couldn't think of the last time she really needed him. Samuel had been there. She sighed. "I know you're right. I just feel like I'm losing my best friend."

Samuel pulled her into his arms, then gently kissed her lips. "Brian is still going to be your friend." He felt her nod, then released her and turned the key in the ignition and pulled off as he said, "If Caitlyn lets him."

Brian walked out to the balcony where Caitlyn and Elliott were sitting. "Is the lady with the beach ball and the giant gone?" Elliott asked.

Picking him up Brian took the seat and placed Elliott on his lap and his arm around Caitlyn. "Yes, Aunt Cynthia and Uncle Samuel just left."

"Wow, Mommy I have an uncle and an aunt."

"It appears so," Caitlyn replied, a little unenthusiastically.

"Tracy and Ashley called, they are on their way over with God only knows what. They are going to love you." He smiled at Caitlyn. "Samuel just called. He and Cynthia would like to host a celebration for us tomorrow in their home."

Caitlyn sighed, "I don't suppose they could postpone that to a later time."

"They could," his fingers twirled in her hair. "But, my friends would like to meet you and show their support." With his finger under her chin, he turned her face to his. "And I would like for you to give them a chance."

Caitlyn exhaled, she knew he was referring to the green eyed wench that just left. Her husband seemed nice enough, but Cynthia, was just as nasty as the first time they met. Caitlyn wasn't sure she could let bygones be bygones."

An hour later Ashley and Tracy stopped by with a truck-load of items. There was furniture for Elliott's room, decorative towels and wash clothes, tableware, including table-cloths, napkins, cups, glasses and silverware. In addition to that, they stocked the refrigerator. "We know you did not have time to get anything prepared for Elliott," Tracy explained, "So we did a little shopping for you. Now, you can exchange any of this and our feelings will not be damaged at all."

"This is all so thoughtful, thank you," Caitlyn replied.

Ashley sat on the floor near the door. "Whew, I have no idea what I was thinking when I got pregnant this time."

"You weren't thinking," Brian laughed, "at least not with your head."

Ashley rolled her eyes at him, "Caitlyn, I realize you don't know us very well, but would you mind very much if I hit your husband up side his head?"

"Actually I like that head," Caitlyn smiled at the woman that was clearly a close friend of Brian's. "Now, you're married to James, right?"

"Yes. The Brook-master is mine, and I'm keeping him."

"How many children do you have?"

"Three. There's James Jr. who is my step-son from James' first marriage and we have a set of twins, Jayden and Jayda."

"Are you expecting twins this time too?"

"Girl, bite your tongue." Ashley laughed.

Tracy laughed at she watched the movers assemble the bed they'd purchased for Elliott. "I don't know why you are laughing. The way you and JD be going at it, you are going to be pregnant again soon." Brian laughed.

"And what about you?" Ashley asked.

"What about me?" Brian frowned.

"Now that you have Caitlyn, when can we expect another Elliott?"

As if on cue, Elliott and JC, Tracy's son came running into the room. "Daddy guess what?" Elliott called out. "JC said they have a big creek near his house. Can we go fishing there?"

"Of course you can." Ashley answered, "And if there aren't enough fish there we can go to Grandmother Gwen's house, they have a river in their yard."

"WOW, for real? Just like Grandfather Jacob's house. I'm going to like it here Daddy."

"I'm glad to hear it son," Brian smiled as the two boys ran back out of the room.

Tracy smiled up at Brian, "Well, how does it feel to be a family man?"

Brian looked up at Caitlyn with love in his eyes. "I love it."

The house was finally quiet. Elliott was in bed, Caitlyn was taking her shower and Brian was leaning on the banister to the balcony of his home contemplating his life. When he left the house three days ago, no one could have told him he would return with Caitlyn. His Caitlyn. He looked up to the heavenly skies. God must be holding him in high regards, for there was no way in hell, he could have done this on his own. "Sorry God, for using the word hell in my thinking." Brian pinched his arm to make sure he was still alive. A few months ago, he wasn't sure the pain he felt a minute ago would have existed. "Big Mom, I'm sure you're up there having the time of your life now. I made it through just like you said I would. Your God kept his word and now I'm keeping mine. I promised Caitlyn years ago I would always protect her. Well, I married the love of my life today." A tear breeched the corner of his eye. "I was afraid I would never find another woman to love me the way Caitlyn did, now it's a mute point. I'm so grateful God has brought her back into my life. Now you know I am not a religious man. I believe in the All-mighty, but the going to church every Sunday and on Wednesday nights like you did was never my thing, Big Mom. But now, I will make a better effort to pay my respects. Your God not only put Caitlyn back in my life, but he gave me a son." Brian stood still thinking how at times after the shooting he was in so much pain that he questioned why God had let him live. Now he knew why, Caitlyn and Elliott needed him. "I will never question you again," he said to the sky.

Turning to walk back into the bedroom he froze. Standing in the door way between the bedroom and the bathroom was Caitlyn in a black lace negligee. The negligee was long with splits up the sides and little bows strategically placed to hold the delicate material together. Her skin was still wet, or maybe it was glistening from the baby oil. That and coco butter was all she ever used on her skin. The memory made him smile. There had never anything frilly about her, she'd always kept it simple. That's what made her so different, so beautiful to him. Where other women were wearing outlandish clothes to show off their bodies, Caitlyn did just the opposite, but her beauty shined through. He continued to watch as she stood there nervously looking off into space. Then she slowly raised her eyes to him and his body instantly hardened, his breathing became shallow and his heart rate soared.

Caitlyn walked out of the shower with one of the negligees' Ashley had given her. This was the first time she had every worn something sexy to bed. When they were in college, she would just wear one of Brian's old jerseys or one of his tee shirts. There was no reason after that to even think about something alluring to sleep in. Now, she had to pay attention to those things, as Ashley said. Women forget the little things that keep a man happy. Like making sure the bedroom is his refuge. This is his kingdom, where he comes for relief from his stressful day. There should be no television in the room, no children and definitely no drama. If you want that man to come home to you every night, you make sure this room, the bedroom is where he finds nothing but love. Caitlyn watched Brian on the balcony and wondered could she keep him coming home? She was not as experienced as the women from his past. The only man she'd ever known was him.

Suddenly she shuddered, her nerves were getting the best of her. The last three days had been so dramatic, she never had a moment to think about now or the day in day out of a relationship with Brian. It's been years, is he the same man— is she the same woman? So many questions were now floating through her mind. Then she felt it, without looking up she knew his eyes were on her.

Slowly she raised her head and looked into his eyes. Her chest heaved, she couldn't seem to catch her breath, her heart began pounding so loudly she was sure he had to hear it across the room. They stood there as the clock on the side of the bed ticked off seconds, one mesmerized by the other.

"Caitlyn." The sound of her name on his lips washed over her like a spring shower, cool moisture rained over her body, then he took a step towards her and the coolness disappeared. Heat took over and seemed to intensify with each step he took. Pulling his tee shirt over his head and dropping it to the floor, he never lost a stride. His intent was clear as soon as he reached her and fell to his knees. Grabbing her behind, he buried his face into the very core of her kissing her there with only the lace barrier between them. Caitlyn could feel the heat of his breath against the opening between her legs. All she could do was close her eyes and grab his shoulders to keep from falling. "Caitlyn," was the only sound she could hear over and over and over again as she began to vibrate from his touch.

The scent of her was the same, the way her behind filled his hands was the same, the soft, smooth velvety feel of her skin was the same. The dream was now a reality. Running his hands slowly from her ankles, to her calves to her thighs, then touching her moist cocoa scented center he smiled, this was where his son came from. The thought sent him reeling. He kissed the top of her feet, the outside of her calf, going under the gown, he kissed the inside of her thigh and placed them over his shoulders. Still on his knees he held her over his head then submerged his tongue as deep into to her as he could go. His mouth covered her completely as he took his fill as if he was dying of starvation. Every inch of her outer core was touched by his lips, while his tongue plunged in and out of her.

There was nothing she could do, no-where she could turn to avoid the sensations that were building at an incredible speed inside her. All Caitlyn could do was hold on and even that was turning out to be a challenge, with Brian's mouth sucking any sense of reality from her. As hard as she tried, she couldn't hold back, he was demanding his due and within minutes she cried out, releasing the love he had pulled from her. "Brian," she screamed as she clawed at his back, but he didn't stop even with her contracting from the first orgasm, he continued to suck on her until she screamed out his name again and again and again.

It wasn't enough, was the only thought running through Brian's mind. He had to have all of her, everything she had to give and more. Her taste was intoxicating and rejuvenating at the same time. When she fell across his shoulder he stood, still inhaling her scent, walked over to the bed laid her down, then promptly kicked off his slippers and removed his pants. As he stared down at Caitlyn still reeling from her last orgasm, he realized nothing was more stimulating than seeing the woman you love in the aftermath of an orgasm—nothing.

The wait for him and Caitlyn was over, he pulled her to the edge of the bed, wrapped her legs around his waist and buried himself deep inside of her. Neither moved. Then Caitlyn opened her eyes, staring right through to his soul. "I love you Brian. The blood that runs through my veins to yours. Always has been, always will be."

Still buried deep inside of her, Brian laid his body over hers and cupped her face between his strong hands, his lips not even a breath away from hers. "I died inside the day I lost you. Now I'm ready to live again." He kissed her gently.

"I love you Caitlyn. I always have and I always will." Tears rolled down her cheeks and he kissed them away. Now it was time for him to seal what was his. Kissing her lips, he pulled out of her slowly, then eased back in. Kissing her again, then slowly easing back, he did it again, repeating the same motion, feeling himself grow thicker in side of her with each emergence. Each movement felt like an airplane when it's slowly picking up speed down a run way, then increasing with power as he pumped deeper and harder into the hot silky feel of her core and it still wasn't enough. Reaching down he captured her hips in his hands, guiding her up and down his shaft.

Caitlyn grabbed the sheets, then she tightened her legs and raised her body up to him, sucking and pulling everything from him. She wanted every inch, every drop of life he had to give and more. This was what had kept her living, the memory of the way he made love to her. Reaching down she grabbed his arms, pulling him even deeper into her as she began contracting around him. She felt him expanding, his hands tighten around her hips as he increased his speed, plunging into her with such power, such strength until they both exploded and he still didn't stop. Slowing down he still eased in and out, slowly gliding her hips over him. They could hear their bodies as they came in contact with each other's. They could feel the juice from their love making flowing down her legs, his thighs, onto the sheets and neither caring. They could smell their scent in the room. All their senses were in full bloom as he eased them back down to reality.

Brian held Caitlyn wrapped securely in his arms, kissing the back of her neck, the top of her shoulders. "In my heart you became my wife the first time we made love Cait. Today we made it official."

"I thought you would have waited."

"I've waited ten years to give you my name. That's long enough."

Caitlyn scooted her butt closer to him, "Girl, you are asking for it, backing that thing up on me like that." He could feel her smile against his arm.

"I know it has to be awkward to have an immediate family. I thought you might need some time to adjust to your life."

"Ask your question Cait?" he said as he played with the ribbons on the side of her gown.

The man knew her too well. After ten years of being apart he could still read her like a book. She shrugged, "Some of your visitors from earlier today seemed a little bothered by the fact that I was here. Your friends may need a little time to adjust."

"I'm waiting."

She turned around facing him, still lying in his arms, but looking into his chest. "I was just wondering, if,"

He put a finger under her chin and brought her eyes level with his. "I'm up here," he said. "Now ask your question."

The soulful brown eyes of his were lethal to her. They killed any thoughts that were forming in her mind. Then his fingers slowly moving up and down her thigh weren't helping her concentration at all. "I was wondering, if," she looked away and he brought her eyes right back. "if there was someone special in your life?"

He held her eyes captive. "Yes, you. It's always been you. Ten years ago it was you. For the last nine years, it's been you. In every dream, it was you, Caitlyn. No one has ever been able to replace you. I'm not going to tell you I've been without sexual encounters, because I haven't. But no one has ever touched my heart. A lost heart has been found Caitlyn." he placed her hand over his heart. "This one Caitlyn, I lost it the day I lost you, and now it's been found."

The feel of his heart beating beneath her hands filled her heart with so much joy and peace. Her heart was finally at peace. But her body was roaring again. The heat from his chest as she roamed slowly over it and his six pack he called a body, began to seep into her soul. She kissed one nipple and his body jerked. It was good to know his body responded so intensely to her touch, so she kissed the other just to give them equal attention. Slowly she slipped one leg over his body to straddle him.

"You're in trouble now," he smiled up at her.

"Do you know one of my favorite past-time is riding?"

"Really," he teased giving her a lopsided grin,

She could feel his manhood increase in size against her thigh. Placing her hands on his chest, she pushed up and placed her center right at the tip of his shaft. He began pulling the ribbon on the side of the gown apart. "Know what I like the most about riding?"

"What?"

Pushing against his chest to balance herself she eased slowly down onto him. Her inner muscles contracted as soon as he breeched her entrance. "I like to feel the sheer power of the animal between my legs." She eased down again, going a little lower this time.

"Hmm." Brian moaned as his eyes rolled back. "Cait you feel so good."

"Do I?" she asked as she slowly rose up, then eased back down slowly taking him in inch by inch, savoring in the feel of the essence of his power inside her. The sensations in her stomach were building with every delicious stroke. Caitlyn held his eyes, for she no longer had to close them to imagine he was here, this was all the way live. She could feel the power in his chest each time she pushed down on it. Her tongue glided across her lips as she moaned, "Hmm Brian, you feel so hard and smooth. So thick." She said as her body contracted every time she lowered herself on him.

He untied the last ribbon on the gown leaving only the shoulder to hold the two pieces of material together. He pulled it over her head exposing her breasts to him, then he placed his hands behind his head and watched his woman get her fill of riding him.

She was a sight to behold as she worked her body over him, taking her time, enjoying the feel of him inside of her. The sight of her face as her body tension began to climb higher and higher with each stroke, was enough to make any man explode, but he refused. He wanted her to get her pleasure the way she wanted it. The closer she came to her satisfaction the more tension built within him. The buildup was killing him, each time she eased down, her inner muscles contracted, squeezing him, calling out to him, but this was for her—her way. He could see it coming on her face, her lips parted, her breathing was shallow as she plunged down with more force. She moved down grinding against him, up, down, grind, then back up, then she simple stayed down, grinding, her body squeezing her muscles around him like a blanket until her head fell back and she screamed out his name, her body contracting around him again, and again, and again.

Moving as fast as a panther, Brian pushed her backwards never breaking contact, pinning her legs over his shoulder, plunging deeper and deeper into the very core of her, relentlessly giving every ounce of himself over to her. "This is yours. All of this is yours."

Reaching out she grabbed his butt and pulled him deeper still inside of her. The explosion rocked both of them to the core. Neither speaking, just Brian spreading kisses on every place on her face, as tears of joy escaped from their eyes.

"Caitlyn, we didn't get off on the best foot, so I'm going to be the bigger person here and apologize for my behavior yesterday." Cynthia began the rehearsed speech. "I was upset and my hormones are completely out of whack. But I should have understood that you may or may not know Brian and I have a special relationship. He's like my over protective big brother and I'm his pain in the ass little sister.

So if I came off a little pouty just chalk it up to being a part of my personality."

Cynthia laughed at her words, but Tracy could see the attempt at apologizing did not go over well with Caitlyn. The small celebration was a wonderful idea, but her friend wasn't executing it very well. "Cynthia is our version of Imelda Marcos. She is used to having her way and we tend to indulge her." Tracy looked to Ashley and Roz to jump in.

"Yeah, we know she can be a pain in the ass, but we love her anyway," Ashley added.

Cynthia frowned at the remark and had a reply on the tip of her tongue, but Roz stopped her. "There are times—many when Cynthia doesn't know what to say out of her mouth." Roz began, "and if she gave me an accurate accounting of what took place at your home yesterday, I would not blame you for not wanting her anywhere near you or your family. In her defense I will offer you this, Brian was the only person that took the time to teach Cynthia what family love was supposed to be. He has been the one constant in her life. We all have come to depend heavily on Brian. Now that he has a family of his own, we have to adjust our lives. Cynthia more so than the rest of us. But we will adjust-right ladies."

"Yes, definitely," Tracy and Ashley agreed.

Cynthia hesitated as she looked from one friend to another. She wasn't ready to let Brian go yet. "Brian has always been a part of my life and he always will. If you are going to be a part of his life you just have to accept that."

The collective moans from Tracy, Ashley and Roz could be heard across the room capturing the attention of the men.

"If being selfish and uncaring is a part of your character and your friends choose to accept it, that's wonderful, I'm happy for you." Caitlyn said. "As for me, I don't particularly care for people that treat others as if they are beneath them. Nor do I want my son to be exposed to such a person. You apparently have a special relationship with Brian and I will not interfere with that, however I want you to understand and accept that I am his wife. Your husband is the person you can demand to do your bidding, not Brian." She turned as Brian walked up behind her, Marco stood next to Roz, James stood behind Ashley, JD stood next to Tracy and Samuel stood behind Cynthia. That did not deter her from getting her point across. "All of you have the benefit of history between you. I don't have that luxury. And I do want to fit in, but I will not allow you," she looked at Cynthia," to have the benefit of your husband and mine. So there will be some lines drawn and if you step across them I will set you back. Nine years of our lives were disrupted because of your personality flaw."

"How did I disrupt your life?" Cynthia angrily asked.

"Calm down Cynthia," Samuel suggested as he rubbed her shoulders.

"Caitlyn," Brian but his hands around her waist.

"Brian," JD stated. "Let them get it out."

"You really don't remember?" Caitlyn asked not believing Cynthia was playing this game.

"Remember what?"

"Nine years ago I came to Richmond to tell Brian about the baby. You told me, Brian had plans for his life. I was just a fling and I should move on. Then you slammed the door in my face. You never asked why I was there. You didn't care."

"Cynthia?" Brian asked hoping Caitlyn was wrong.

"I don't remember that," Cynthia regretfully replied.

"I do," Caitlyn replied with tears streaming down her face. "I remember as if it was yesterday. Your uncaring actions set off a string of events that changed my life. So forgive me if I'm not so eager to just accept your ways."

Samuel and Brian gathered their teary wives into their arms to console them. "I'm sorry" Cynthia said into Samuel's chest.

Samuel kissed her forehead, "Not to me sweetheart, to Caitlyn." He turned her back to face Caitlyn, as Brian did the same. Cynthia wiped the tears away from her cheeks. "I was a very cruel and selfish person back then. I had no idea what my actions did too others. But I've changed a lot since then. For the better I hope. It may not seem that way to you but I have."

"She has," a teary eyed Ashley nodded.

"She doesn't curse anywhere near as much as she used to," Tracy added wiping tears away.

"That's right, she doesn't." Roz said as she looked around at all their friends for acknowledging the fact. "Last week she let me make a decision at the office."

JD grunted. Tracy turned and frowned at him just as Calvin and Jackie walked up. "Why are we standing around singing Cynthia's praises?" Calvin asked.

"We're trying to get Caitlyn to like her," Tracy replied.

"A daunting task."

Jackie turned to her husband, "Calvin." She exclaimed then sighed. "I have one. She talked to Carolyn nice one time, last week when she said she looked like a little whale."

Everyone glared at Cynthia who actually was the size of two whales. "I said a little whale." She cried out.

Caitlyn chuckled first then Brian and the rest followed. The irony was too much to let slip away. "There are times that we don't know how our actions affect others." Samuel said. "We all should be mindful of one another's feelings."

Cynthia turned to Caitlyn, "I'm not asking you to like me." Groans went around the group, "I'm just asking you to tolerate me a little."

The group held their breath as they waited for Caitlyn's response. Wiping tears from her eyes Caitlyn looked down and smiled. "I don't think that is more important than getting you to the hospital. I believe your water just broke."

Everyone eyes went to the floor as surprised expressions appeared on their faces.

"Well don't stand there gawking while I'm pissing on myself. Somebody get me to the hospital."

Samuel picked her up. "Cynthia Antoinette you're about to become a mother."

"And you, Samuel Lassiter are about to become a father," Cynthia smiled and kissed her husband.

"Now is not the time for all of that." Brian stated as he grabbed Caitlyn's hand, "We'll bring the car around."

"A wedding and a baby, who could ask for anything more?" Tracy exclaimed smiling as she hurried around the room gathering Cynthia's things.

James smiled at Ashley as they rushed to follow the others, "You're next."

"You wouldn't be smiling if you were the one that had to push something out between your legs."

"No, but I always smile while I'm between them," James smiled brightly at his wife.

Brian got in to the car with Caitlyn as soon as Samuel and Cynthia were on their way to the hospital. "Well, looks like we are going to have another baby around soon," he said grinning as he pulled away from the curb.

Caitlyn shook her head. "If I didn't know better I would swear Cynthia planned it this way."

Brian turned to his wife before starting the car. "You are holding her responsible for things she had no control over."

"That's not true. She could have simply given you the message or given me a number to contact you. There were options." She huffed then turned to the window.

Brian reached out taking her chin in his hand turning her face back to him. "Then I'm just as much to blame. You know how I was back then Caitlyn. No woman held any ground with me and Cynthia knew that. JD and Calvin were the only ones that knew how much I loved you. So to her you were just another woman chasing after me. Cynthia had no way knowing I would have wanted that message from you. Now if you can forgive me, why can't you forgive Cynthia?"

Caitlyn looked away. "I don't know." She whispered.

"I know why," Brian said as he turned the key in the ignition. "Jealousy. Pure and simple."

"What?"

He pulled out of the parking lot. "Yep, you thought Cynthia wanted a piece of your chocolate cupcake." Caitlyn stared at him with an incredulous look. "That's right. You know the women love me, they can't help it, cause I'm the man."

Caitlyn smiled at him, "You are so full of yourself."

"No baby, I'm full of love for you." he continued driving not seeing the tears on the verge of dropping from her eyes. "And now you are what you should have been ten years ago—my wife. It took us a while to get here, but baby we made it. Cynthia's actions are a part of the past. I don't know about you, but my mind is on the future. Care to join me?" He put his hand out and waited.

Caitlyn took his hand and he closed it around hers. "I still say she went into labor on purpose."

Brian looked over at his wife and smiled. "You're probably right."

"So you finally decided to let the whale out," Brian smiled at Cynthia from the door-way.

"Hey," She smiled from her bed in the hospital suite. "Where have you been? She asked as she sat up.

"Waiting for the crowd to die down. The hospital had to build another elevator to handle the overload of Lassiters that's been coming out of the woodworks visiting you."

"Hey now, that's my family you are talking about."

"Well there's a hell of a lot of them. You don't have to worry about ever being alone, again." Brian said as he sat on the side of her bed.

"That doesn't mean you get to disappear out of my life now."

"I have no plans on doing that. But now you have responsibilities to your husband and baby girl. Just like I have a responsibility to my family."

Cynthia threw her head back. "Do we have to talk about that?" She sighed.

"If by that you mean Caitlyn, the answer is yes. We have to talk about her." Brian pushed a curl from her face, then smiled. "You have always had these unruly curls." Cynthia smiled. "You know I will always be around whenever you need me. Caitlyn is not your rival. She's my wife and I love her more than life itself. The fact the she gave birth and cared for my child all these years only enhances my love for her." He hesitated "You asked me once why no one loved you. I wondered the same thing about myself. I never imagined it was because I couldn't love them in return. My heart was already taken. Now look at us, you have Samuel to love and I have Caitlyn." He tilted his head and gave her a teasing frown. "You're not going to make me choose are you?"

"Would you choose me over her?"

"A consoling smile touched his lips, "No, it would be like cutting my heart out again."

"How do you know she is not going to do that again? I was around during that time Brian. I know how hurt you were. I didn't know what happened but I know it changed you. I don't want you to be hurt again."

The fog had cleared. He now understood. Cynthia had a problem with Caitlyn because of the past. He sighed, that he could fix. "Cause you love me. Go ahead admit it," he joked.

"Yes I do Brian, Cynthia replied seriously. I love you just as much as I love Blake. And just like with him, I will have serious problems with anyone that hurts you."

The words touched Brian's heart. "I love you too. But I need you to love me enough to accept the woman I choose to make my wife."

"If Elliott did not exist, would you have married Caitlyn?"

"Yes, because I love her. What happened to us ten years ago was not her doing. But none of that should matter to you. Your only question should be am I happy. And I can tell you, my life has changed dramatically in the last week and I would not change one minute of it. That's how happy I am."

Cynthia smiled, "Oh alright I'll accept your wife and son." She said as she wiped a tear away.

"Well don't do me no favors now," He laughed.

"You always have been a smart ass. Does Caitlyn know that about you?"

"Yes she does and she loves me anyway."

A knock sounded at the door and they turned.

"Hey," Tracy called from the door with JD, James, Ashley, Roz, Marco and Caitlyn, "Can we come in yet?"

Smiling brightly Cynthia replied, "Another herd of people. The hospital staff is going to put me out. Come on in."

"It's your winning personality," Brian winked as JD grunted.

"We saw the baby," Roz said smiling, "she is beautiful."

"Just like her mother," Samuel said as he walked in the door with the baby in his arms. "Here you go little Mommy," he put the baby in Cynthia's arms then kissed her temple. "Thank you."

Brian stepped back and pulled Caitlyn into his arms. "What's her name? Caitlyn asked as everyone cooed and awed around the room.

She held the baby up. "Her name is Samantha Brianna Lassiter. She is named after my two favorite men."

Caitlyn felt Brian's body shiver. She kissed his cheek. "I think that's a perfect name."

"I agree," Samuel smiled.

"Me too," Tracy added.

"It's alright," Joshua said from the doorway. "I think Joshuanna would have been better."

Samuel threw a pillow at him as everyone else booed him. Brian and Cynthia looked at each other and shared a smile of mutual acceptance as their friends talked around them.

The Epilogue

The celebrations were still going strong a week after the inauguration of Governor Jeffrey Daniel Harrison. This was a private celebration taking place at what was now known as the complex, but was the private home of the now Governor and First Lady. The official home being the mansion that, Gavin and Carolyn Roberts and their son Gavin Jr. had just vacated.

This celebration was open to family, friends and a few political power players. But tonight's concentration was on the core friends that had been by his side from the very beginning, the ones that believed in him before he believed in himself. This night, for JD, was about Calvin, Brian, Douglas, James, and Senator Roth. This night was for his wife Tracy, his sister Ashley and his mother, Martha Harrison. This night was about family and friends.

The political heavy weights were here because they were now a necessity in his life. Stanley Covington who had recently relinquished his role as Chairman of the Democratic National Committee would remain on staff in an advisory capacity. Newly retired Senate John Roth was the new Chairman.

"Life has certainly changed," Brian grinned as he watched Caitlyn and Tracy laughing in the distance.

"Man, stop looking at that woman as if you were going to jump her bones any minute." JD teased as he took a drink. "It's been five months now. Aren't you over it yet?"

"I'll never be over her."

"Now you understand why I can't keep my hands of Tracy. That woman just does something to me."

"It's been five years. Aren't you over it yet?"

JD smiled at his friend, "I'll never be over her."

"Touché," Brian and JD tap glasses.

"What are you two talking about?" James asked, "No, let me guess, the women."

"What else would they be talking about?" Calvin asked as he joined them. "The only time we talk about anything else is at work."

"Speaking of work," James extended his hand, "congratulates Mr. Chief of Staff."

Calvin beamed, "Thank you, thank you. I have to say, I was surprised."

"Why?" JD asked, stunned at the revelation.

"Man, I'm an advisor. I like being behind the scenes. When you need me to research and keep you honest, I'm there. But, Chief of Staff, well that's for somebody like James that knows how to motivate people to get things done."

JD patted Calvin on the back, "I have all the confidence in the world in you. You will excel as you always have."

"Well, well, well. Look who's here?" Brian said pointing towards the entrance.

The men turned and Calvin, grunted. "You know you are in danger when your rival attends one of your political functions."

"Who are they?" Douglas asked.

"Senator Jeremiah McClintock," Samuel replied.

"And his son, Jerry McClintock, number IV." Brian added, "He is the Republican presumptive nominee for President in four years."

"Neither one of them is my concern," James pointed. "It's the grandfather, Jeremiah McClintock, Jr. better known as Mac. He would stop at nothing to get his grandson elected."

"Not even espionage," Samuel stated. "Ah my brothers, I think we need to start recruiting more men to the security detail."

"Wise men once said keep your friends close, and your enemies closer." Brian set his glass down. "Come on," He said to JD, "Let me introduce you." The men walked off with Samuel following.

James turned to Calvin, "Don't for one minute allow JD to take those two lightly. You're his Chief of Staff, watch his back at every turn." James walked off to join his wife and friends on the dance floor.

And just as the small group of men had just discussed, everyone at the event was not there to celebrate the occasion. Some were there to assess the competition.

"I want you to look around boys, Senator McClintock instructed."What do you see?" He asked in his famous Texas drawl.

"I see a good man celebrating a well deserved victory," his son and Governor of Texas, Jerry warmly replied.

The warmth in his grandson's words angered Jeremiah McClintock Jr., who was known to all of Texas as Mac. The thought of a person that shared his blood admiring a Black man's rise in power sent a surge of anger through him. "My father would turn over in his grave at the warmth you express for these people," he seethed.

Jerry bent down to his grandfather, who was a few feet shorter than he. "I, for one, am grateful times have changed. These people, as you call them, are Americans with families and dreams no different from yours or mine."

"Jerry," his father called out in a warning tone.

"Yes father," Jerry replied mockingly, "I know, Don't speak to my grandfather in that tone, he holds the key to my future. I've heard it for years."

"Then show some respect son. Your grandfather is doing his part to assist you in achieving the Presidency. You would be wise to heed his words. After all it was his wisdom that got me where I am today."

It was more like his money and connections, Jerry thought, but did not dare speak the words. "You're right father." He turned to his grandfather and plastered on that winning smile. "Forgive me grandfather. I know you want the best for me and I certainly welcome your wisdom in all things. What we want to accomplish is a monumental task and I need you with me. We just have very different philosophies on how to get there."

"If you are not careful your philosophy will have you making a concession speech while Harrison is making an acceptance speech. Look around, the people in the room supporting this man are from both sides of the aisle. This man is dangerous to our plans with his ability to unite people. Humph. He even has a good old fashion American name for a President. We need to take action now to eliminate him or Jeffrey Daniel Harrison will be President of the United States."

"Good evening gentleman," JD extended his hand. "Welcome to our celebration. I'm JD Harrison."

"Governor Harrison," Jerry took his hand. "It's an honor to meet you. Congratulations on your victory."

"I appreciate that Governor McClintock. We look forward to working with you on a couple of issues."

"I look forward to it," Jerry replied. "Allow me to introduce my family. My mother Barbara, and my father Senator Jeremiah McClintock and my grandfather, Mac, McClintock."

"It's nice to see you all." JD turned on the winning smile as he shook hands. He managed, but it was hard not to flinch at the coldness he felt when he shook the grandfather's hand.

Jerry turned to Brian and gave him a bear hug. "Thompson, it's good to see you. How in hell have you been?"

"Doing good Jerry," Brian replied. "Good evening Senator, Mrs. McClintock, it's good to see you again. How is the family?"

"They are doing well."

"It's good to hear. Jerry, where is Eleanor?"

"My wife was unable to join us tonight." Jerry answered losing a little of that carefree attitude he seemed to always have. "What about you Thompson?" His playfulness returning, "If I remember correctly you were hanging pretty tight with Caitlyn Montgomery. Whatever happened to her?"

"I married her," he nodded towards the center of the room. "That's my wife in the red gown."

The group turned, "Why she looks familiar," the Senator said.

"You sly fox," Jerry laughed, "You married Caitlyn Montgomery. "

"Yes, I did." Brian smiled, "Caitlyn is my wife."

"Speaking of wives, I think I'll take mine for a twirl around the dance floor." JD stated. "Governor, thank you for coming. I hope you and your family enjoy the festivities."

"We'll catch up later Jerry," Brian said then followed JD to the dance floor.

Samuel followed behind JD, but slowed his step to ensure Mac McClintock got a good look at him. He knew the old man recognized him the moment they walked up. *That was good*, Samuel thought. *I want you to know what you are up against if you come after the Governor.*

With the new Governor and his wife on the dance floor the crowd gathered around. Mac watched Samuel Lassiter walk away. His eyes twitched. Eliminating JD Harrison may not be as easy as he originally thought.

Brian held Caitlyn close as they danced around the room. He knew his life had changed, for dancing was not his thing, but at the moment he loved it with a passion. "Do you have any idea how much I love you?"

"It's slowly becoming a reality to me now," Caitlyn smiled as she moved closer to her husband.

"I'm afraid our life is about to change in so many ways." Brian held her tight. "Your mother has decided to stay with her people in South Carolina now that your father is incarcerated. Damn, I wish you would have let your mother have him castrated." He laughed, "But hey, we are about to have a baby."

She smiled into his eyes, "This one we're doing together."

"Together Caitlyn, together," he said holding her a little tighter. "You know, in eighteen months JD is going to become a candidate for President of the United States. That means my time at home will be limited."

"As long as you come home to me. I'll take what you have to give." Brian kissed her temple. "You know, it's funny. I look around and see everything that my father wanted. And it was granted by the one man he tried to keep out of my life. If he had just let us be, he would be here amongst the rich and powerful."

"That's what happens when you judge people before taking the time to get to know them. You are a perfect example."

"Why me?" Caitlyn asked.

"I didn't judge you based on the prim and proper look you were sporting in college. I looked beyond and found the woman that stole my heart. For I was lost, but now I am found."

Staring deeply into his eyes Caitlyn's heart was lost forever. "If you keep looking at me like that I'm going to make love to you right on this dance floor."

"Let's get our son and go home," Caitlyn smiled seductively.

Brian took her hand and led her off the dance floor. "You don't have to tell me but once." Caitlyn laughed as she followed him. "You say goodnight to the girls, I'll handle JD and get Elliott. Meet you at the door in fifteen."

Elliott Thompson and JC Harrison sat in the window seat in JC's room while their parents celebrated downstairs. Their feet hanging over the edge with Elliott's extended longer than JC's and a bowl of M&M's between them, both reaching in and popping a few in their mouth. "You know what?" Elliott said to the little boy sitting next to him."

"What?" JC replied excitedly, ready to hear anything his new best friend had to say.

"Because you are littler than me I have to protect you like my daddy do your daddy."

"Ok. Why?"

"That's just how things go. But you know what else?"

"No, what?"

"You gonna be President one day too. You know why?"

JC shook his head no. "Cause you are smart like your mommy and like people like your daddy. That's what my daddy says."

"You going to be big and strong like Uncle Brian."

"Yep, see." He held up his arm to let JC feel his biceps.

"Wow!" JC said as he felt his friend's muscle. "You going to stop the boys from calling me a mommy's boy at school."

"No that's not a bad thing. I'm a mommy's boy too."

"But I want to be a big boy like the other boys at school."

"But you're not like anybody else, that's what my mommy says. There is only one you. God made us like we are and he don't make mistakes,"

"My daddy says that too," JC nodded. "You really think I can be President like my daddy is going to be?"

"Yep." Elliott nodded in agreement.

"Elliott what's a president supposed to do?"

Elliott thought for a minute, then put his arm around JC's shoulder and said, "I don't know. But we'll figure it out together."

JC reach up and put his arm over Elliott's shoulder. "Ok, cause that's what friends do right?"

"Right friends figure out things together."

James Jr. and Little Calvin came over and joined the two friends. "What you doing?" James Jr. asked as he grabbed a few M&M's and put them in his mouth.

"Talking about being friends." Elliott replied.

"Will your mommy let you be our friend too?" JC asked.

"I don't know maybe, but my daddy will." James Jr. replied.

"I thought we were already friends?" Little Calvin said as he took a seat next to JC.

"We are," JC said to his kindergarten school-mate. Now we have big friends and nobody at school will mess with us."

"That's right," James Jr. said as he sat next to Elliott. "Cause we won't let them."

"Are you going to be around all ways?" Little Calvin asked.

Elliott put his hand out palm down, "Friends forever.

James Jr. put his hand on top of Elliott's. "Friends forever."

Little Calvin smiled and placed his hand on top of James Jr., "Friends forever."

JC stood and put his hands on the top. "Through thick and thin, Friends forever."

The boys all smiled, then took a seat and continued eating the M&M's. "What do friends do?" JC asked.

Elliott shrugged his shoulders and said, "I don't know but we'll figure it out."

JD and Brian stood in the doorway staring at each other, shaking their heads. "The next generation," JD said with a smiled.

Brian shrugged, "And so it begins."

The Heart
Prologue

Jeffrey Daniel Harrison stood at the podium, as a sea of people looked on. The Convention Center in downtown Richmond was lined with red, white and blue banners, balloons, posters, hats and any other peripheral available to mankind. The atmosphere in the room was more than electrifying, it was explosive. He looked to his left and saw his wife Tracy beaming with love and pride in her eyes. The unspoken message that passed between them was more intensified than he could handle. He stepped away from his podium, placed his arm around Tracy's expanded waistline then proceeded to give her the most passionate kissed ever witnessed on national television. The crowd cheered louder, as they reveled in the knowledge that they had just elected, a family man, a loving man and another African American as President of the United States. The White House on Pennsylvania Avenue will be filled with a loving family and young children.

The wonderful thing about the moment was when the cameras scanned over the crowd, it was an array of what America had become, truly one nation under God. Every ethnic group imaginable stood side by side cheering at the prospect of having a better future under the leadership of Jeffrey Daniel Harrison, President of the United States.

A hush came over the crowd as they waited to hear the words of the new leader of the free world. Every eye was looking toward the stage with the first family of the United States and their friends smiling brightly with the attendees anticipating the words of encouragement and hope they have become accustomed to receiving from the young man facing them.

JD returned to the podium, smiled and looked at the eager faces in the crowd. Turning to the people on the stage he shook hands with, Calvin Johnson and James Brooks. He kissed his sister Ashley and his mother Martha. He smiled and began, "Marrying my wife was the smartest thing I have ever done." He bowed his head and chuckled, "Her love has made me rich beyond my imagination in so many ways. The most prominent of which is being able to stand before you today and accept the faith you have placed in me, to be President of the United States of America." The crowd cheered widely, almost frenziedly as JD scanned to room smiling.

One of the secret service agent whispered to another, "It's been a long time since we had a President with rock star status, we need to tighten up." At the command more agents entered into the room and spread throughout the crowd. JD continued with his speech as the agents moved about unnoticed. Midway through the speech, JD reached down to picked up his two-year-old daughter, Gabrielle who was tugging at his pants. She captured his cheeks between her small hands and kissed her daddy. As the crowd clapped, Gabrielle joined in smiling. JD smiled at his daughter and turned back to his speech. She then laid her head on his shoulder and listened as he talked.

Moments later, shots rang out, with center stage as their targets. The loud sound continued to flow through air like shock waves. Secret Service sprang into action, covering the children, then Tracy as ordered by the newly-elected President. JD protectively covered Gabrielle's head as an agent covered his body immediately propelling him forward. He hit the floor with Gabrielle beneath him. That's when he heard the sound. A sound that would awaken him drenched in a deep sweat, for years to come. The heart-wrenching scream filled the air and he was certain it came from Tracy. With agents' bodies surrounding him, his movement was limited and his line of sight was blocked. "Seal the room," he heard an agent command as he reached out and grabbed her hand. "Tracy!" he yelled out, to no avail. Chaos had broken out around the room. "Ashley," he heard James panicked voice penetrate his mind.

When the firing stopped, the crowd was still buzzing and the room was half-empty. JD looked down at Gabrielle, who was now crying. He held her tightly as he scrambled to stand. Tracy was pulling her hand from him reaching for something. When he looked over he saw blood on the stage and his heart literally stopped. Is it possible his dream and worst nightmare had all occurred on the same night? Looking around at bodies on the floor and stage, he thought how would he live his life knowing he was responsible for the events happening at that moment? How many lives would come to an end on that night, trying to accomplish a dream?

CPSIA information can be obtained at www.ICGtesting.com
Printed in the USA
LVOW10s1623170715

446649LV00002B/297/P